DEADLY INFERNO

A DETECTIVE JANE PHILLIPS NOVEL

OMJ RYAN

INKUBATOR
BOOKS

Published by Inkubator Books
www.inkubatorbooks.com

Copyright © 2024 by OMJ Ryan

OMJ Ryan has asserted his right to be identified as the author of this work.

ISBN (eBook): 978-1-83756-337-1
ISBN (Paperback): 978-1-83756-338-8

PROLOGUE

There was a bitter evening wind blowing in from the east, and the temperature had dropped close to freezing as he took up his position opposite the Wythenshawe Social Club, just after 9 p.m. Luckily for once, the suburb – located five miles south of Manchester – had managed to escape another wet autumnal evening. Good news for him considering what he had planned tonight.

Staring across at the single-storey building now, its wide windows cloaked in condensation, it appeared that a large number of police officers and staff had braved tonight's cold conditions in order to join Sergeant Armstrong in celebrating his retirement from the Greater Manchester Police. Slinging his small backpack over his shoulder, he walked briskly across the quiet road towards the double-doored entrance of the club. The nylon wig he was sporting under a grey beanie was making his head itch to the point of distraction, but he knew only too well how important it was he wasn't recognised at this evening's party. After all, he was no stranger to the police.

A moment later as he pulled open one of the entrance doors, he was hit by the heat emanating from within, his clear-glass spectacles fogging up instantly. 'Shit,' he mumbled as he stepped into the entrance hall and attempted to clear the lenses with his scarf.

Glancing around at his sparse surroundings – careful to hide his face from the CCTV camera fitted opposite the front door – he could see the building itself was split into three different sections: the Sports Bar to his left, the Members Lounge straight ahead, and the venue for tonight's party, the Function Suite, to his right. Muffled music was playing behind the double doors that led through to the event, and he could hear raised voices, laughter and what appeared to be several women singing bleeding through from the other side. Returning his spectacles to his face and making sure to keep his head down, he strode at pace across the hall, stopping just before he reached the door to take a breath as he attempted to calm his racing pulse. A second later he yanked it open and stepped inside.

As he had anticipated, the room within was packed full of men and women of varying ages, as well as states of intoxication, and the party appeared to be well under way. Immediately to his right, three women, their arms locked together as they huddled around a single microphone, delivered their own tuneless karaoke rendition of 'We Are Family' by the Pointer Sisters. To his left, the main bar was filled with men huddled together in a pack, gulping down pints of lager and laughing hoarsely at one of the group who appeared to be holding court.

God, I hate cops.

Walking slowly across the room so as not to draw any attention to himself, he found an empty spot at the bar and ordered himself a Diet Coke. He'd never really had much of an appetite for alcohol; he preferred to stay sharp and focused at all times, but especially so on an occasion such as this.

A few minutes later, two men in wrinkled suits lumbered next to him at the bar, one of them catching him on the shoulder, causing him to spill some of his drink, much to his chagrin.

'Sorry, mate,' slurred the man who had bumped into him, patting him on the shoulder with fat fingers.

'Can't handle his drink,' said his equally inebriated partner.

'Can I get you another?' asked the first man, nodding towards the spillage.

'Don't worry about it,' he replied through gritted teeth. 'I'm fine with this.'

'Please yourself,' the first man mumbled before shouting his own order at the woman working behind the bar, just a few feet away.

As the two men waited for their drinks to be served, their voices seemed to grow in volume, and he was forced to listen to them plotting their prolonged assault on the free bar tab that had been set up for the evening.

With his jaw clenching as he grew increasingly irritated by their drunken mumblings, he was tempted to find a quieter spot in the bar, but that would risk drawing attention to himself, which was the last thing he wanted. So, instead, he decided it was best to stay where he was and keep his head down for the time being.

About thirty minutes later – with the room full to the brim with drunken cops and other police staff – he decided now was as good a time as any to make his move. So, after draining the remainder of his drink, he picked up his backpack, turned away from the bar and, with his head lowered, made his way out of the Function Suite and back out into the cold night air.

Moving quickly to the rear of the building, he spotted two industrial-sized waste bins, which he wheeled next to the club's fire exits. Thankfully the area around him was cloaked in darkness and had not been afforded any CCTV coverage, meaning he could work away unnoticed. Opening the backpack, he reached inside and retrieved a heavy-duty wrench, then dropped to his knees. A couple of minutes later, with two of the four wheels removed from the first bin, it lurched backwards against one of the fire doors. After repeating the process with the second bin, he stood back and admired his handiwork; no one would be escaping through those exits anytime soon.

Carrying his backpack in his right hand, he walked back to the front of the building, where he stood for a moment staring back at the club. The party had remained in full swing, and he allowed himself a wry smile. 'They haven't got a fucking clue,' he muttered to himself.

Reaching into the bag once more, he pulled out the wine bottle filled to the brim with petrol, the neck stuffed with a fuel-soaked rag, and with his back to the wind, he flicked open his antique Zippo. Firing it up, the flames began to dance in front of his torso. His pulse quickened as he allowed the rag to catch fire; the flames flickered slowly at first before suddenly enveloping the material. With just a few seconds left before the whole thing caught fire, he spun round and, with all his might, launched the Molotov cocktail at the double-doored entrance to the club.

With an audible whoosh, the bottle exploded on contact,

and a split second later the entire doorway was engulfed in flames. Standing just a few feet away, his eyes widened as the flames spread around the entrance and into the building beyond.

Slinging his backpack over his shoulders, he moved back across the street, activating the video on his smartphone as he did. Turning to face the club, he couldn't help but laugh out loud as its drunken inhabitants began to realise what was happening, their shouts and screams suddenly audible from inside.

'I'm a firestarter, twisted firestarter,' he began singing to himself as a chair smashed out through one of the windows, immediately followed by thick plumes of black smoke.

Standing in the shadows now, he repeated the song lyric over and over as men and women fought to free themselves by climbing out through the smashed windows, and he once again marvelled at his handiwork.

It was only when he heard the sound of sirens in the distance that he realised it was time to go.

As more and more partygoers clambered out the windows, he ended the filming before turning away and slipping off into the night.

1

I t was just after 11 p.m. by the time Phillips pulled the British racing green Mini Cooper alongside the array of police patrol cars, ambulances and fire trucks that littered the street around the Wythenshawe Social Club – the night sky illuminated by their flashing blue and red lights. Jumping out, she pulled the collar of her charcoal winter coat up against the cold night air and made her way towards the building, which was now cordoned off with the ubiquitous blue and white police tape. Her second in command, DI Jones, was already on-site. His thinning hair, which was fighting a losing battle against the bitter wind, accentuated his bony features.

As she moved closer, Phillips was more than a little surprised to see Jones talking to their boss, Chief Superintendent Carter, standing by his side. In contrast to Jones, Carter was broad and muscular and, despite being in his mid-fifties, had the physique of a man twenty years his junior.

She nodded as she caught Jones's eye.

'Evening, guv,' he said in his South London accent.

Carter turned to face her. 'Jane.' His warm, rich North-eastern tone was in stark contrast.

'It's not often we see you at a crime scene, sir,' she said as she moved to stand next to them both.

He shook his head. 'I was just finishing up at the Lord Mayor's charity dinner when I saw the alert on my phone. It's on my way home and based on the fact that some of those injured were on the job, I figured I'd better take a look.'

Phillips felt her brow furrow. 'I thought those types of functions were strictly Fox territory.' Referring to the head of the Greater Manchester Police, Chief Constable Fox.

'Ordinarily, yes, but she's away at a police conference in Florida this week, so I got the short straw.'

'Lucky you.' Phillips turned her attention to the blackened doorway of the club. 'So what exactly happened here?'

'Based on witness statements and the fact the place stinks of petrol, it looks like someone threw a petrol bomb into the doorway around ten o'clock.'

'A Molotov cocktail?'

'That's the one,' replied Jones.

'And who do we think was being targeted?'

'Well, there was a retirement party happening inside at the time for a Sergeant Tom Armstrong from the Wythenshawe uniform team.'

Phillips shook her head slightly. 'Don't know him.'

'Everyone calls him Tommo, it seems.'

Phillips was none the wiser.

Jones continued, 'Anyway, after the fire started, it spread pretty quickly, and once people noticed, they tried to escape through the rear of the club, but it seems the doors were blocked by two large wheelie bins.'

'Well, that was a disaster waiting to happen,' Carter cut in.

'We can't be sure just yet, but it looks like they were placed there deliberately, sir.'

'What makes you think that?' asked Phillips.

'Two wheels from each bin had been removed so they wouldn't budge.'

'So do you think someone was intentionally targeting Armstrong?' asked Phillips.

Jones shrugged. 'Too early to say at this stage. Most of the people I've spoken to were in shock, so I've not been able to get much out of them as of yet.'

'You mentioned on the call earlier that there'd been no fatalities. Is that still the case?'

'As far as I know, yes, but a couple of people have since been admitted to ICU, including Armstrong, who was in a bad way due to smoke inhalation. From what I've been told, I'm afraid it's not looking good.'

'Poor fella,' said Carter. 'He managed to survive a lifetime on the force and then gets seriously injured at his own retirement party.'

'And,' Jones continued, 'I thought you'd want to know that DCI Cleverly was also injured at tonight's party.'

'As in Serious Crimes Unit Cleverly?'

'Yeah, suffered quite bad burns to his hands and arms, apparently, so he's on his way to the burns unit at Wythenshawe as we speak. Hopefully his injuries aren't too serious though.'

Phillips fell silent as she stared at the club and the firefighters moving around the now soaking wet entrance. 'Oddly, I can remember something like this happening before.'

'How'd you mean?' asked Carter.

'Some nutter targeting police officers back in the mid-noughties, setting fire to cop shops and police houses, etc. There were a fair few fatalities, as I recall. I was just out of uni back then, but it was big news and all anyone was talking about at the time.'

'Did they ever get anyone for it?' said Jones.

Phillips nodded. 'I don't remember his name, but the guy got life. So unless he's since been paroled, he should still be in Hawk Green.'

'I'll get one of the guys to see if he's still there, first thing in the morning,' added Jones. 'And if he's not, then he's the first person we need to speak to.'

'Agreed,' Phillips replied.

Just then a large white van pulled up on the other side of the police cordon, and a tall well-built man jumped out of the driver's seat.

'Aye, aye.' Jones turned to face him. 'Who's this fella?'

'Someone from the media maybe?' asked Carter.

'Well, if it is, they can stay the hell out of the way,' said Phillips. 'The last thing we need is the press lumbering around and getting under people's feet.'

The man strode confidently towards the police tape now.

'I'll deal with him.' Jones took a few steps forward to intercept him. 'Sorry, mate, this is a crime scene. I need you to stay behind the line.'

The man stopped, and a thin smile flashed across his handsome face. 'I'm not press, buddy. I'm your new senior CSI.' The accent was cultured Irish and rich in tone as he locked his piercing blue eyes on Phillips. 'I'm Evans's replacement. Cormac O'Shea, but everyone calls me Mac.'

'Shit, sorry, mate.' Jones immediately lifted the tape so

Mac could step under before offering his hand. 'DI Jones, and this is DCI Phillips and Superintendent Carter,' he added.

'Good to meet you.' Mac extended his hand to Phillips and Carter in turn.

'We weren't expecting you for another week,' said Carter.

'I finished up my last job early, and I'm not big on taking holidays and doing nothing, so I thought I may as well get started straight away.'

'Well, in that case, I should probably bring you up to speed,' said Jones.

Mac waved him away. 'No need. I like to look at a crime scene without contamination.'

Jones's brow furrowed. '*Contamination?*'

The same thin smile returned. 'You know, someone else's ideas of what happened. I prefer to keep my own counsel on how things played out.'

Phillips felt herself recoil slightly. It seemed their new senior CSI was nothing if not confident.

'Well.' Mac clapped his hands together. 'This crime scene isn't going to figure out what happened itself, so I'll just grab my gear and get cracking.'

With that, he turned and stepped back under the police tape before striding off towards his van.

'Confident bugger, isn't he?' said Carter.

'Arrogant, more like,' Phillips shot back as she watched Mac opening the rear doors to the van.

Jones chuckled. 'He's no Evans, that's for sure.'

Phillips turned her attention back to Carter. 'Look, sir, I think we've got everything covered here. Why don't you head home, and I can debrief you tomorrow on anything we find tonight.'

Carter nodded. 'Sounds like a plan, but my phone will be on and next to the bed, so call me if you need anything.'

'I will,' Phillips replied.

'Very good,' said Carter, then headed off towards his car.

Five minutes later Mac returned carrying a large toolbox and fully suited up in forensic overalls, latex gloves and shoe coverings.

Jones lifted the tape once more so he could pass under it without bending.

'A couple more of my guys will be here in the next half an hour or so,' said Mac. 'Let them know where they can find me, will you?' Without waiting for an answer, he headed inside.

'Looks like it's gonna be a long night, guv,' mumbled Jones.

'Yeah,' Phillips replied. 'It sure does.'

2

First thing the following morning, Phillips and Jones sat down to debrief on the events of the previous night with the other core members of the Major Crimes Unit, Detective Constables Bovalino and Entwistle. In light of the early hour, Phillips had provided bacon rolls and hot drinks for everyone. Unusually, the man-mountain that was Bovalino was showing little interest in his sandwich.

'You feeling all right, sweetheart?' teased Entwistle – Whistler, as he was known in the team – as he took a seat opposite the big man on the bank of four desks. 'You've hardly touched your food.'

'Bugger off, you idiot,' Bovalino replied in his Mancunian accent. 'I'm just not hungry this morning, that's all. It's not a crime, is it?'

Entwistle smiled widely, which accentuated his chiselled mixed-race features. 'I never thought I'd live to hear you say that, big lad!' he said before taking a bite of his own sandwich.

Phillips allowed herself a smile, watching the two of them bickering like brothers as per usual, but noted that it *was* very unlike Bov to be off his food. Still, there was a lot to do, and she was keen to move on, so she got straight down to business. 'Right, what insights can we garner from the uniform reports logged last night?'

Entwistle placed his sandwich down on the desk before opening a file on his laptop. 'I had a quick look earlier, and it appears that several people saw a man they didn't recognise come into the function room bar about an hour before the fire started. One of the witnesses, DS Hart from Serious Crimes, apparently bumped into the guy at the bar and spilled some of his drink, but it seems the conversation was quite short-lived. Hart offered to buy him a replacement drink, but the guy wasn't interested, and that was that.'

'Any kind of description?' asked Jones.

' Nothing of note,' Entwistle replied. 'By his own admission, Hart was a bit pissed at the time.'

'Of course he was,' said Phillips sardonically. 'Like most of the people in there last night, no doubt.'

'Which will only make our job harder,' added Jones through a mouthful of bacon.

'Speaking of Serious Crimes, is there any update on Cleverly?' Phillips asked.

'I called the burns unit before the meeting,' replied Bovalino. 'They said he was stable, but wouldn't give me any details.'

Phillips turned to Jones. 'We should head over to the hospital later. If he's up for talking, he could be a decent witness.'

Jones nodded. 'As long as he wasn't pissed as well.'

'Bov.' Phillips focused on the big man. 'Go through the

witness list and speak to anyone who can remember the mystery party guest. Let's see if we can get a photofit together.'

'I'll get straight onto it, guv.'

Jones passed Bovalino a pen drive. 'And take a look at that, will you? It's the CCTV footage we managed to pull off the system at the club last night. Thankfully the drive was in the back office, so it escaped damage, but the feed from the camera at the front door will no doubt cut off once the fire takes hold. Still, we may get lucky and catch him on the earlier footage when he first arrived.'

Bov made a note in his pad.

'We'll also need the council cameras checking,' Phillips cut in. 'From what I could see last night, there should be at least one camera on the street that faces the club. As long as it's working, that is.'

'I'll look into that, guv,' said Entwistle.

'There's something else I need you to look at as well.' Phillips took a sip of her black coffee. 'Back in the mid-noughties – at least I think it was around then – there was a spate of arson attacks on police stations and officers' houses.'

Entwistle sat back in his chair. 'Really? You thinking they're linked?'

'I don't think so, because the guy they picked for it got a life sentence, but we need to find out if there's a chance he got parole. Because, on the slim chance he is out, then he's our first port of call.'

'I'll look into that first.' Entwistle scribbled down the details.

Bovalino's thick brow was furrowed, and he appeared deep in thought.

'Something on your mind, Bov?' asked Jones.

'Just wondering who Armstrong must have pissed off to have his retirement party torched.'

'If he was the intended victim, that is,' Jones shot back. 'There were an awful lot of coppers in that room last night. Any one of them could be the target.'

'True,' Phillips cut back in, 'but before we spread ourselves too thin, let's at least start with Armstrong. See if anyone on his recent arrest sheet might have reason to take a pop at him.'

'I know plenty of the lads in uniform,' replied Bovalino. 'I'll ask around.'

'And one more thing.' Phillips folded her arms before sitting forward and resting them on the desk. 'It seems our new senior CSI started a week early. Jones and I had the pleasure of meeting him last night.'

Jones's eyes widened as he stifled a chuckle. 'I think it's fair to say he's *very* different from his predecessor.'

'Night and day,' said Phillips flatly. 'Cormac O'Shea is his name, *but*, as he was at pains to tell us last night, everyone calls him Mac.'

'Bit of a prick was he, guv?' asked Bovalino.

'Let's just say he's not what you call a shrinking violet,' she replied.

'Arrogant arsehole springs to mind,' Jones chimed in.

'You've always had a way with words, Jonesy,' said Phillips. 'When you get a mo, Whistler, do some digging and see what you can find on this guy. I don't like surprises, and I don't like people descending on my crime scenes unannounced.'

'I'll see what I can find, boss.'

At that moment, the main door to Major Crimes opened behind them as Carter strode in.

Phillips turned. 'Morning, sir.'

'Have you got a minute, Jane?' His expression was grave.

'Of course.' Phillips stood before following him to her office. 'What's up?' she asked as she closed the door.

'Fox has been on the phone from the US. She's not happy.'

'So, what's new?'

Carter ran his fingers through his thick salt-and-pepper hair. 'She wanted to know why she was hearing about the fire last night from social media as opposed to through me. Of course, I explained we had it all under control, and I didn't want to disturb her conference, but she wasn't having it.'

Phillips exhaled loudly. 'Damned if you do, damned if you don't, right?'

'Quite. And the upshot is she wants me to make a statement to the press to try to get out in front of this one, especially given the similarities to the Archie Pearson case in 2006.'

Phillips clicked her fingers. 'That's the guy's name! I remember it now.'

'Yeah. It seems Fox was already a DCI by then, so she's familiar with the case and is very keen to play down *any* links between him and last night's fire. In her words, "The last thing GMP needs right now is mass hysteria from the public thinking there's a copycat fire setter roaming around Manchester."'

'Sounds like a bit of an overreaction, sir. Even by her standards. I mean, it's been such a long time since the Pearson case, I doubt many people would connect the two.'

'I agree, but you know Fox as well as I do, and she was

very clear that we need to be mindful of whom we talk to about this case outside of the immediate team.'

Phillips frowned. 'It's an active police investigation into a firebomb attack on a bunch of cops. It's hardly something I can keep under wraps.'

Carter raised his hands in surrender. 'Look, you're preaching to the converted here, Jane, but she's the boss, and we have to at least *try* to follow her directives.'

'Very well, sir.' Phillips sighed. 'But it's not going to be easy to keep this one low-key. You know as well as I do, cops are the biggest gossips on the planet.'

'I do, yes, and I also know how good you and the team are, so I'm sure you'll do what you can to minimise any fallout.'

'Of course, sir.'

Carter checked his watch. 'I'm due to meet with Rupert Dudley in half an hour to plan the press briefing, so if you've got a few minutes, I could really do with an update on anything you got from the scene last night.'

'Sure,' said Phillips, thumbing out towards the office. 'Just give me a second to update Entwistle with the name of the historical fire setter, and I'm all yours.'

3

With a rolled-up cigarette nestling between his lips and smoke wafting up in front of his face, he turned the volume up on his phone resting on the table next to him. A music app was playing 'Firestarter' for the umpteenth time this morning, which boomed out of a small but powerful Bluetooth speaker he'd recently purchased from the local pawnshop. He'd lost track of how many times he'd heard it in the last hour as he'd watched the video footage taken from last night's fire. Despite the dark skies that filled the background of the video – and maybe even *because* of them – the flames appeared brighter than he remembered. After all, it had been some time since he'd set a fire of that size, and he'd almost forgotten how good it felt to bring such a beast to life. To create something so powerful yet so delicate it could simultaneously creep through the eye of a needle while ravishing an entire building. It truly was a sight to behold.

At that moment, the local lunchtime news flashed up on the TV, which was muted in the corner of the small living room. Pressing pause on the music, he activated the volume on the TV and watched on as the top story played out.

The typically good-looking news anchor stared out into the camera, his expression as grave as the tone of his voice. 'Police are appealing for witnesses after it appears a fire was deliberately started in a social club in Wythenshawe last night...'

He took a long drag on the cigarette. 'I bet they are.' He chuckled before exhaling through his nostrils.

The presenter continued, 'Several people were taken to Wythenshawe Hospital and treated for burns and smoke inhalation. The senior officer leading the investigation had this to say.'

Much to his disappointment, a man he had never seen before appeared on-screen now. A tall man in full uniform with a serious expression, reading from a script directly into a sea of logo-ed microphones from radio and TV networks. Photographic cameras fired and flashed around him as he took up his position in front of the main entrance of the police HQ. The caption underneath gave his name, Chief Superintendent Carter, and the location as Ashton House, a place he himself was yet to be acquainted with.

'Last night at approximately 10 p.m., officers from the Greater Manchester Police, as well as the Greater Manchester Fire Service, attended a blaze at the Wythen-shawe Social Club in what appears to be a deliberate act of arson. A number of serving, as well as retired, police officers were attending an event at the time. Several people were taken to hospital, suffering with smoke inhalation and burns, while others received treatment for minor injuries at the scene. We are appealing for anyone who may have been in the area last evening to come forward, as they may have information that could help our enquiries. There will be no further questions at this time.'

Despite his final statement, a flurry of questions erupted around him as camera bulbs flashed like strobes, but true to his word, Chief Superintendent Carter turned his back and strode quickly towards the revolving doors visible in the distance.

'Fucking pricks,' he growled at the screen as he muted the TV again and squashed the remnants of the roll-up into the overflowing ashtray. He wasn't interested in a bloody *superintendent*. He wanted the top boss: that bitch, Fox. Where the hell was she? He had attacked her own people, yet she chose to hide away? Well, that was all about to change; he would make sure of that. By the time he was finished, Fox would be on her knees, staring down the camera, begging him to stop. Grabbing his phone, he hit play once more, and 'Firestarter' blared out through the Bluetooth speaker as he gathered his things and headed out to the small yard at the back of the house.

As ever, it was another dark, rainy autumn day in Manchester, but as he knew only too well, that meant nothing when it came to setting a fire. Throwing the black nylon wig and beanie hat from last night into a makeshift fire pit he'd constructed using a few stray bricks he'd sourced from a nearby demolition site, he doused them in lighter fluid. Then, pulling out his trusty Zippo, he dropped to his haunches and fired it up before touching the flame against the nylon. In an instant the small fire erupted, and he watched on as the flames devoured last night's disguise. 'Dance, my pretty, dance,' he said, a satisfied grin spreading across his face.

4

As Phillips returned from the ladies', Entwistle beckoned her over.

'What you got for me?' she said, moving next to the bank of desks where Jones and Bovalino were also hard at work.

'Archie Pearson was denied parole three months ago, and so far he's served seventeen years of a life sentence.'

'In Hawk Green?' asked Jones, listening in.

'Yeah,' Entwistle replied. 'And looking at his file, he'll be in there for at least another eighteen months more, which is when he can apply for parole again.'

'So he *definitely* didn't start the fire, then,' said Phillips.

'No, guv.'

Jones leaned back in his chair. 'So *could* we be looking at a copycat, then?'

'It's always a possibility,' replied Phillips, 'but if it is, why copy Pearson in the first place? And why do it now, after all these years, when so many people have forgotten all about him and his crimes?'

Jones shrugged. 'I've got no idea.'

'Me either,' added Entwistle.

'Beats the shit out of me,' mumbled Bovalino.

'So what about Armstrong?' Phillips asked. 'Any updates on his arrest records? Anyone who might have a grudge?'

Bov tapped his pen on his pad. 'I'm still waiting for the files to be sent through. Apparently, the admin team are short-staffed.'

'Typical,' bemoaned Jonesy. 'Fox's budget cuts slowing things down yet again.'

Phillips was keen to avoid going down a police financing rabbit hole, so she ignored the remark. 'Any insight on Armstrong from your pals in uniform?'

'I've asked around, and it seems you'd struggle to find a nicer bloke on the entire force,' said Bovalino. 'Popular with his colleagues and respected in the community. There's certainly nothing coming back that would suggest he's the type of bloke whose party deserved to be firebombed.'

Phillips said nothing for a moment as she processed what he was saying. 'So, in that case, it's time to start looking at who else was at the club last night.'

'Such as Serious Crimes,' said Jones.

'Exactly,' Phillips replied. 'They deal with nasty bastards on an hourly basis. When we're done here, you and I should head over to Wythenshawe Hospital and see if Cleverly's fit enough to talk to us yet.'

'Sounds good to me.'

'And with a bit of luck, DS Hart's memory might have improved overnight now the booze has worn off.' Phillips turned to Entwistle. 'Can you call the governor's office at Hawk Green for me? I'd like to meet with Archie Pearson.'

'Sure. When do you want access?'

'This afternoon ideally.'

Jones folded his arms across his chest. 'Why? What you thinking, guv?'

'I don't know, to be honest. Due diligence, I guess. I mean, as far as I'm aware, this is the first direct arson attack on police officers since Pearson was convicted back in 2006 – on this scale at least.' She shrugged. 'Maybe he's involved somehow.'

'From inside?'

'Why not? We know plenty of convicted gang bosses doing life who are still connected to their empires on the outside. Why not Pearson? He could easily have put someone up to it.'

Jones nodded. 'I guess that's possible, but if he is involved, why now, after all this time?'

'I don't know,' replied Phillips. 'We'll just have to ask him.'

'But do you think he'll want to talk to the police?' Bovalino asked.

'If it breaks up his monotonous day-to-day routine, he'll definitely talk to us. Whether he'll share anything of value is another thing entirely, but it's worth a shot.'

'Fair enough,' replied the big man.

Phillips continued, 'And what about our newest colleague, Cormac O'Shea? Any intel on him?'

'A few bits.' Entwistle clicked open a window on his web browser. 'According to his profile on the National Forensic Society website—'

'That sounds like a fun group to be part of.' Bovalino's tone was laced with sarcasm.

'Does, doesn't it?' Entwistle chuckled. 'Anyway, according to their website, our boy O'Shea is a bit of a star in the forensic world. Originally from Dublin, he studied medi-cine-biophysics at Queen's College over there, then did a master's in forensic science at King's College, London. After graduating from King's, he went to work for the Police Service of Northern Ireland. He worked as part of the forensic team there for five years before he was hand-picked for a twelve-month secondment to the FBI, where, it seems, he spent several months studying at their world-famous body farm in Knoxville, Tennessee. He then returned to Belfast and the Police Service of Northern Ireland as a senior CSI, where his work was instrumental in securing convic-tions in a long list of political killings and gang murders.'

'Sounds like he wrote that bloody profile himself,' scoffed Jones.

'Having met him, I'm quite sure he did.' Phillips felt her brow furrow. 'So if he's been *that* successful over the water, and with such high-profile, big-hitting cases, why move to Major Crimes in Manchester where there's zero glamour?'

'No idea,' said Entwistle, 'but if I keep digging, I'm sure something will come up.'

Phillips patted him on the shoulder. 'Do that. I'm not sure why exactly, but something's telling me there's a lot more to our Irish friend than meets the eye.'

'I'll see what I can do, boss.'

Phillips turned to Jones now. 'You ready to head to the hospital to see Cleverly?'

He nodded as he stood. 'You want me to drive?'

'Please,' she replied. 'I'll just get my coat.'

5

Forty minutes later Phillips and Jones walked through the entrance to the burns unit located in A Ward adjacent to the A&E department. As they had experienced previously, the area was incredibly quiet, and their footsteps echoed around them as they made their way along the corridor to the nurses' station at the far end.

'Doesn't seem that long since we were last here,' said Jones.

'No, it doesn't,' Phillips replied, her mind wandering back to the recent case he was referring to. The victim had been trapped in his car after a homemade bomb had been detonated under it. Mercifully, the oversized SUV had protected him to some degree, but he'd still suffered life-changing injuries.

'I wonder how Grayson's getting on.'

'Last I heard, he'd been moved into a rehab ward, with the plan being to get him home in the next few months.'

Jones shuddered. 'It still gives me the willies thinking about him being locked inside that burning vehicle.'

'Me too,' said Phillips absentmindedly as they reached the nurses' station.

A face they'd become familiar with during the previous investigation glanced up at them from behind the desk, ward sister Agata Dabrowska. 'Detectives. I did wonder if any police would be paying us a visit today.'

Phillips offered her a faint smile. 'We promise we're not trying to make a habit of getting in your way.'

Dabrowska matched her smile as she nodded softly.

'We're hoping to speak to Ricky Hart and Steve Cleverly if they're well enough,' said Phillips.

Dabrowska craned her neck to check the whiteboard fixed to the wall behind her as she scanned the list of patients' names and their allocated room numbers before turning back. 'Mr Hart is in room five, and Mr Cleverly room eight. They've both been fitted with morphine PCA pumps so should be okay to talk to you, but only for a short time if they need more pain relief. Once that kicks in, they'll be out of it.'

Phillips nodded. 'We'll be as quick as we can.'

A minute later they stepped through the door to room five, where they found Detective Sergeant Hart sitting up in bed, his bandaged hands and arms connected by tubes to the host of machines that surrounded his bed. His eyes were closed, and a TV attached to the wall opposite played on low volume.

'Ricky?' Phillips asked softly as she moved to stand next to the bed with Jones at her side.

Hart opened his eyes and glanced to his left.

'It's DCI Phillips and DI Jones.'

'Hiya,' he said in a low, husky voice.

'How you feeling?' Phillips asked.

Hart's eyes closed again momentarily. 'I've been better,' he said, opening them again.

'I bet,' she replied. 'Are you up for answering a few questions about the fire?'

He took a moment to clear his throat as he attempted to shift his weight further up the bed. 'Sure.'

Jones pulled out his notepad and pen.

'We understand from your statement that you may have bumped into the firestarter at the bar,' said Phillips.

He nodded.

'Do you remember what he looked like or his build perhaps?'

Hart took a moment before answering. 'He was leaning against the bar, so I can't be sure, but he looked quite short to me. But then again, I was pretty pissed, like.'

'Was there anything else you can recall about him?'

'He had a beanie hat on, which was weird, as the place was roasting, and I'm not sure if I imagined it, but he looked like he was wearing a wig underneath.'

'What kind of wig?' Jones asked.

Hart shrugged. 'Dunno. All I remember is it was black and shiny.'

Phillips cut back in. 'Did he speak to you at all? Did he have an accent?'

'Yeah. Mancunian.'

'Did you notice any distinctive marks or tattoos?'

'No. Sorry.'

'Was there anything else you can remember that might help us?' she probed.

'He was wearing glasses.'

'Can you describe them?'

'Metal frames, I think,' replied Hart. 'Nothing that stands out.'

'Anything else?'

'Yeah, he had a backpack by his feet. I remember cos I caught my foot on it, which was how I ended up falling on him.'

'Do you remember what brand it was?' said Phillips. 'Or the colour?'

'No. It was dark, and like I say, I was pissed.' Hart grimaced in pain and shifted his weight in the bed again as he grabbed at the PCA pump release. 'I need some more.' A second later his eyes closed.

Phillips watched on as his head sank back into the pillow. She turned to Jones. 'Let's see if Cleverly has anything to add.'

DCI Cleverly was Phillips's opposite number in the Serious Crimes Unit, an elite squad that spent the majority of their time dealing with organised crime. Despite the fierce rivalry that existed between the two units, SCU and MCU had successfully collaborated on several occasions over the last few years.

As they strode into room eight, just a few doors along the corridor, they found Cleverly lying down, his torso at a 45-degree angle against the bed. Even on his back, it was evident that he was a tall man with long, awkward limbs, and in his current condition – and much to Phillips's amazement – his face appeared even gaunter than normal. Like Hart, the burns on his arms and hands had been dressed, and he was hooked up to an array of machines monitoring his vital signs.

'How you doing, Steve?' she said as she moved next to his bed with Jones at her side.

He offered a faint smile. 'I'll live.'

'Looks like you've really been in the wars,' said Jones.

'Yeah. Hit directly by the backdraft when I opened the door to see what was going on.'

'Can you tell us what happened?' Phillips asked.

Cleverly exhaled slowly. 'I was a bit worse for wear, so it's all quite hazy, but from what I can recall, everything was normal; Tommo and I were giving Dennison some stick about the state of United's back four the other night – how they'd spent billions and won bugger all – and then, all of a sudden, someone shouted fire and pointed towards the door. I turned to look and could see smoke in the entrance hall. I ran out towards the main entrance, where it looked like the smoke was coming from. Without thinking, I yanked open the door, and next thing I know, I'm lying on my back, with Ricky slamming his hands onto my arms and legs, trying to put the flames out. The heat and the pain were incredible. Seriously, I thought I was a goner for a second.'

Jones scribbled in his pad.

'Any ideas who did it?' Phillips asked.

'No, not at all.'

'The thing is, Steve,' said Phillips, 'we've looked into Armstrong, and we can't seem to find anyone with a bad word to say about the guy.'

'Yeah. He's a top bloke,' Cleverly replied. 'He was my sergeant when I was first starting out.'

'Whereas you and Ricky,' Phillips continued, 'you deal with proper villains on a daily basis.'

'What?' Cleverly recoiled. 'You think the guy was after us?'

'Maybe. I mean, Serious Crimes has put a lot of nasty bastards away over the years,' she replied. 'Can you think of any gangbangers out there who might want to burn down the club with you two in it?'

Cleverly chuckled and instantly grimaced. 'Take your pick.'

Phillips waited a moment to allow his pain to subside, and when it looked like he was ready, she continued, 'Any crews with a history of setting fires or using petrol bombs to send their messages?'

Cleverly nodded. 'Now you mention it, there is one, the Road Czars, a Russian neo-Nazi biker group who claim allegiance to Putin.'

Phillips did a slight double take. 'Putin? Who the hell supports Putin?'

'A bunch of head-bangers looking for a convenient excuse to wage war on their competitors, that's who,' said Cleverly. 'Rumour has it they've been setting fire to shops, restaurants and clubs run by rival Ukrainian gangs – and they know their way around a Molotov cocktail. We've been monitoring the Road Czars for about six months now – looking at them for money laundering and racketeering – but so far we've not found enough proof to warrant a full-scale operation.'

'So who's the gaffer of this lot?' asked Jones.

'A guy called Maxim Podgorski. He's filled some of the space left by Bahmani and runs a bunch of car washes across north Manchester called Revolution Valeting. The biggest is in Ardwick, where he keeps his office.'

'Sounds like a good place to start,' said Phillips.

Cleverly closed his eyes now.

Just then, Phillips's phone rang. She could see from the screen it was Entwistle. 'Whistler, what's up?'

'Your meeting with Pearson is all set for two p.m. The team at Hawk Green are expecting you at one thirty.'

She glanced at her watch; it was just after midday. 'Okay. We'll head over there now. Thanks.' After hanging up, she glanced over at Cleverly, who was evidently in a lot of pain. 'We'll leave you to it, Steve. You take it easy. Rest up and make sure you don't rush back. Okay?'

He nodded as he closed his eyes once more.

Phillips turned to Jones and gestured for him to lead them out.

6

HMP Hawk Green, Manchester's maximum-security men's prison, was located twelve miles southeast of the city centre, a sprawling mass of buildings constructed at the turn of the millennium to house some of the country's most dangerous prisoners.

Thanks to roadworks and long queues of traffic, the journey from Wythenshawe Hospital took longer than the expected thirty minutes, and it was approaching 1.15 p.m. by the time Jones pulled into one of the police vehicle bays outside the main entrance to the prison.

The heavens had opened not long before their arrival, and with no signs it would stop any time soon, Phillips and Jones jumped out of the car and rushed across the carpark to the relative safety of the reception block.

After signing in, they were escorted through the first set of security barriers, where they were met by a senior prison officer, Tracy Scott, a short woman with greying hair, whom Phillips placed in her late forties.

'I'll take you through security and then on to the visitors

building,' said Scott as she ushered them through a thick door at the rear of the reception area.

Scott walked at pace in front of them, and as she did, the keys connected to her belt by a heavy chain jangled against her sturdy legs. A couple of minutes later she used the same bunch of keys to open the heavy metal gate that led out into an empty courtyard, where the rain continued to lash down. Security was located in a purpose-built Portakabin on the opposite side of the courtyard, surrounded on all sides by towering metal fences topped off with loops of razor wire.

After moving quickly through the rain, they rushed up the steps inside, where they found a body scanner and an X-ray machine similar to those found in any airport around the world.

'I'll need your mobile phones and any smart watches,' said Scott, very matter-of-factly.

Phillips and Jones handed them over as requested and then, after removing their coats and placing them on the conveyor belt, stepped in turn through the body scanner.

A few minutes later, with all the checks complete and their coats returned, they followed Scott back out into the rain once more, reaching the shelter of the entrance to the visitors block a few seconds later, where Scott stopped once again to open a locked door.

'Gotta love the Manchester weather,' muttered Jones as they finally escaped the rain.

'Yeah, there's nothing quite like a wet Thursday in October, is there?' Phillips shot back sardonically.

Finally, almost twenty minutes after they'd first entered the prison, Scott unlocked the door to Visitor Room Two and switched on the lights. Holding the door open, she gestured for them to enter.

'Pearson'll be here in a minute,' she said as they stepped inside. 'He's a pretty quiet fella, all told, but if you get into trouble, press the panic strip along the wall, and we'll be right with you.'

Phillips scanned the room, which contained a small plastic-topped table, a single ashtray and four plastic chairs, and made a mental note of the panic strip's location in relation to the seats she and Jonesy would be occupying.

'Enjoy,' said Scott finally before stepping away and allowing the door to close behind her.

Jones shuddered. 'This place gives me the creeps.'

'The room or the prison?' Phillips enquired.

'The whole bloody place. I'm claustrophobic at the best of times, so I hate prisons, that feeling of being locked inside, the walls closing in on you.'

'They're only an issue if you break the law, Jonesy.' Phillips flashed a wry smile. 'Is there something you're not telling me?'

Jones laughed as he waved her away. 'God. Don't even joke about it. Can you imagine a cop being stuck in here with these animals?'

At that moment the door opened, and a second prison officer, a large man with a sharply trimmed beard and razor-shaved head, stepped inside, his name badge identifying him as Officer Dooley. He was closely followed by a wiry, balding man, no taller than five feet five, with an ashen face and sunken dark eyes.

'Prisoner 45894, Pearson,' said Dooley, glancing towards Phillips. 'I'll wait outside,' he added before retreating to the corridor.

Phillips presented her ID – which Pearson seemed to

have little interest in – then gestured to the desk and four chairs. 'Please take a seat, Archie.'

'Calling me by my first name?' said Pearson. 'You obviously want something.'

Phillips allowed him to sit before she and Jones took up their positions opposite. 'Do you know why we're here?'

'Ms Scott said it had something to do with the fire on the news.'

'So you heard about that?'

He laughed. 'A bunch of cops getting set on fire? What do *you* think?'

'How did you hear?'

'TV. Plus there's more smartphones in here than there are screws.'

'But they're banned, aren't they?' Jones cut in.

'So's spice and ecstasy, but you can still get as much of those as you want *if* you've got the means to pay for them.'

'So what exactly did you hear about the fire the other night?' asked Phillips.

'Just that a bunch of cops were getting pissed at a party in Wythenshawe, and some guy set the place on fire.'

'Do you know who the guy was?'

'Why would I?'

Phillips shrugged. 'He's a fire setter; you're a fire setter—'

'I'm no fucking arsonist,' Pearson spat back before she could finish.

'Really?' Phillips feigned shock. 'Then how come you're serving a life sentence?'

'Because I was set up,' he shot back.

'Of course you were,' added Jones.

Pearson glared at him for a moment. 'Believe what you want; makes no difference to me.'

Phillips was in no mood to debate Pearson's guilt, so she chose her words carefully now. 'Has anyone ever contacted you about the fires you were convicted of setting?'

'How do you mean?'

'Well, you know, any fan mail? People asking how or why you did it?'

'I told you, I *didn't* do it.'

'So you say, but that doesn't stop people with an interest believing that you *did*, does it?'

He shrugged. 'I've had one or two letters over the years.'

'Who from?' asked Phillips.

'Can't remember.'

'Did you keep any of them?'

'No. Why would I? Bloody drivel, written by lunatics most of the time; asking me to write back and tell them what it was like to kill cops. How the hell should I know? I never killed any. Nope, they held absolutely no interest for me, so I chucked 'em.'

'All of them?' asked Phillips.

'All of them.'

'You didn't maybe keep one or two back?' she prodded. 'To read every now and again?'

'Like I said, I had no interest in them.'

Phillips could feel her frustration mounting. It was evident Pearson had no interest in talking to them, and while he continued to lie about setting the fires in the first place, what he had to say had little value anyway. She suddenly realised it had been a mistake coming, and she was more than a little annoyed at herself for wasting valuable time that could have been better spent elsewhere. Exhaling loudly, she stood. 'Right. Well, I think we've got all we can from this little chat.'

Jones flinched next to her and appeared momentarily startled by her declaration.

'Is that it?' Pearson was incredulous.

'Yes,' she said flatly.

'What a waste of bloody time.'

'Well, thankfully, that's one thing you've got plenty of,' Phillips shot back before opening the door to find Dooley, who had remained standing just outside. 'We're done. You can take him back.'

'Out you come, Pearson,' the burly guard bellowed.

Getting up from the chair, Pearson shuffled slowly across the room, stopping just as he reached the door and locking his sad eyes on Phillips.

'I really didn't do what they said, you know.'

'Nobody in here ever did,' she replied without feeling before watching him follow Dooley out.

'That was quick, boss,' said Jones, standing.

'I know,' she replied. 'We should never have come.'

At that moment Scott opened the door. 'Well, that didn't take long,' she quipped.

Phillips stared back without responding, in no mood for the guard's input.

'If you could escort us out, that would be great,' added Jones.

'Back the way we came,' Scott said as she held the door open and gestured for them to step through.

Twenty minutes later, and finally free from the confines of the prison, they strode side by side across the carpark. Thankfully, the rain had finally stopped.

'He could be telling the truth, you know, guv,' said Jones.

'About what?'

'About the fact he's innocent. I mean, what if they got the

wrong guy back then, and the real arsonist is still out there and has started setting fires again?'

'I hear what you're saying, but I'm not sure I buy that,' she replied as they approached the squad car. 'If he *is* innocent, why not do something about it? Why not appeal? Shake things up and make some noise now the fires have started again? He pretty much mentioned it in passing back there.'

'Maybe that's what he wants, though, to stay inside?' Jones deactivated the central locking, which beeped as the doors released. 'I've heard it said before that it's hard for some lifers to imagine living on the outside after so many years in prison. Maybe he's one of them and doesn't actually want to be released?'

'Yeah. Maybe.' Phillips pulled open the passenger door. 'I mean, in truth, at his age, what's waiting for him out here? A halfway house full of junkies and then, if he's lucky, a bedsit in a shitty part of town?'

Jones held her gaze before glancing back towards the prison. 'When you put it like that, maybe prison isn't so bad after all.'

7

Early the next morning the team debriefed in the MCU conference room. Entwistle's laptop was connected to the big screen fixed to the wall at the end of the long conference table where they had each taken seats, nursing steaming hot drinks recently collected from the canteen.

'How did it go yesterday?' Entwistle asked as he took a sip of his coffee.

'Bit of a mixed bag, really,' said Phillips. 'We spoke to Hart first, and as we thought, his memory is a bit sketchy thanks to the fact he was pretty drunk when the fire started, but he did give us some sort of description.'

Entwistle's face creased. 'How do you mean?'

'He seems to think the guy he bumped into at the bar was wearing metal-framed glasses and a black wig under a beanie hat.'

'As in a toupee?'

'He's not sure,' Phillips replied. 'He said it was shiny and black, which would potentially make it conspicuous and kind of goes against the point of having a toupee in the first place, so it may be more likely it was the kind of thing you'd get in a fancy dress shop.'

'You said he was wearing a beanie hat and glasses?' Bovalino interjected.

'That's right.'

The big man passed a pen drive to Entwistle. 'Open that, will you.'

As Entwistle connected the drive, Bov explained what they were about to see.

'I've been going through the CCTV from the club, and one of the guests captured going into the party around the time of the fire matches that description. And now you mention it, I think he had what appeared to be black hair too.'

The video file began to play on-screen.

Bovalino continued, 'This is from the camera just inside the entrance hall that faced the main doors to the club. The camera and everything it captured was destroyed just before ten o'clock, but the feed was backed up to a hard drive in the club office up until that point. It starts at eight thirty p.m., so you'll need to fast-forward to around nine.'

Entwistle did as instructed, and a moment later the grainy footage played.

They watched on for a few minutes in silence as several people moved through the entrance hall until eventually Bov told him to stop the tape. 'There. That's him.'

Frozen on the big screen was a man fitting Hart's description of the suspect to a tee, a backpack slung over his right shoulder.

'Hart mentioned he fell over his bag,' said Phillips.

'That's how he ended up bumping into him in the first place.'

'Looks like that could be our guy, then,' Jones added.

The room fell silent for a time as they each scrutinised the image on the screen.

'Are there any other cameras in the club?' Phillips said eventually.

'Nope. Just this one, I'm afraid.'

'No expense spared,' said Jones sarcastically.

'What about the footage from the council cameras?'

'I haven't started on that yet, guv,' replied Bovalino.

'Was there a delay in it coming through?'

The big man shook his head. 'I just haven't got to it yet. I'm a bit behind.'

Phillips frowned. 'In that case, we need to pick up the pace, don't we?'

'Yeah, sorry. I'll get straight onto it this morning.'

'And how did you get on with Armstrong's arrest records?' asked Phillips.

'Nothing that I could see would warrant him being the target,' Bov replied. 'He was an old-school community officer, so he spent most of his time trying to support the locals in the area rather than nicking them.'

'Which is what we expected anyway,' said Jones.

'Yeah.' Phillips took a mouthful of coffee. 'On that, Jonesy, why don't you bring the guys up to speed on the Road Czars?'

'Road Czars?' Entwistle's brow furrowed. 'What the bloody hell are they?'

'Not what, Whistler, *who.*' Jones sat forward in his chair. 'We asked DCI Cleverly if Serious Crimes had ever had issues with any gangs with a penchant for using petrol bombs, and he seemed to think a group called the Road Czars were worth a look – and more specifically the head guy, Maxim Podgorski. They're supposed Russian loyalists and have been suspected of firebombing Ukrainian businesses across the city since the war broke out. By the sounds of it, they know their way around a Molotov cocktail.'

'And so SCU have been looking at them for money laundering through Podgorski's chain of car washes,' said Phillips. 'It's called Revolution Valeting, and Cleverly says he keeps his head office at the outlet in Ardwick. We're going to need the address over there so Jonesy and I can pay him a visit.'

'I can sort that.' Entwistle scribbled in his pad.

'Great.' Phillips drained her cup and placed it on the table. 'And as for our visit to Hawk Green, I'm afraid that was a pointless exercise.'

'Really, how come?' Bov asked.

Phillips folded her arms across her chest. 'Pearson gave us nothing of any value. In fact, he still claims he's innocent.'

'Don't they all?' Entwistle chuckled.

'Exactly what we said,' added Jones.

Just then Carter popped his head through the conference room door. 'Jane, can I borrow you?'

'Of course,' she said as she stepped up from her chair. 'Lots to do, guys, so let's get cracking, hey?' she added, then followed her boss out.

Carter's expression was grave.

'Everything all right?'

'Fox wants to see us both on a Zoom call at midday.'

Phillips felt her shoulders sag. 'God. That's all we need.'

'Tell me about it.' He checked his watch. 'I have a few

meetings this morning, but if you come to my office for about eleven fifty, we can do it there.'

'Of course. Can't wait.' Her tone was laced with sarcasm.

Carter offered a knowing smile, then turned and walked away.

8

As the time approached midday, Phillips took a seat next to Carter at the small conference table in his office, which was positioned in front of a large TV screen attached to the opposite wall. As the hosts of the Zoom meeting, they could see themselves reflected on-screen as they waited for Fox to join. Carter had purposefully muted their microphone so they could continue to talk without risk of anything they said being heard at the other end.

'What time is it in Florida?' asked Phillips as she shifted in her seat.

Carter glanced at his notes on the large pad in front of him. 'Five hours behind, so just before seven a.m. over there.'

'I didn't think she left her coffin when the sun was up,' she quipped.

Carter chuckled. 'Now, now, Jane.'

Just then Fox's name appeared on-screen, requesting to be admitted to the meeting.

'Here we go,' said Phillips with a sigh.

Carter accepted the request, and a moment later Chief Inspector Fox appeared on the screen side by side with them. 'Good morning, ma'am,' he said enthusiastically.

'Is it?' Fox's skin appeared even more tanned than usual; her bleached blonde hair was almost white now from exposure to the sun. Her expression, however, remained the same as always: austere and agitated.

'How are things?' Carter continued with his charm offensive.

'*Busy.* I'm preparing to give a talk tomorrow on the rise of cybercrime and the challenges of policing social media, so if it's all the same to you, let's dispense with the small talk and get on with the meeting, shall we?'

Phillips nudged Carter's knee under the table with her own in a hidden show of solidarity.

He nudged hers back, then continued, 'Of course, ma'am.'

'So what's the update on this fire in Wythenshawe?' quizzed Fox.

Phillips cleared her throat as she sat forward now. 'We have a number of witnesses who say they saw a man wearing a beanie hat and glasses – and what we believe might have been a wig – entering the premises carrying a backpack just before the fire started. He was also seen leaving the premises not long after. We believe he's very much a person of interest.'

'Any ideas who he is?'

'Not as yet, no, but we're going back through CCTV as we speak, trying to piece together his movements.'

'Anything else?' said Fox.

'I don't know if you're aware of the fact, ma'am, but a couple of the Serious Crimes team were at the party,' said

Carter. 'Notably DCI Cleverly and DS Hart, who are both being treated in hospital for burn injuries and smoke inhalation.'

Fox shook her head. 'No, I wasn't aware of that. Are their injuries serious?'

'Serious enough, but it looks like they'll both make a full recovery.'

'Any idea how long they'll be off work?'

'No,' replied Carter flatly. 'I'm afraid I don't.'

Fox exhaled loudly. 'That's all we need. Paying long-term sickness when the budget is already in deficit.'

Phillips curled her toes in her boots as she tried to stop the utter disdain she felt for the chief constable reaching her face. Two of GMP's hardest-working officers were being treated in hospital after trying to save their colleagues and friends from an arson attack, and all Fox could think about was her precious bloody budgets. She really did care about nothing and no one but herself.

Carter continued, 'DCI Phillips and DI Jones also spoke to Archie Pearson in HMP Hawk Green, ma'am. He was convicted of setting similar fires against police personnel back in 2006 and received a life sentence.'

'I'm fully aware of who Pearson is, chief superintendent,' spat Fox. 'The thing I don't understand is what the hell he has to do with this investigation?'

Phillips cut back in now. 'I thought it made sense to see if anyone had been in contact with him about his own crimes, a superfan if you like. Maybe if they had, they might be worth looking at.'

'And had anyone?'

'No, ma'am. They hadn't,' replied Phillips.

'Well, it seems you had a wasted trip, doesn't it?'

'Yes. I'm afraid it does.'

Fox continued, 'Do us all a favour and stay the hell away from Archie Pearson, will you? The man is a pathological liar and a menace to society.'

'He still claims he's innocent,' said Phillips.

'Nonsense,' Fox spat back. 'Pearson killed and seriously injured many good officers, Jane, coppers like you and the guys in your team. Don't ever forget that. He deserves to die in prison, and if I have my way, that's exactly what'll happen. I want to hear nothing else said about him or any potential links to copycats. That's a wild goose chase waiting to happen, which we can ill afford budget wise, not to mention a PR nightmare we can well live without.'

Carter glanced at Phillips and then back at the screen. 'We understand, ma'am.'

'Good,' said Fox firmly. 'Any other *actually* worthwhile leads?'

Phillips felt her jaw clench as she struggled to maintain her composure. 'One theory we're looking at is the fact that DCI Cleverly and several of his team members may have been the intended targets, victims of a disgruntled gang.'

'I can certainly see that would make more sense than your other theories,' said Fox.

Phillips ignored the sly dig. 'He's given us the name of a Russian biker gang called the Road Czars, who he believes have a history of using petrol bombs. The head guy is a man called Maxim Podgorski. Serious Crimes have been looking at them for money laundering and potential racketeering.'

'Podgorski?' said Fox.

'You know him, ma'am?' Carter asked.

'Only what I've seen in various reports.' She nodded. 'I

think he would be a good shout for it, actually. So what's your plan for him?'

'Jonesy and I will be paying him a visit this afternoon. See if he can account for his movements on the night of the fire.'

'Sounds like a sensible option. Anything else?'

'Not for the moment, ma'am,' Phillips replied.

'Very well,' said Fox. 'I'll be landing in the UK on Tuesday next week and back in the office on Wednesday afternoon. I'm expecting a lot more progress by then.'

Do you ever expect anything else? thought Phillips as frustration gnawed at her gut.

'Rest assured, we're fully focused on the job in hand, ma'am,' Carter said confidently.

Fox glared out from the big screen. 'I do hope so, Chief Superintendent.'

At that moment, a loud knocking sound filtered through the speakers.

Fox glanced to her left. 'That'll be my breakfast.'

'Well, in that case, we'd better let you go, ma'am,' said Carter.

'Keep me posted on any updates,' Fox replied absent-mindedly before leaning forward and leaving the meeting.

'Room service and sunshine,' Phillips muttered. 'How the other half live.'

Carter closed down the Zoom app before turning his attention to Phillips. 'I know she's pretty unpleasant at times, but try not to take what she says personally. I mean, look at her comments about Cleverly and Hart. She treats the other teams just as badly as MCU.'

'Well, when you put it like that, sir.' Phillips chuckled.

Carter matched her. 'Sorry, that wasn't meant to sound

quite how it came across. All I'm saying is that we know what Fox is like and how she operates. I wouldn't want her lack of support to knock your confidence or dampen your morale.'

'It doesn't.' Phillips sighed. 'Of course it pisses me off, but I've worked with her long enough now to let it wash over me as much as possible. I've got a job to do, and nothing she says is going to stop me doing it.'

'That's the spirit.' Carter flashed a wide grin.

'And on that note, I'd better be going. I've got a Russian nasty bastard to interrogate. Was there anything else you needed?'

'No. I think we've covered everything.'

'Very good, sir.' Phillips stood. 'I'll let you know as soon as I have anything to update you on.'

'Great. Thank you.'

With that, Phillips headed for the door.

9

The Revolution Carwash site in Ardwick had been set up on what looked to be an old petrol station. The pumps had long since been removed, but the telltale signs of its former use were evident for all to see, like the free-standing canopy roof that covered the old forecourt. Large vinyl signs bolted to the perimeter fence advertised the various services available, from a standard wash at £5 to a full valet of a large 4x4 or motorhome for £50.

As Jones steered the squad car through the gates, Phillips spotted the shabby Portakabin to the left of the site that, according to Cleverly, housed Podgorski's office. A black Harley-Davidson Fat Boy was parked up outside, the chrome twin-exhausts, engine block and wheels gleaming in spite of the overcast sky.

As they jumped out of the car, Phillips scanned the empty site, noting the couple of guys wearing jeans, sweat-shirts and wellington boots who were sitting in silence on fold-up plastic chairs, smoking as each of them stared into their phones, plastic buckets at their feet.

'Business is booming, then,' said Jones sarcastically.

'I can see why Cleverly is looking at this place for money laundering,' Phillips replied. 'I mean, it's perfect for it, isn't it? Everybody pays cash, there's no receipts, and at the end of the day you can claim you've washed five hundred cars at a tenner each, when in truth you've probably done a tenth of that. If my maths is right, that's a quarter of a million quid a year, and according to Whistler, Podgorski has ten of these places across the city.'

Jones whistled. 'Wow. That's a lot of money, guv.'

'Yeah. It is. So I'm guessing that he must be very good at hiding what he's up to; otherwise Cleverly would have had him by now.' Phillips set off walking towards the Portakabin. 'Come on, let's go and see what he has to say for himself.'

A minute later, she pushed open the flimsy door to the office with Jones at her back. Stepping inside, she was immediately hit by the smell of stale tobacco and the sound of Podgorski's deep, growling voice as he spoke on his mobile in what sounded like Russian, as he sat behind the old desk at the opposite end of the office.

Even sitting down, it was clear he was a big man, with broad shoulders and huge hands. His shaven head was wide, the brow thick over a large nose that had evidently seen more than its fair share of fights.

As he locked his dark eyes on Phillips, he muttered something into the phone, then ended the call. Reclining in the leather office chair, he folded his arms across his barrel chest. 'And to what do we owe the pleasure of a visit from Manchester's finest?' Bizarrely, his accent was now suddenly broad Mancunian with just the slightest hint of Russian.

'Maxim Podgorski?' Phillips asked.

'Who's asking?'

Phillips stepped forward and presented her credentials. 'DCI Phillips and DI Jones from the Major Crimes Unit.'

Podgorski's expression never changed, and he appeared unmoved. 'Need your car washing, do you?'

Phillips smiled sardonically. 'Where were you on Wednesday night between nine and ten p.m.?'

'Why do you want to know?'

'Because we're investigating a petrol bomb attack on a social club in Wythenshawe that took place at around that time.'

'And what's that got to do with me?'

'Well,' she said, 'as we understand it, you're a man who's very familiar with Molotov cocktails.'

'Ha,' Podgorski scoffed. 'And who told you that?'

'Our colleagues in the Serious Crimes Unit.'

'I'm afraid they're mistaken. Just cos something has a Russian name doesn't mean anything, you know. It was the Finns who invented them, not us,' he added with a smirk.

'You still haven't answered the question,' Jones cut in.

Podgorski recoiled slightly, feigning shock. 'Oh, so it speaks, does it?'

Jones held his gaze but remained silent.

'So again, where were you on Wednesday night?' Phillips continued.

He shrugged his heavy shoulders. 'Dunno off the top of my head.'

'Well, could you perhaps have a think?'

Podgorski took a moment and appeared deep in thought as he stared back at Phillips. 'Playing poker with the boys.'

'I see. And where was that?' she asked.

'The Comrades Club.'

'Which is where, exactly?'

'Cheetham Hill,' he replied.

'And can anyone vouch for you?'

He nodded. 'Everyone at the table.'

'We're going to need names,' said Jones, pulling out his notepad and pen.

Podgorski let out an audible sigh before sitting forward in his chair. 'Alex Vasilyev, Matvey Petrov and Daniil Lebedev.'

Jones scribbled them down.

'We'll need their phone numbers too,' added Phillips.

'Really? I'm a busy man, Chief Inspector. I've got things to do.'

'And we appreciate all your help,' said Phillips without feeling.

Podgorski opened his phone, then took a moment to dictate the numbers of his three alibis.

Jones scribbled furiously in his pad once more.

'Anything else I can do?' Podgorski asked eventually.

'I think we have everything for now,' replied Phillips.

'Well, like I say, I'm a busy man.' Podgorski checked his watch. 'I need to be getting on.'

Phillips turned to glance out the window. 'Yeah. Your boys look like they're rushed off their feet out there.'

'I'm expecting the post-lunch rush any minute now.' Podgorski produced a wide grin as he reclined in his chair once more.

'Of course you are,' said Phillips before turning and heading for the door. 'We'll be seeing you, Mr Podgorski.'

'Not if I see you first,' he shot back with a chuckle.

Outside and out of earshot, Phillips and Jones debriefed.

'Well, he's a piece of work,' Phillips said as she dropped into the passenger seat of the squad car.

'Yeah,' replied Jones. 'But he's also not the wig guy from the club either. I mean, he's twice the size of the fella we're looking for.'

'True, but as we know from bitter experience, these gang bosses rarely do the dirty work when it comes to dishing out punishment.'

'You thinking the wig guy could be one of his crew?'

'Maybe.'

'And what about his alibis? They could be an issue, guv.'

'A bunch of his gang mates?' she scoffed. 'Hardly cast iron.'

'True, but as long as there's reasonable doubt, he's pretty much in the clear as far as the CPS will be concerned.'

Phillips remained silent for a moment as she cast her gaze back to the Portakabin. Jones was right, getting the CPS – or Crown Prosecution Service – to consider charges without hard evidence to counter the claims of three alibis would be nigh on impossible. She sighed. 'No doubt he'll be on the phone to each of them in turn, getting their story straight, but check them out anyway.'

'Will do.'

'And in the meantime, I'll get Whistler to do a full background check on Mr Podgorski. See what skeletons he can find.'

Jones fired the engine. 'Well, if anyone can, Whistler can.'

10

B ack at Ashton House, Phillips and Jones updated the team on their meeting with Podgorski and his apparent alibis for the time of the fire, which Whistler and Bov were tasked with verifying. She also ordered a full background check on Podgorski himself, as well as all known members of the Road Czars, in case any of them were a potential physical match for the wig guy. With all that in train, she headed for her office, where she spent what remained of the afternoon catching up on the decision logs for the case, as well as a raft of other paperwork she'd fallen behind on. It was her least favourite thing about the job, but in modern policing, where every detail could be scrutinised by a defence barrister in court, sadly a necessary evil.

After the rest of the team had drifted off one by one for the weekend and the time approached 7 p.m., she decided to call it a night herself. Adam would be waiting for her when she got home, and she was looking forward to a rare weekend off together. Thanks to his new job as a doctor with

HEMS – Helicopter Emergency Medical Service – coupled with her recent spate of weekend shifts as on-call senior investigating officer, aka SIO, they'd spent precious little time together of late. And so, after packing up her things, she switched out the lights and headed for the carpark where her Mini Cooper was waiting to whisk her home.

The journey from Ashton House to the boho suburb of Chorlton took just over thirty minutes, and it was approaching 7.45 by the time she pulled the car onto her drive, parking it next to Adam's pride and joy, a red Jaguar F-Type. A minute later she opened the front door, where she was met by her cat, Floss, who snaked around her ankles, purring loudly as she did. Reaching down, Phillips scooped the cream Ragdoll up and carried her into the kitchen, where she found Adam sitting on a high stool at the island. The TV on the wall to his left was playing at a low volume, but he didn't appear to be watching it. Instead, his eyes were fixed to the phone in his hand.

'Hey, babe,' she said as she wandered into the large open-plan space.

He looked up immediately and smiled. 'Hiya.'

'You okay?' she asked.

He nodded enthusiastically. 'I was out with Tony today, and we had such a good laugh.'

The Tony he was referring to was one of the helicopter pilots who flew Adam and the rest of the HEMS team to serious emergencies across the northwest of England. As Phillips was now only too aware – mainly because it was all Adam could talk about at the moment – different pilots worked different shifts, so he wasn't always paired with the same people. Tony, however, was Adam's favourite flyer because of his previous experience as a pilot in the army, and his love of flying low and fast through the hills and valleys that surrounded the cities of Manchester and Liverpool.

'You should have seen how low we got flying over Lady-bower Reservoir. It was brilliant. I felt like I was in *Airwolf*.' He was of course referring to the hit eighties TV show about a supersonic helicopter captained by a rogue pilot.

Phillips nodded without feeling as she placed Floss back on the floor. As happy as she was to see Adam enjoying his work again, she was getting a little tired of him talking about it constantly.

'How was your day?' he asked eventually.

'Frustrating,' she said as she opened the fridge and pulled out a bottle of Pinot Grigio. 'We seem to be getting nowhere fast with this firebomb attack, and as ever, Fox is getting restless.'

'I thought she was in the States?'

'She is,' replied Phillips as she grabbed a glass and poured herself a large measure. 'Carter and I had the plea-sure of being berated on a Zoom call from her hotel room.'

'Sounds like fun.'

Phillips nodded as she took a mouthful of the ice-cold wine, which tasted like nectar on her palate. 'I'm just glad we've got a couple of days off to try to forget about work for a change.'

Adam winced slightly. 'Erm, about that...'

Phillips placed the glass down on the island. 'Please don't say what I think you're about to say.'

'Look, I'm sorry, but Jonny asked if I could fill in for Dom tomorrow and Sunday, and I couldn't say no.'

Jonny was Adam's new boss.

'Oh, for God's sake, Adam. This is the first weekend we've had off in at least a month.'

'I know it is, but I'm the new boy. I have to show willing.'

'By working every weekend? This'll be the fourth in a row.'

'That's the job, babe,' he shot back. 'Shit doesn't suddenly stop happening on a Friday night. You should know that better than anyone.'

'I do! But it doesn't stop me being pissed off that I'll be spending the weekend with just the cat for company.'

'It's not as if we had plans, is it?' Adam shrugged. 'I mean, we were only going to be hanging round the house.'

'Which is exactly what I was looking forward to doing after the week I've had.'

Adam threw his arms in the air. 'Right,' he exclaimed petulantly. 'If me working an extra shift in my new job is such a problem for you, I'll call Jonny and tell him I can't do it.'

'Oh, spare me the drama,' said Phillips as she grabbed the wine bottle in one hand and picked up her glass in the other. 'You're not putting this on me,' she added as she turned and began walking away.

'Where are you going? I thought we could head down to the Jockey for a couple of drinks.'

'You can go where you like,' she replied without looking back. 'I'm going for a hot bath and an early night.'

fter an early morning trip to the DIY superstore to collect supplies – paid for in cash, of course – he wandered slowly home, taking in the world around him. He'd never been one for lying in bed on a Saturday morning, even when he had the rare opportunity to do so, and it always amazed him how many people in the world preferred to sleep until lunchtime, as opposed to making the most of the day. What a waste of precious time.

As soon as he arrived back at the flat just after 9 a.m., he made a cup of sweet tea and rolled himself several cigarettes to smoke at his leisure, before settling down at the kitchen table ready to work. Connecting the Bluetooth speaker to his phone, he hit the play icon on-screen, and the distinctive opening chords of 'Firestarter' by the Prodigy boomed through the air as he lit the cigarette now perched between his lips. *Bliss.*

As he worked away constructing the small incendiary device, the song continued to play on loop. Cranking up the volume as far as it would go, he continued to be impressed with just how much noise the little speaker could make. It had been a sound investment, he thought, then chuckled to himself. 'No pun intended.'

Just then, what sounded like a loud knock coming from the direction of the front door drew his attention. Stopping what he was doing, he remained motionless for a moment as the music continued to boom around him. He heard another knock, louder this time. It was definitely coming from the front door. He shrugged his shoulders and got back to work, but a second later, the banging started again, and this time it continued unabated.

'Fuck's sake,' he muttered as he stubbed out his latest cigarette before covering his work with a tea towel. Then, after jumping up from the chair, he strode towards the front door and the source of the banging.

'I know you're in there!' he heard someone shout from the other side of the door.

Yanking it open, he came face to face with a tall, muscular man with bright red hair, whom he recognised as one of his neighbours. Despite living next to him for the last two months, they had never spoken.

'Turn that bloody racket down, will ya?' the big man growled in his nasally Mancunian accent over the music, his nostrils flaring.

'Why?' he asked, glaring back.

'Because it's fucking early, and I'm trying to sleep.'

He felt his brow furrow. 'It's *ten* o'clock.'

'Exactly, and I only got to bed a few hours ago,' the big man replied. 'So turn it down!'

'No,' he said, folding his arms across his chest.

The big man took a step forward, towering over him now. 'Turn that fucking music down or—'

'Or what?' he spat back.

The big man leaned closer so their faces were level. 'Or I'll smash your fucking head in, you little shit.'

Holding the Neanderthal's gaze, he took a moment to respond. 'I'll tell you what I'm gonna do, shall I?' He thumbed over his shoulder. 'I'm gonna go back in there, carry on what I was doing, and keep listening to whatever the bloody hell I like, as loud as I like. And do you know what *you're* gonna do?'

A snarl formed on the big man's top lip.

He didn't wait for a reply. 'You're gonna piss off back to your flat and stay the fuck out of my way.'

'Oh, I am, am I?' The big man's eyes bulged as rage oozed from every pore.

'Yeah, you are. Because if you don't, tonight, when you and your missus are sound asleep, I'll pour a gallon of petrol through your letter box. And then I'll use this' – he pulled the Zippo from his pocket and held it in front of the man's face before firing up the flame – 'to set you pair o' cunts on fire.'

The big man raised his eyebrows as he straightened and took a step back.

Seeing this quite violent reaction made him chuckle, and as the chorus of the song boomed out behind him, he began to sing along at the top of his voice, 'I'm a firestarter, twisted firestarter!' All the time glaring at his opponent and waving the lighter back and forth.

'You're bloody nuts, you are,' the man mumbled before turning on his heel and heading back along the walkway towards his open door.

He waited until his unwanted guest had disappeared out of sight, then stepped back inside and closed his own door behind him before wandering back towards the kitchen, singing at the top of his voice as he did. 'I'm a firestarter, twisted firestarter!'

12

By 7 a.m. Monday morning, Phillips was already at her desk, keen to get a head start on the week ahead.

It was an hour later when Jones appeared at her open door carrying two steaming cardboard cups. 'Morning, guv,' he said as he placed her black coffee on the desk in front of her. 'Good weekend?'

'Not really,' she replied flatly as she reached across and grabbed her cup.

'Oh dear.' Jones took a seat opposite. 'Trouble in paradise?'

Removing the lid, she took a tentative sip. 'Don't ask.'

'Like that, is it?' He chuckled.

'Thanks for this, by the way,' she replied, ignoring the question. 'How about you? How was yours?'

Jones crossed his left ankle over his right knee as he took a mouthful of his favourite, peppermint tea. 'Uneventful to say the least. I spent most of it being dad's taxi to the girls.'

'The joys of teenage daughters, huh?'

Jones blew through his lips. 'Tell me about it. If they're not emptying my bank account, they're draining my petrol tank. They're a blooming nightmare.'

Just then Entwistle and Bovalino walked past Phillips's open door in unison as they headed for their desks in the main office.

Phillips nodded in their direction as she stood up from the chair. 'Let's see what the troops have been up to, shall we? Hopefully they've had better luck than the pair of us this weekend.'

Jones matched her. 'Can't have been any worse,' he said as he followed her out.

'Nice weekend, guys?' asked Phillips as she approached their desks.

Entwistle flashed a knowing grin. 'You could say that.'

'Another hot date, was it?' said Jones.

'Something like that,' Entwistle replied.

Phillips shook her head. 'MCU's very own Casanova.' She turned her attention to Bov now. 'How about you? Did you do anything of note?'

If Bovalino was listening, it didn't show, and he appeared lost in his own thoughts as he stared down at his phone.

'*Hello?*' said Phillips loudly. 'Anybody home?'

Still no response.

'Bov!' added Jones.

'What?' The big man suddenly looked up, his brow furrowed. 'Sorry, I was miles away.'

Phillips laughed softly. 'So we can see. I was asking if you had a good weekend.'

'Er, yeah,' Bovalino replied without conviction.

'Well, I'd hate to see you after a bad one,' said Jones sardonically as he took a seat.

Phillips dropped into the chair at the spare desk, and a moment later, with everyone now paying full attention, got down to the business of the day – keen to know if the guys had come up with anything of value she could share with Carter and Fox.

Bov was first up as he passed across a series of black-and-white printouts, narrating what Phillips was looking at as he did. 'These are stills from the council CCTV cameras that came through on Friday afternoon. I've managed to track the wig guy from outside the club to Wythenshawe park and gardens about half a mile away, where sadly he disappeared into the trees.'

'Can you pinpoint where he went in?' Phillips asked.

'Yeah. It's an entrance used a lot by dog walkers near Baguley Brook Bridge.'

'Great. Let's get a uniform team down there and see if they can find any souvenirs he may have left behind.'

'Sure thing. I'll do it now.'

'And get in touch with the bus companies that run the routes in that area. Let's see if we can find him on any of their services within a two-hour timeframe of him leaving the club.'

Bovalino nodded as he made a note in his pad.

Phillips continued, 'I know the fact he was wearing a wig and a beanie hat doesn't help, but get in touch with DCI Flannery. See if they can find a match for him on their facial-recognition software.' Flannery was a senior detective in the counter-terrorism unit and, based on the work they'd done together previously, a man of infinite resources.

'Will he be all right with that?' asked Bov. 'It's not as if we're working together on this one, guv.'

'He'll be fine.' Phillips waved him away. 'One team, one

dream,' she added as she turned her focus to Entwistle. 'Where are we at with the Maxim Podgorski alibis?'

'They're first on my list this morning, boss,' he replied.

'And don't forget we also need a full background on the man himself as well as anything you can find on the Road Czars gang, too.'

'They're on my list.'

'Good stuff. Sounds like we're making some headway.' Phillips drummed her fingers on the desk in front of her. 'Fox is back from the States in three days and expecting progress, which means we have lots to do, guys. So let's get on with it, shall we?'

A chorus of 'yes, guv' filled the air, matched with a flurry of nodding heads.

Pushing back the chair with her legs, Phillips stood now. 'Speaking of which, I'd better get upstairs and update Carter,' she said before turning and making her way towards the door.

13

Wearing a hi-vis waistcoat over a set of blue overalls with a matching cap to help hide his face from any CCTV, he strode confidently through the front doors of tonight's venue, carrying his large canvas tool bag in his right hand. The pub in question – the George and Dragon – was located in the Hazel Grove area, about five miles south of the city. With the fake ID he'd created hanging loosely on a lanyard around his neck, he made his way to the function room bar, where he spotted a petite, dark-haired woman he placed in her mid-twenties, restocking the fridges.

'Where's your gas shut-off valve, love?' he asked cheerfully.

She turned to face him, exposing the name badge on her chest, which suggested she was called Rose. 'You what?'

'Your gas shut-off valve. Someone's reported smelling gas.' He lifted the tool bag above the bar level so she could see it, then smiled. 'I need to do a full diagnostic on your system.'

Rose's eyes widened; her face suddenly filled with panic. 'How long will that take? I've got a hundred and fifty thirsty coppers landing here at seven.'

'Depends what I find,' he said as he checked his watch. 'If there's no leak, then hopefully no longer than half an hour. If that's the case, I'll be out of your hair by six.'

'And what if there *is* a leak?' Rose asked.

'Well, that's a whole different story.'

'Jesus, that's all I need.' Moving briskly along the bar, she stepped out through the hatch. 'Come with me,' she added, her tone urgent.

Falling in behind her as Rose walked at pace, he followed her along the corridor and in through a door marked 'Staff Only'.

Once inside, she moved quickly across the small room, past a battered old desk and decrepit office chair, and yanked open a thick cupboard door located in the far wall. 'It's in here.'

He fixed his gaze on the large metal handle attached to the gas valve. 'That's the one. I can take it from here, luv.'

'Good,' said Rose before heading for the door, 'cos I'm way behind as it is.'

Alone now in the heart of the pub, he allowed himself a smile. 'It's too easy,' he muttered as he pulled out the old chair and took a seat. Closing his eyes, he breathed deeply and began to visualise what lay ahead.

Fifteen minutes later, he picked up his tool kit and headed back to the function room, where Rose was now setting up a long table against the wall on the far side of the room that he assumed would carry tonight's buffet.

'Looks like there's nothing to worry about,' he said as he approached.

She turned and let out an audible sigh of relief. 'Oh, thank God.'

'I'll need to check a few of your ventilation points in here before I sign you off though,' he added. 'Just to make sure you've got a good flow of air moving through the building.'

'Yeah, sure, whatever,' Rose replied without conviction before turning her attention back to the buffet table.

According to the Facebook posts he'd seen advertising tonight's event – a fundraiser for a charity that rehouses police dogs – there would be a local DJ as part of the entertainment, a man by the name of Carl C. Making his way to the small stage that would most likely house Carl along with his decks and speakers, he dropped to his knees and opened the tool bag. Checking over his shoulder and happy he wasn't being watched, he pushed the change of clothes to one side of the bag, then located the small device. With another furtive glance over his shoulder and confident Rose was none the wiser to his movements, he pulled it out and positioned it out of sight where it was unlikely to be discovered behind a thick pair of curtains attached to the wall. Next, he pulled out a can of BBQ firestarter spray before surreptitiously giving the carpet and curtains around the small stage a good covering in the accelerant. With everything in place, he zipped up the tool bag and got back to his feet. Next, holding a yellow digital voltmeter in his hand, he walked casually around the room.

'Everything all right?' Rose asked as he moved past the buffet table.

He gave her a flash of the voltmeter, but not enough so she could actually see what it was. 'Just checking the atmospheric pressure in the room,' he lied, confident she was unlikely to have any idea what he was talking about.

Her blank expression confirmed his suspicions.

'Won't be long,' he added as he made his way over to the fire exit close by, where he made a mental note of the colour of the large emergency release handles fixed to the middle of each door; *black*, just as he had hoped. Turning back into the room, he smiled. 'That's me done, luv. All good.'

Rose's posture physically softened. 'Brilliant. That's such a relief.'

'I'll be away, then,' he said as he set off towards the door. 'And good luck for this evening. Hope it all goes well.'

'Yeah, should be a big night,' she replied before going back to her current task in hand.

'You have no idea,' he whispered to himself as he strode out of the room.

———

To pass the time over the next few hours, he headed to another pub nearby, the Black Horse, where he treated himself to steak and chips, washed down with a couple of pints of bottomless Coke. When he was finished, and feeling thoroughly satisfied, he picked up the tool bag and headed for the disabled toilet located at the rear of the pub. Once inside, he removed his overalls, the hi-vis waistcoat and blue cap, then pulled a hooded sweatshirt and a pair of jeans from the tool bag and quickly got changed. As a final touch, he slipped on a black New York Yankees cap, which was fitted with a flat, oversized brim. After checking his reflection in the mirror, he felt satisfied he would not immediately be recognised by Rose if he bumped into her again later. And given the fact she was expecting to cater for a hundred and fifty people at the event tonight, it seemed highly unlikely she'd have time to worry about anyone other than the people standing in the queue for the bar.

A few seconds later, with his fake gas-man outfit packed away in the bag, he unlocked the toilet door and, keeping his head low, marched to the exit.

After making the short walk back up the hill to the George and Dragon, he arrived at the pub just after eight. Standing across from the venue now, he took a few steps back into the shadows of the overhanging trees and dropped to his knees before unzipping the tool bag. Despite his darkened position, he found the cable ties in just a few seconds, which he transferred to the front pocket of his jeans. Then, after ensuring no one was watching, he hid the bag in the thick shadow of the large oak tree he was kneeling next to and got back to his feet. Then, with his head down and the brim of his cap covering his eyes, he headed for the main door of the pub and back to the function room. As he moved closer, he could see the party was already in full flow, the room filled to the brim and in stark contrast to the empty space he'd left behind just a couple of hours ago.

Slipping inside, he walked quickly past a small table that had been placed en route to the bar, upon which sat a host of raffle prizes, including a food hamper, a signed football shirt donated by Stockport County FC, a large teddy bear wearing a kilt and sporran, along with a host of other smaller items people could win, all for the price of a £5 raffle ticket. Careful not to make eye contact with the two older ladies staffing the table, he moved deeper into the room.

He soon found the perfect spot in a darkened corner, where he dropped into an empty chair next to an equally empty table. Scanning the space now, his eyes narrowed as his gaze moved from person to person, each having what appeared to be a lovely time at their precious fundraiser, and each blissfully unaware of what was about to unfold in the next thirty minutes. He felt a rush of adrenaline as he imagined the changes in their expressions once they realised what was happening. He was going to enjoy this.

Unsurprisingly for a police fundraiser, the bar itself was packed with people desperate to drink as much as they could, all in the name of raising money for charity.

'Pah,' he muttered to himself. 'They couldn't give a monkey's about bloody police dogs. All they want to do is get shit-faced.'

Right on cue, a long-legged young woman with an ample bosom, which had been packed into a *very* low-cut top, and looking a little worse for wear, took a tumble on the dance floor, shrieking as she went down. This was closely followed by raucous laughter as she found herself sitting on her backside on the ground, surrounded by what appeared to be her equally inebriated friends, all standing over her, laughing heartily at her misfortune. Quick as a flash, a flurry of burly men with chests sticking out like peacocks appeared from all sides, rushing to her aid, fussing around her as they jostled for her attention.

He couldn't have planned a better distraction if he'd tried, and he was up from the chair without missing a beat, pulling the cable ties from his pocket as he walked. A few seconds later with everyone in the room seemingly focused on the melee on the dance floor – or with their eyes locked on the bar as they waited impatiently to recharge their glasses – he strode towards the fire door. A second later and in one fluid movement he locked the black plastic ties securely in place across both handles, rendering the doors impenetrable without some form of time-consuming intervention.

He quickly turned back to the room and was relieved to see not a single person was paying him the slightest bit of attention. With his adrenaline spiking now, he took a couple of deep silent breaths, then set off in the direction of the stage, where the DJ was touching his fingers to his right headphone and nodding his head to the beat, totally lost in the moment. *Perfect.*

Knowing enough about forensics, and not wanting to leave any trace evidence behind, he had swapped his Zippo lighter for a small box of matches, which he pulled from his jeans pocket now. Without stopping or slowing his pace, he opened the box and picked out a single match, striking it a split second later. Then, as nonchalantly as he could, he tossed it in the direction of the accelerant-soaked curtains just a few feet away with the tiny incendiary device hidden beyond them.

Despite the fact music was booming out through the nearby speakers, he swore he could hear the unmistakable *whoosh* he'd come to know and love as the match landed and the fire instantly burst into life. Glancing over his shoulder, he smiled seeing the glorious glow that had appeared as the flames greedily took hold. It was time to leave.

With his head down and the cap pulled low over his brow, he marched quickly in the direction of the main exit. By the time he passed the raffle table for the second time tonight, much to his delight, he could already hear the sound of panic filling the air behind him as the fire began to spread. Moving through the double doors at the entrance to the function room, he pulled them closed behind him before quickly locking the handles together with a second set of cable ties. Then, after one last look through the glass at the chaos now erupting on the other side, he left the building.

A minute later he once again bent down in the shadows as he retrieved his tool bag from the side of the oak tree before straightening and turning back towards the pub to admire his handiwork. By now, the partygoers had evidently realised they were trapped inside, and their terror-filled screams and shouts punctuated the sound of music still bleeding out from the fundraiser.

Pulling his phone from his pocket, he opened the video app and pressed record, relishing the rush of excitement coursing through his veins as a window smashed from the inside out and smoke began billowing from within, the screams and shouts instantly louder now.

A broad grin spread across his face. Everything had gone just as he'd planned, and now the police were suitably distracted, it was time to hunt down the real target.

14

With Adam working the night shift, Phillips once again found herself alone for the evening, and as the opening titles of the eleven o'clock news boomed out from the TV, she found she was struggling to keep her eyes open as she lay on the couch with Floss already fast asleep on her lap. The raging heat from the open fire was making the skin on her cheeks feel tight, and the two glasses of wine she'd demolished earlier, along with a bowl of pasta, were starting to take their toll. She felt so comfortable and relaxed for the first time in ages, she was tempted to let sleep envelop her.

Just then her phone burst into life, instantly jolting her from her slumber and causing Floss to wake up and jump down onto the floor. Sitting up, she grabbed the phone, and her heart sank as she spotted Jones's name on-screen; it was unlikely to be good news at this time of night.

'Jonesy,' she said, trying to hide the fact she still felt half asleep but failing miserably.

'Sorry, guv. Were you in bed?'

'No, no, just dozing on the couch. What's up?'

'There's been another arson attack.'

Phillips sat to attention now. 'Where?'

'The George and Dragon in Hazel Grove.'

'Were the targets cops again?'

'Yeah. Looks like it was a police fundraiser of some sort.'

'Any fatalities?' she asked, fearing the worst.

'We're not sure at this stage, but the place was packed, and it sounds like the firefighters and paramedics are dealing with a lot of serious injuries on scene.'

'Shit.' She checked her watch. 'I've had a drink, so I'll need to get a taxi over.'

'Don't be daft,' Jones replied. 'I'll come and get you.'

'But that's taking you right out of your way.'

'It's not a problem, guv. I'll be with you in twenty minutes.'

'Cheers, Jonesy, I'll see you then,' she said, then ended the call.

THEY ARRIVED at the George and Dragon just before midnight and were confronted by a scene reminiscent of a Hollywood disaster movie, with fire trucks and ambulances, plus a host of emergency service workers, littering the street outside the now-smouldering function room, the sky blue from flashing lights. Mercifully, the section of the building that housed the main pub had been saved from the effects of the fire, but the function room to the side was a mass of blackened timber roof joists and charcoal-covered brick-work, a mixture of steam and smoke rising into the night.

After passing under the blue and white police cordon,

Phillips and Jones approached the firefighter who appeared to be in charge.

Phillips presented her ID. 'DCI Phillips and DI Jones from Major Crimes.'

'Watch Manager Billy Dunn,' he replied.

'Any ideas how or where it started?' said Phillips.

'As far as *how,* it's too early to say, but in regard to *where,* my best guess at the moment is around the stage area. That's where the fire damage seems to be worst and would indicate the point of ignition.'

'Was it set deliberately?' Jones cut in.

'Certainly looks that way,' replied Dunn. 'And you should know the only fire exit in the room had been cable-tied shut.'

'Could that be an oversight by the staff?' Jones continued. 'Being overcautious around security?'

Dunn shook his head. 'I doubt it, given the fact the same thing had been done to the entrance doors to the room once the place was set alight.'

'Bloody hell,' muttered Phillips.

'So, sadly, it looks like another deliberate attack on the police,' added Dunn.

'You heard about Wythenshawe, then?' she asked.

'Who hasn't?' he replied.

Phillips glanced at the blackened building and then back to Dunn. 'Any fatalities?'

He nodded sombrely. 'An elderly woman, died in the ambulance from the effects of smoke inhalation before the paramedics had even left for the hospital.'

Jones pulled out his notebook. 'Do you know her name?'

'No, sorry, your uniformed teams were dealing with that.'

'So when will it be safe to get forensics in?' said Phillips.

'Should be fine by the morning,' Dunn replied. 'As long as there's no danger of what's left of the structure collapsing, that is.'

Phillips exhaled sharply. 'Okay, thanks.'

A few minutes later, as they stood next to one of several ambulances, the police officer in charge of the scene, Sergeant Brooks, debriefed them on events so far. 'A hundred-plus guests from what we know, ma'am, attending a charity do to raise funds to help rehouse retired police dogs. As it stands, twenty have been taken to A&E at Wythenshawe Hospital, five directly to the burns unit there, and sadly one lady passed away in the ambulance before we could move her.'

'Can you give us her details?' Phillips asked.

'Violet Williams, aged seventy-one. She was a part-time cleaner at the local nick, apparently.'

'Address?'

Brooks glanced down at his notebook. 'Forty-seven Rowntree Lane, Hazel Grove. It's just round the corner.'

Jones scribbled in his pad. 'Any idea on next of kin?'

'According to the electoral roll, looks like she lives with her daughter, Esther Williams.'

'Has anyone spoken to her?' Phillips asked.

'Not yet, we were just about to head over there now.'

'We can go,' she said. 'Seeing as there's nothing else we can do here until the building is secure.'

'If you're sure?' said Brooks.

'Yeah, I'm sure,' she replied as she turned and headed back to the car.

FIFTEEN MINUTES LATER, Phillips rapped her knuckles on the front door of the small semi-detached house located on the very quiet Rowntree Lane. Even with the curtains to the front room closed, it was evident that someone on the other side was watching television. A few seconds later the hall light flicked on before the lock was released, and the front door was opened by a tall, auburn-haired woman wearing a dressing gown, pyjamas and slippers. It was hard to say for sure in the relatively low light, but Phillips put her age at around fifty.

'Can I help you?' she asked, her brow furrowed.

'Esther Williams?' said Phillips, flashing her credentials. 'DCI Phillips and DI Jones. Is your mother Violet Williams?'

Esther's eyes widened now. 'Yes. Oh God. Has something happened to her?'

'It'd be better if we can talk inside,' Phillips replied softly.

'Okay.' Esther swallowed hard, then nodded and opened the door wide before heading back inside.

Phillips stepped in first with Jones at her back as they followed Esther through the first door on the right into the small living room.

Esther muted the TV but remained standing as she turned to face them, fear etched on her face.

'Please, take a seat,' said Phillips.

Esther did as asked and dropped tentatively into the armchair to her right.

Phillips and Jones sat down next to each other on the sofa opposite her, a glass coffee table between them.

'What's happened?' Esther's tone was desperate now.

'Did your mother attend an event at the George and Dragon pub this evening?' asked Phillips.

'Yes.'

Phillips took a silent breath, knowing the impact of what she was about to say. 'The function suite of the George and Dragon pub was severely damaged by fire earlier this evening, and I'm sorry to tell you that your mother died as a result of the injuries she sustained in that fire.'

'Oh my God.' Esther touched the fingers of her right hand to her open mouth, blinking furiously as she began shaking her head from side to side. 'No. No, that can't be true.'

'I'm afraid there was nothing the paramedics could do,' said Phillips softly.

Esther stared into space for a long moment before suddenly bursting into tears.

Phillips glanced at Jones, who instinctively knew what to do, jumping up from the chair and grabbing a box of tissues from the mantlepiece above the fireplace, which he handed straight to Esther.

He had remained standing. 'I'll make us some hot sweet tea,' he said before leaving the room.

For the next minute or so, Phillips sat silently, allowing Esther's tears to flow, knowing from experience it was the best thing for her in that moment and that nothing she could say would be of comfort to the woman.

'Here we are,' said Jones a few minutes later as he returned carrying a tray of hot drinks, which he handed out before retaking his seat.

Esther wiped her nose with a tissue. 'Can you tell me what happened?'

'We're not sure at this stage,' said Phillips.

'How did the fire start?'

'I'm afraid we won't know for certain until the fire investigation team have had a proper look at the scene.'

'Mum told me about the fire in Wythenshawe last week,' said Esther. 'It was big news down at the station, apparently. Was this the same sort of thing? Arson?'

'We'll be following all lines of enquiry.'

With Fox's orders ringing in her ears regarding limiting any hyperbole around the fire setter targeting cops specifically, she changed the subject. 'We've been told your mum was a cleaner at Hazel Grove police station, is that right?'

Esther nodded as she wiped her nose on the tissue again. 'Been there for almost twenty years, now. She loves it—' Esther caught herself in the moment. 'Sorry, *loved* it.'

'And was that why she was in attendance this evening, at the charity event?'

'Yes. She didn't get out much and so was really looking forward to going. She told me she was involved with the raffle tonight, either collecting money or giving out the prizes to the winners. I can't remember which it was, but she was excited about the whole thing, whatever it was she was doing.'

Phillips nodded softly as she placed her drink down on the coffee table. 'Look, I know this is the last thing you'll want to do, but we're going to need someone to officially identify your mum.'

A tear streaked down Esther's cheek.

'Would you be able to do that for us?'

'Yes.'

'Thank you,' said Phillips. 'One of our family liaison officers will be in touch tomorrow to organise a time and transport.'

Esther's bottom lip trembled. 'Okay.'

Phillips's heart went out to her. No matter how many times she'd broken this kind of news, it had never gotten any easier. 'Is there anyone else you'd like us to talk to about what's happened?' she asked. 'Any siblings or close relatives?'

'No.' Esther's shoulders sagged. 'Since Dad died a few years ago, it's just been the two of us.'

'Well, is there anyone who can come and stay with you tonight?' asked Jones. 'You've had an awful shock; you really shouldn't be on your own.'

'My cousin, Liz, lives down the street,' Esther replied. 'I can probably call her.'

'Or we can call her if you'd prefer?' said Phillips.

'No, it's fine.' Esther shook her head. 'I'll do it once you've gone.'

Phillips pulled a business card from her coat pocket and handed it across. 'If you need anything, or if we can help in any way, please call the family liaison team, day or night.'

'Thank you,' said Esther, returning her smile.

'We'll be on our way now,' Phillips said as gently as she could as she got up from the chair – Jones following suit a second later. 'We'll see ourselves out.'

Just as they reached the door to the lounge, Esther called after them.

'If it was deliberate, what kind of monster would set a fire at a charity event, Inspector?'

'I don't know.' Phillips turned to face her. 'I really don't know.'

15

The following morning Phillips paid a visit to Carter's office to debrief him on the events of the previous evening.

'So we're looking at a second arson attack inside a week?' Worry was etched on his forehead as he sat forward in his leather chair before resting his elbows on the desk.

'Looks that way, sir,' she replied.

'Was it the same guy?'

'Too early to say for certain, but if I were a gambler, I'd have to say yes. We'll have a clearer idea once we get hold of CCTV from the venue and surrounding council cameras.'

'Any eyewitnesses?'

'Uniform are working through witness statements as we speak. There were over a hundred people in that room last night, so it's taking a bit of time to get through them all, but from the few reports I saw briefly this morning, nobody saw anyone in particular who stood out. Probably because there were so many people in the room.'

'What about forensics?' he asked.

'The fire crew gave them the green light to go in just after dawn, once they were sure the building wasn't going to fall in on top of them. I'll be heading down to the site later this morning to see if they've managed to find anything yet.'

'I understand the woman who died worked at Hazel Grove nick.'

'Yes, sir. Violet Williams. She was a cleaner over there.'

'Poor thing,' he muttered, shaking his head. 'This is a bad business, Jane.'

'I know, sir, and I wish I had better news with regard to leads, but I'm afraid we don't have anything concrete.'

'What about the biker gang guy?'

'Podgorski? I'm hoping for an update in the team meeting straight after this, but he seemed pretty confident in his alibis for the first fire.'

Carter exhaled heavily. 'Fox flies back this afternoon. No doubt she'll be back in the office tomorrow, demanding answers.'

'I know, and I'm dreading it. I have to admit, sir, it's been a lot easier doing this job without her around. A lot less stressful to say the least.'

'I have to agree,' he replied. 'That said, she's never really been too far away thanks to the wonders of modern tech. I had the pleasure of a second Zoom call in the early hours of this morning to brief her on the second fire.'

'Oh, God. How did that go?'

'Better you don't ask, Jane.'

Phillips shifted in her seat. 'I know I'm probably clutching at straws here, sir, but as she's been in the job for such a long time, is there any hope she might retire soon? I mean, she must have an enormous pension.'

Carter sighed. 'No doubt, but it's not about the money

with Fox. It's the job itself that drives her; what matters is being the top dog – and I can't see her giving that up anytime soon. In fact' – he chuckled – 'I suspect the only way she's leaving this office is in a box.'

'Or in handcuffs.' The words came out before Phillips could stop them.

He didn't react.

'Sorry, sir. I shouldn't have said that.'

Carter sat back. 'Look, Jane, I understand how hard it is for you taking orders from her knowing that she hasn't always played with a straight bat – and believe me, I struggle with it myself at times – but unless we can come up with proof that she ordered Entwistle to get rid of the sex-party videos we found at Duval's house, we're stuck with her.'

'That's just it, sir. No matter how hard we look, we can't find *anything*. Apart from Whistler's admission that she forced him to hand over those tapes, we've got diddly squat.' Phillips sighed. 'Are you sure it's not worth talking to the PCC about it? Especially given the fact that Entwistle is willing to go on record to say she essentially blackmailed him into destroying vital evidence? Evidence that could well have implicated her in Todd and Venables's dodgy dealings?'

'I'm afraid not,' said Carter. 'Without concrete proof that she interfered with the chain of evidence in the Crowther case, Fox would simply deny it. It'd be the word of a highly decorated chief constable with thirty years on the job, versus a detective constable with less than five. And we both know how that would go.'

Phillips shook her head in frustration. 'It makes me so angry, sir. Especially given the rumours that she's likely been bending the rules to suit herself for most of her career.'

'I know, and I get it, Jane, I really do, but like I say, we need the evidence to prove it. If we can find that, then trust me, I'll take it to the Home Secretary myself if I have to.'

Phillips nodded in silence.

Carter continued, 'But for now, and for the sake of your own sanity, do yourself a favour and put Fox's past indiscretions to the back of your mind. We need to focus on catching this fire setter before he strikes again.'

'Of course, sir.' Phillips offered a faint smile. 'You're right; believe me when I say it has my full attention.'

'Never in doubt,' he replied.

'If there's nothing else, I'll get back down to the team.'

'I think we've covered everything.'

She stepped up from the chair. 'I'll let you know as soon as we have something of value.'

'I know you will, Jane. And remember, it works both ways. I'm here if you need anything too.'

'Thank you, sir,' she replied before striding out of the room.

16

By the time Phillips marched into the main office, it was approaching 9.30 a.m. As she approached Jones and Entwistle, both of whom appeared hard at work – their eyes locked on their computer screens – she noted the empty chair at Bovalino's desk.

'Where's the big fella?' she asked.

Jones looked up. 'No idea. He's not come in yet.'

Phillips frowned. 'That's not like him.'

Jones glanced at his watch. 'God, is it half past nine? I'd totally lost track of time.'

Just then the door opened heavily behind her.

'Here he is,' said Entwistle.

Phillips turned to see a flustered Bovalino rushing towards her, his face red and sweating, a shirt tail hanging over his belt buckle.

'Sorry I'm late, guv,' he said, sounding harassed. 'I got stuck in traffic.'

'Well, that's a first for you, big man,' said Jones with a grin.

It was widely known that Bovalino knew every back road and shortcut in the city, and if anyone could get through rush hour without delay, it was him.

Phillips sat down at the spare desk and watched on in silence for a moment as he took his seat opposite and readied himself for the briefing. 'Good to go?' she asked finally.

'Yeah, yeah. All good,' he replied.

'Right,' she said as she looked at each of them in turn. 'Where are we at?'

Entwistle was first up. 'I've just had an update from the uniform team who checked the Wythenshawe Park and Gardens near Baguley Brook Bridge, and their search has drawn a blank. No trace of our guy anywhere in the area.'

'Hardly surprising,' said Jones. 'Still, it was worth checking.'

'Anything else?' Phillips asked.

'Podgorski,' Entwistle read from his laptop screen. 'According to our records, he's a Russian who came to the UK when he was two years old along with his mother, Kira, his father, Artem, and his older brother, Ryszard. They settled in Cheetham Hill in the late eighties, and he's been here ever since with full British citizenship, which he got when he was seven. He has a record of delinquent behaviour as a young teenager, mainly for fighting, and by the time he was fifteen, he had already served six months in a youth custody centre.'

'And what specifically was that for?' asked Phillips.

Entwistle searched for the info in the file for a second. 'Football violence as part of the Red Army, Manchester United's football hooligan gang.'

'The Red Army?' said Jones. 'Seems quite appropriate for a Russian thug.'

Phillips nodded. 'Anything else on his record?'

'A few short sentences for drug possession in his late teens and early twenties, but nothing longer than six months each time. After that, he's as clean as a whistle.'

'Or learned how to cover his tracks better,' Jones mused.

'Sounds about right.' Phillips folded her arms across her chest. 'Did you get anywhere with his alibis for the night of the first fire?'

'I spoke to them all yesterday, and each of them confirmed he was with them playing cards at the Comrades Club at the time of the fire.'

'And let me guess,' said Phillips. 'They all gave *exactly* the same story. Am I right?'

'To a man, guv. They were identical in every way.'

'Of course they were,' she scoffed. 'Which means they're *all* lying.'

It was Bov's turn to speak now, his brow creased. 'How old did you say he was?'

Entwistle glanced at his notes again. 'Er, forty-five.'

'Which means he would likely have been involved in the infamous nineties iteration of the Red Army,' said Bovalino. 'I remember my uncle, Marco, used to go to the United away games for years, but he stopped around that time because things were getting pretty hairy thanks to the Red Army. Apparently, they got a taste for chucking petrol bombs at opposing fans on the way to games.'

Jones shook his head. 'I'll never understand why football fans can be so violent. I mean, it's just a bloody game, after all.'

'Me either,' continued Bov, 'but if we can prove Podgorski

was part of that group, maybe that could link him to the petrol bomb attack at the club?'

'It's certainly worth looking into,' said Phillips, turning to Entwistle. 'Can you do some more digging?'

'Of course, boss. I'll have a look at it after this.'

'As for his alibis for the night of the Wythenshawe fire, what do we know about them?'

'Not a lot at this stage,' said Entwistle. 'Other than they're all of Russian descent, and each of them got into trouble with the police around the same time as Podgorski – and all for similar offences: violence, disturbing the peace, drug possession, etc.'

'Comrades in arms,' quipped Jones.

'Any of them a match for the wig guy?' Phillips asked.

'Hard to tell from their mugshots. I'll need to have a proper look online and see what other photos I can find of any of them.'

'Do that.' Phillips sat forward, linking her fingers together on the desk. 'Podgorski is definitely a person of interest and someone we should be keeping an eye on, but unless we can link him to either fire directly, he'll end up running rings round us.'

'Shall we pay him another visit?' asked Jones. 'See where he was last night?'

'No point,' she replied. 'He'll just spout the same shit that he did on Friday with alibis to match. Better to check his mobile records and see if we can track any vehicles registered to him through the ANPR cameras.'

'I'll add it to the list.' Entwistle scribbled in his pad.

'And speaking of cameras,' said Phillips, 'any joy with the bus cameras on the routes surrounding the fires?'

Bov shook his head. 'I checked them all, and there's no sign of the wig guy.'

'That's annoying.' Phillips drummed the fingers of her right hand on the desk. 'Well, let's do a full sweep of cameras around last night's fire. As long as the main hard drive survived the fire, Jones and I will be able to collect the CCTV from the club later this morning when we meet with the fire investigation team. In the meantime, Bov, you check council cameras and put a request into the bus company for all routes around that area within a two-hour timeframe of the fire starting, like last time.'

'Sure thing, boss,' the big man replied.

Phillips checked her watch as she turned to Jones. 'I've got a couple of emails I need to send, and then you and I can head out to the George and Dragon. See what Mac and the fire investigation team have to say.'

'Sounds good to me,' said Jones.

'Great.' She focused on Bovalino once more. 'You got a minute?'

Bov flinched slightly. 'Me?'

'Yeah. Won't take long.'

'Er, yeah. Sure.'

'Let's chat in my office.'

A minute later, after closing the door behind him, Bov took a seat opposite Phillips, who was now sitting back behind her desk.

'So, what's going on with you?' she asked.

He shifted his weight in the chair. 'How'd you mean, boss?'

'I mean you're not yourself at the minute.'

'If this is about me being late, look, I'm sorry, and it won't happen again.'

'It's not just that. I understand that can happen, and I'm not worried about any of you being late from time to time. God knows we all put enough hours in to make up for it.' Her eyes narrowed. 'No. It's *you* I'm worried about. You've not been yourself at all this last week, and I'm concerned there might be something going on that you're not telling me.'

Bovalino dropped his chin to his chest for a few seconds and exhaled loudly before looking up again. 'It's Izzie.'

'What about her?'

'She found a lump in her breast last week.'

'Oh, shit, Bov, I'm so sorry. Has she had it checked out?'

He nodded. 'The GP had concerns it could be cancer, so he's referred her for a scan. She'll be having an MRI as we speak. That's why I was late. I got caught in traffic after dropping her off.'

'She's having a scan now?' Phillips recoiled. 'What the bloody hell are you doing here, then? Why aren't you at the hospital with her?'

'I couldn't face it, guv. Not after what happened in the Hawkins case. I still get panic attacks every time I go into a hospital.'

'But what about Izzie? She's really going to need you at a time like this.'

'Her sisters are with her, all three of them.'

'Okay, that's something at least.' Phillips glanced out in the direction of Jones and Entwistle, who appeared focused on their tasks in hand. 'Why didn't you say something?'

'I didn't want to,' he replied. 'I know this is going to sound weird, but in my head, if I don't think or speak about it, it's not real. Does that make sense?'

Phillips had spent enough time in hospital herself over the last few years to completely understand where he was coming from. 'It does, yeah,' she said. 'Look, I get the fact you can't face being in the hospital, but I really think you should go home and look after your wife.'

He shook his head. 'I'd rather stay here if it's all right with you, boss. If I'm working on the case, then I'm not thinking about what might happen *if* it is a tumour.'

'I get that, Bov, I really do, but what about Izzie? You can't just leave her at home.'

'Her sisters have practically moved in.' He gave a wry smile. 'To be honest, I can't get near her.'

Phillips took a moment before responding. She'd met Izzie's sisters when Bov had been seriously injured during the Hawkins case, and could easily imagine how hard it might be for him at home with them all right now. 'Look, in the end,' she said, looking him in the eye, 'you've got to do what's right for you, but please promise me that you'll go home at the first sign that she needs you, okay?'

'I promise, guv.'

She nodded. 'So when will she get the results?'

'The next few days. And if there is something there, then she'll need a biopsy, which could take a few weeks to sort out.'

'Seems a long time to wait, given the circumstances.'

'That's the reality of the NHS for you. There's a backlog of cases at the moment, apparently.'

'Well, if you really want to keep on working, then I'll respect your decision, but I mean it, Bov, if it all gets too much and at any point and you need to go home, go. Right?'

'Yeah, I will.'

'Likewise, if I feel you're not able to do the job, I'll be sending you home. Understood?'

'Yes, guv.'

'Okay. In that case you can crack on if you must, but please know I'm here if you need to talk at any point.'

'Thank you,' he replied before heading for the door. Just as he reached it, he stopped and turned back to face her. 'Can we keep this between us for now, guv? I'd rather the guys didn't know. I don't want them treating me any differently.'

'Sure,' she said softly.

He smiled weakly, then opened the door and walked back to his desk.

17

A few hours later Phillips and Jones set off to the George and Dragon with Jones at the wheel of the squad car.

'What was all that about this morning?' he asked.

'What was all what about?'

'Your little one-to-one with the big man. Is everything all right?'

'Yeah, fine,' she replied as she glanced out the window. 'I just wanted to check he was okay, as he's not been himself of late.'

'Yeah, I thought that, too,' he replied. 'And was it? All right, I mean.'

Phillips hated keeping things from Jonesy, but she'd made a promise to Bov. 'Yeah, a few things going on at home, but hopefully nothing that can't be sorted out pretty quickly.'

'Really?' Jones glanced to his left for a second. 'As in trouble between him and Izzie?'

'No, no, no,' she said. 'Nothing like. Just an issue with her sisters. I'm sure it'll be fine, and to be honest, he didn't seem all that keen to talk about it.' Phillips was desperate to change the subject. 'So what's the name of the fire investigator we're meeting today?'

'Jock Simpson,' Jones said boldly. 'As luck would have it, it seems he worked on the original Archie Pearson fires back in the day.'

'Really? How do you know that?'

'I'm a detective.' Jones grinned. 'I did some *detecting*.'

Phillips laughed. 'Touché.'

'From what I've heard about him, he's a good bloke and really knows his stuff.'

'I'm glad somebody does.' Phillips's tone was facetious. 'I feel like a fish out of water when it comes to fire setters.'

'I know what you mean,' said Jones, then accelerated into the outside lane of the dual carriageway.

It wasn't long before they were parking up in the same spot outside the function room they had used the previous night, but the scene looked very different in the cold light of day. The large fire engines and ambulances had long since gone, and only a couple of patrol cars and four or five uniformed officers had remained in place to secure the scene, which was cordoned off with blue and white police tape.

Positioned just outside what was left of the function room was a large white and yellow forensic tent.

Phillips glanced out the window as the car came to a complete stop. 'Looks like our man Mac is still on site.'

'Ooh, goody. Maybe he can tell us all how to do our jobs again,' said Jones sarcastically.

'Saucer of milk for Jonesy,' Phillips shot back playfully before opening the door and jumping out.

As they approached the police cordon, they presented their IDs to the uniformed officer standing next to it.

'Ma'am, sir,' he said as he lifted the tape so they could step under.

Making their way to the CSI tent located just a few metres away, they found their new senior CSI, Mac. He was guzzling greedily from a bottle of water, his hood pulled down to reveal a soaking wet mop of wavy dark hair.

'Looks like hot work,' said Phillips.

'You could say that.' Mac locked eyes with her and smiled as he held her gaze. 'But sure, a little bit of sweat never hurt anybody, now did it?'

Phillips cleared her throat as she felt her neck flush. 'Er, so what have you found?' she asked, eager to move things along.

Jones stifled a grin next to her.

Mac shrugged. 'We're about a quarter of the way through the room, but nothing of note so far, I'm afraid. As expected, the fire has left us very little to work with, but we'll keep on searching. We may get lucky.'

'I see.' Phillips suddenly felt very unsure of herself. 'Well, I guess we'd better leave you to it, as we need to speak to the fire investigator.'

Mac thumbed over his shoulder. 'He's inside.'

'Right,' said Phillips. 'We'll let you crack on.'

Mac nodded as he took another mouthful of water. 'No rest for the wicked,' he said, smiling broadly now.

Without responding, Phillips set off towards the entrance to the function room.

Jones was at her side in a flash. 'I think he fancies you, boss,' he said under his breath.

'What?' Phillips did a double take. 'Don't be ridiculous.'

'It doesn't take Sherlock Holmes to see he was flirting with you back there.'

'Oh, shut up,' she shot back, feeling her cheeks blush. 'He was doing nothing of the sort.'

Jones raised his arms in mock surrender. 'Just saying what I saw, guv.'

'Give over,' she replied, waving him away.

Mercifully, a short stocky man wearing forensic overalls with a fire service crest on his chest emerged from the burned-out shell of the function room, his face covered with a mask.

'I'm guessing this is our guy,' Phillips said, relieved of the distraction, as she retrieved her ID for a second time. 'Jock Simpson?'

The man nodded as he removed his face mask.

'DCI Phillips and DI Jones from Major Crimes.'

'How you doing?' he said as he pulled down the hood of his overalls before running his right hand through his sweat-soaked grey hair, which was matched by his thick, soggy beard.

'How's it looking in there?'

'Well, the fire was definitely set deliberately.'

'What makes you say that?' Phillips asked.

'This.' Simpson held up a blackened tangle of metal and wire in his left hand.

Phillips leaned closer to get a better look. 'What the hell's that?'

'An incendiary device. Homemade and what you might call *a classic*.'

'How do you mean, "a classic"?' said Jones.

'I mean the last time I saw one of these was over seven-

teen years ago, during the Archie Pearson murder investigations.'

Phillips felt her adrenaline spike as she glanced first at
Jones, then back to Simpson. 'We'd heard you were part of
the investigation team on those fires.'

He nodded sombrely as he looked down at the tiny structure in his hand. 'I thought I'd seen the last of these when
that bastard got life.'

'Are you telling us that this device is similar to the ones
Pearson used back in 2006?'

'No. It's not similar. It's bloody *identical*.'

Phillips paused as she processed what he was saying.
'Identical?'

'Yep. I worked extensively on deconstructing the mecha-
nisms he used and matching them with the evidence left
behind at each fire, and I'm telling you, these are exactly the
same.'

'So what are you saying?' Jones cut in now, his face crum-
pled. 'That Pearson somehow set these fires – from inside his
prison cell?'

'Of course not, no,' he replied. 'But whoever did set them
has seen his work and was able to copy it perfectly.'

'And you're sure of that?' Phillips asked. 'You're sure
they're identical and not just a very close match.'

'I spent months in the lab presenting the evidence for
that case, and I'll never forget the composition of those
devices.' He held up the tangle of metal in front of them now.
'And this is a carbon copy.'

Phillips's mind was flooded with questions. 'Was Pearson's handiwork ever made public?'

'Nope,' Simpson replied. 'The judge ordered a media

blackout on that part of the trial, so it was redacted from all the public files.'

'How come?' asked Jones.

'She was worried they could be copied by any lunatic with an internet connection. You see, all the parts come from household electrical items like kettles and toasters, for example. They're incredibly effective and very, very easy to make. She didn't want that kind of information in the public domain.'

Phillips's eyes narrowed. 'So the only people who knew the details of their construction were Pearson and people who were connected to the investigation?'

'Exactly.'

'Holy shit,' muttered Jones.

Phillips turned to her second in command. 'If that's the case, then it would seem our friend Pearson may not have been telling us the truth the other day when he said he'd never responded to his fan mail.'

'You've spoken to Pearson?' said Simpson.

'A few days ago,' Phillips replied. 'Still claiming he's innocent.'

Simpson shook his head. 'He's a stone-cold killer, that one. I wouldn't believe a word he says.'

'Sounds like good advice,' added Jones.

Phillips pointed at the small device. 'When will you be able to send through composite details of what you've found?'

'Depends. I'm working through a bit of a backlog, but hopefully I can get you a preliminary report over within forty-eight hours.'

'Okay,' said Phillips. 'If that's the case, we'd better not delay you any further.'

Standing to her right, Jones's eyes suddenly darted over Phillips's shoulder. 'Oh shit. Scumbag alert.'

She span round to see veteran *Manchester Evening News* reporter, Don Townsend, walking towards them. A tall man with greased-back dark hair and the permanent tan of a sunbed user.

'DCI Phillips and DI Jones,' he said as he approached, his lopsided grin revealing tobacco-stained, crooked teeth. 'Fancy meeting you here.'

Townsend had been a thorn in Phillips's side for years now, and she was in no mood to play his games. 'What do you want, Don?'

'The exclusive, of course, Jane. Always the exclusive.'

Jones nodded towards the main building. 'I'll go and get the CCTV,' he said before walking away.

'I'll leave you guys to it too,' added Simpson and was gone a second later.

Phillips turned her attention to Townsend. 'We've just started the investigation, Don, so there's nothing to tell you.'

'*Au contraire*,' he shot back. 'The very fact you're here says so much. That coupled with the fact this fire started at a police charity fundraiser – the second fire at a police event in the space of a week – and I think the story is beginning to write itself.'

Phillips could only imagine the reaction from Fox if she returned to front-page headlines declaring that arson attacks were deliberately targeting Manchester cops, so she was doubly keen to shut down Townsend's theories. 'The fact it was a police function has nothing to do with it being assigned to us. We're here because sadly someone died as a result of the fire last night.'

Townsend pulled out his mobile and activated the voice

note app before thrusting it towards her face. 'Can you give us a name?'

'The family have yet to formally identify her, so I'm afraid not,' she said flatly.

Townsend flashed a thin smile. 'Okay, well, what can you tell the public about the fact this fire *and* the fire last week at the Wythenshawe Social Club look to have been specifically targeting police personnel?'

'That's an unfortunate coincidence, that's all.'

'Okay. So you're not worried that you may have a copycat killer on your hands?'

Phillips recoiled slightly, feigning shock. 'A copycat? I haven't the faintest idea what you're talking about.'

'The fires set by Archie Pearson in the mid-noughties.' Townsend looked her dead in the eye. 'They look awfully similar.'

'Still don't know what you're talking about,' Phillips lied just as her phone began to ring. Pulling it from her pocket, she could see Carter was calling. 'If you don't mind, I need to take this,' she added before stepping away to answer it out of earshot.

'Jane, where are you?' Carter's tone oozed tension.

'On site at the George and Dragon. Why?'

'I need you back here ASAP. There's something you have to see.'

'Really? What is it?'

'I can't say on an open line. You'll understand why when you get here.'

'On our way,' she said, then ended the call.

18

An hour later, Phillips arrived at Carter's outer office, where she found his smartly dressed dark-haired assistant, Diane, sitting behind her desk, working away on her computer.

'Hello, Jane,' she said, looking up. 'You can go straight in; he's waiting for you.'

'Thanks,' Phillips replied without breaking stride.

Carter was standing with his back to the room, looking out through the window, his hands covered in blue latex gloves.

'Is everything all right, sir?'

He turned to face her, his face pained. 'Thanks for coming so quickly, Jane,' he said as he returned to his desk, where he picked up a pair of gloves that matched his own. 'Put these on and come and have a look at this.'

Phillips did as requested as she moved to his shoulder in order to see his computer screen.

Carter leaned forward and pressed play on the paused video displayed on it.

It took a moment to recognise what she was watching unfold, and then it suddenly became clear; it was a video of the fire at Wythenshawe Social Club, filmed at close quarters, likely on a mobile phone. The blaze had taken hold at this point in the film, and people could be heard screaming and shouting in the distance, mixed with the sound of raucous laughter, evidently coming from whoever was holding the phone camera.

'Where did you get this?' asked Phillips.

'Came in the post this morning.' Carter pointed to the USB drive attached to the front of his PC. 'This drive and this note.' He handed her an A4 piece of paper.

Phillips read the printed words aloud. 'I'm back! *The Real Firestarter*.' She felt the deep creases forming in her brow. '*The Real Firestarter*? What on earth does that mean?'

'There's more,' added Carter as he closed the window and opened a second video, which played a moment later.

Phillips recognised the location instantly, the George and Dragon, and like the first video, the footage had been taken while the blaze was in full flow, and once again, people could be heard screaming inside the pub in between bouts of laughter from the cameraman.

'This guy's a bloody psycho,' she growled.

'My thoughts entirely,' replied Carter.

Phillips said nothing for a long moment as she recalled her earlier conversation with Jock Simpson. 'The fire investigator at the George and Dragon said he believed that the incendiary device used to start that blaze was an exact copy of those used by Archie Pearson back in 2006. Not a likeness, a complete duplicate.'

Carter frowned. 'How does he know that?'

'Because he was part of the team that worked the Pearson cases.'

'So what does that actually mean, then?'

'It means that whoever set the recent fires had to have an intimate knowledge of those original devices. You see, it turns out that the details of those incendiary devices were never made public. So either someone connected to Pearson constructed this new device, or' – Phillips paused as the enormity of what she was about to say dawned on her – 'or someone involved in the Archie Pearson investigation made it.'

'As in *someone on the job*?' Carter was incredulous.

'Yeah,' replied Phillips. 'As in someone on the job.'

Carter exhaled loudly. 'God, that's all the GMP needs, more bloody police corruption.'

'Although there is still a *third* option, sir,' added Phillips.

'Which is?'

'Pearson's always claimed he was innocent, right?'

'As far as we know, yes.'

'And even after *all* this time – seventeen years of prison – he still won't admit his guilt despite the fact it could mean the difference between him getting parole or eventually dying inside.'

Carter folded his arms across his chest. 'I have a horrible feeling I know where this is going.'

Phillips nodded. 'What if he is *actually* telling the truth? What if we got the wrong man back then, and the *real* fire setter – as this guy claims to be – has been out there all along?'

'But if that's true, then why wait seventeen years to pick up where he left off?'

'I don't know,' said Phillips. 'That's the bit I'm struggling to understand too.'

'Could he have fled the country, and he's been overseas, maybe?' suggested Carter.

'Maybe.' The room fell silent for a moment before another thought dawned on her. '*Or* maybe the Real Firestarter has been inside himself for a different crime, and these two displays are about him celebrating his freedom now he's out and back in the world.'

The colour appeared to drain from Carter's face. 'Holy shit, can you imagine if that was the case and it ever got out? The press would crucify us.'

'Not to mention Fox,' added Phillips.

'Oh shit, and she's back tomorrow. She'll go ballistic.'

Phillips pulled her phone from her pocket and took a photo of the note sent by the so-called Real Firestarter. 'Any chance you can email me a copy of the videos, sir?'

'Of course, let me just take a seat,' he said before dropping into the chair.

Phillips remained standing at his shoulder as she watched him locate the files on the drive and open a new email.

'Sent,' he said a few moments later.

As she waited for them to land in her inbox, she explained what she was planning to do. 'First things first, I think we need to speak to Archie Pearson again. See what he has to say about the note and these videos.'

'What? You're going to show them to him?'

'Yes. Why not?'

'Well, because they're evidence in two live investigations for a start.'

'I know they are,' Phillips replied. 'But I can't help feeling

Pearson is somehow connected to this guy, and I think if we confront him with the videos, then his reaction will give us a much better idea of what he knows.'

'I hear what you're saying, but I'm really not sure about this, Jane. Taking unlogged evidence into a maximum-security prison; not exactly following protocols, is it?'

Phillips shrugged. 'No, I guess it's not, but when has that ever stopped me?'

Carter opened his mouth to speak.

Phillips cut him off. 'Plus, it might just give us a nugget we can feed to Fox when she rolls back into the office tomorrow.'

'You make a good point.' Carter chewed his bottom lip for a moment before nodding. 'Okay. Do what you need to do.'

Phillips was already on the move. 'Thank you, sir,' she said, then strode out of the room.

19

Two hours later, Phillips and Jones found themselves being ushered into the governor's office at HMP Hawk Green by his secretary, Mrs Hollins, an image of conservatism if ever there was one, dressed as she was in a mix of greys and browns with an austere expression fixed to her face and sturdy thick-rimmed glasses hanging on a chain around her neck.

'Mr Morrell will see you now,' she said as she opened the door.

Phillips led the way with Jones at her back.

Morrell, a tall, well-built man in his fifties with greying curly hair, stood up behind his desk and offered his thickset hand. 'Welcome to Hawk Green.'

Phillips and Jones shook it in turn.

'Please have a seat.' Morrell gestured to the two chairs opposite his desk.

'Thanks for arranging our visit so promptly, Mr Morrell,' said Phillips, with forced deference. It was widely known across Manchester law enforcement that Morrell had an ego as big as the institution he managed.

'Please, call me Jim,' he replied with a toothy grin. 'Now, I hope you don't mind me asking you to drop in for a quick chat before you speak to Pearson, but I wanted to flag something that I thought might be important.'

'Oh, yes?' said Phillips. 'And what might that be?'

'It would seem that the media have a sudden renewed interest in his case—'

'The media?' Jones cut in.

'Yes.' Morrell leaned forward in his chair. 'The *Manchester Evening News* has reached out to me personally to ask for permission to interview him.'

'Can I ask what they want to talk to him about?' said Phillips.

'From what I can gather, they're looking to publish a piece around his continued claims that he's innocent, even after all these years.'

Phillips drew in her breath. 'Let me guess, the journalist in question is called Don Townsend.'

Morrell raised an eyebrow. 'You're familiar with him?'

'Unfortunately, we are, yes.'

Morrell continued, 'Well, like I say, I received an email from Townsend earlier today, seeking approval for the interview.'

'And what time was that?'

'Er, about an hour before your request to visit came through.'

'I see.' Phillips felt her brow furrow. 'I didn't think Pearson's claim that he's innocent had ever been made public.'

'Neither did I, which is why I was quite surprised when

Townsend suggested this article on him. To be honest, I'm not really sure anybody would care that much anymore.'

While Phillips herself wasn't sure of Townsend's motives, she could hazard a guess – he was likely trying to join the dots between the recent fires and those Pearson was serving time for.

Morrell continued, 'And I must admit, my interest was certainly piqued when you *also* requested to speak to him for a second time in a week, a mere few hours later.'

'Of course.' Phillips decided it best to continue with her own charm offensive. 'I'm sure I'd feel exactly the same way if I were in your position, Jim.'

'Can we speak freely, Chief Inspector?' said Morrell.

'Please do.'

'Is there something going on with Pearson that I need to know about?'

Phillips flinched slightly as she feigned surprise. 'How do you mean?'

'Well, he's been locked up in here for the best part of two decades without the slightest murmur of press or police interest, and now, after two arson attacks on police functions, everyone wants to talk to my prisoner, a man convicted of committing exactly the same crimes. I mean, it doesn't take a genius to put two and two together.'

Phillips smiled thinly. 'Clearly there's no flies on you, Jim.'

'I run a tight ship here at Hawk Green, but I also make it my business to know what's going on *outside* of these walls.'

'Ordinarily I'm not permitted to share the details of an ongoing investigation beyond those involved in the case itself,' said Phillips, 'but as you're already one step ahead of us, then I guess I have no choice but to level with you.'

Morrell sat to attention now, his chest proud as his eyes danced in his head.

'We do see similarities in the methods of fire setting between those attacks perpetrated by Pearson and the two fires set in the last week, and we believe Archie may be able to offer us valuable insight into the person responsible for them. That's why we're here today.'

A satisfied grin spread across Morrell's face. 'I thought as much.'

'As for Don Townsend,' Phillips continued, 'I can assure you that nothing he writes will be of benefit to either yourself, Jim, or the institution of HMP Hawk Green. That man – that *journalist* – is far more interested in headlines and clickbait than delivering balanced, unbiased news. And far be it for me to tell you how to do your job, but if I were in your position, there's no way I'd let someone like Townsend anywhere near my inmates. Not today, not any day.'

'I see.'

'Trust me. It would be like letting the fox into the chicken coop. Through the front door.'

Morrell pursed his lips for a moment before responding. 'Well, I appreciate the heads-up, Chief Inspector. The good news is, Pearson would need permission from the Home Office in order to take part in any kind of interview with the media, and only I can sanction such a request on his behalf. Based on your insight, I'll make sure he speaks to no one, aside from yourselves, of course.'

'That sounds like a very sensible course of action,' said Phillips.

'Well, then.' Morrell stood up from his chair. 'This prison isn't going to run itself, so I'd better let you both get on.'

'Thank you.' Phillips stepped up with Jones closely behind.

'I hope you get what you need,' Morrell added with a knowing tilt of his head.

'So do we,' said Phillips before turning and heading for the door.

———

MORRELL HAD ARRANGED for the interview to take place in the same room as their first visit, and for a second time, Officer Dooley delivered Pearson to Visitor Room Two, then proceeded to wait outside the door in case he was needed.

Pearson's complexion appeared just as grey as last time as he took his seat.

'Back so soon?' he asked.

Phillips's mobile was sitting on the table between them. Picking it up, she opened her email and, when she located the file she was looking for, hit play and turned the screen to face him.

Pearson's eyes locked on the phone now as the video taken at the Wythenshawe fire rolled out in front of him, and he took a deep breath in.

Phillips explained what he was looking at. 'We believe the man who filmed this video also set the fire you're looking at.'

Pearson didn't respond as his eyes narrowed, and he continued staring at the screen.

'Do you recognise the building?'

'Should I?'

'It's Wythenshawe Social Club. The one we talked about during our last visit.'

Pearson simply curled his lip.

Phillips turned the phone around momentarily as she took a moment to locate the second video, then turned it back. 'We also think the same guy set a second fire two days later in Hazel Grove, where a woman died. Do you recognise the person laughing?'

'No. Why would I?'

'Well, it might surprise you to know the incendiary device that was used to start the second blaze was a carbon copy of the ones *you* used to set your fires back in the day.'

Pearson paused, picking at his torn fingernails. 'What did you say?'

'I said the incendiary device that was used to start *this* fire was a carbon copy of the ones *you* used when you set fire to those police houses.'

'Like I told you last time.' Pearson angrily pointed a nicotine-stained finger at the officers. 'I never set those fires. I never set any fires.'

Phillips sat back in the chair and folded her arms. 'That's right, you're innocent, aren't you?' Her tone was facetious.

He glared back at her now. 'Yes. I bloody am.'

'So if you didn't set those fires you were convicted of, *who* did?'

He scoffed. 'Do you think if I knew that, I'd be sitting in here now?'

Phillips remained silent for a moment before responding, 'Here's how we see it, Archie. Someone out there is targeting police, using a device *identical* to the ones that you created. Not similar, not nearly the same, identical. *Identical.*'

Pearson sniffed defiantly.

'But here's the thing,' Phillips continued. 'You've been in here for seventeen years now, so the only way someone would know how to copy your design was if you gave them the blueprint yourself or if they were involved in the original fire setting. Which, either way, means you know who this guy is. And that, my friend, makes you an accessory to murder.'

'I have no idea what you're talking about,' Pearson said flatly.

Phillips glared at him in silence.

'Come on, Archie,' Jones cut in now. 'We'll find out in the end. We always do. So why not do us all a favour and drop the innocent-man bullshit, hey?'

Pearson locked eyes with him. 'I can't tell you what I *don't* know. I never made those devices in the first place, so I don't have any blueprints to pass on.'

'Oh, change the record, will you?' Phillips growled as she sat forward. 'Just admit you set the fires and tell us who this guy is, and we can make sure you get the minimum term added to your sentence. You may even get parole in the next ten years.'

'No,' he replied, his voice surprisingly resolute. 'The only way I'm walking out of here is with a pardon.'

Phillips let out an involuntary laugh. 'A pardon? I've heard it all now.'

'That bitch set me up, and she knows it.' Pearson fixed her with a steely gaze. 'That's why my parole was declined. She's worried I'll get out and tell the world what she did to me. That's why she wrote to the Parole Board to recommend I rot in here forever.' He looked down at his hands for a moment before continuing. 'I've been a model prisoner throughout my sentence; why else would my parole have been denied?'

Phillips flinched, casting her mind back to the Zoom call

with Carter and Fox while the chief constable was away in Florida. 'Who are you claiming set you up?'

There was no hesitation from the grey-skinned man in front of her. 'Detective Chief Inspector Fox.'

Phillips glanced at Jones, whose expression suggested his mind was racing almost as quickly as hers.

'DCI Fox was the officer in charge?'

'Yeah, and from what I heard, the bitch got promoted off the back of my conviction.'

'But why would she want to set you up?' Phillips probed. 'And more importantly, how did she do it?'

'The press was giving her shit about not catching the real killer,' he replied with an urgency in his tone, as if glad someone was listening, finally, to his version of events. 'She needed someone on the hook, and I had form for arson, so she planted my DNA at the scene.'

'Oh, come on,' said Jones, leaning back in his chair, eyes cynical. 'You expect us to believe that?'

'It's true. Forensics went over that crime scene for a week and came up with nothing. Then she shows up, and before you know it, she's found my DNA all over the lighter that started the fire. It was bullshit, but the jury bought it hook, line and sinker.'

Phillips took a moment to process what Pearson was saying. Up until now, she'd believed he was just another con trying to pull the wool over everyone's eyes, but she couldn't shake the feeling there might actually be some grain of truth to his allegations. 'Have you talked to anyone else about this?' she asked.

'Nah,' said Pearson. 'Who'd listen?'

'Well, if you really do want to get out of here any time

soon, I'd suggest you keep it that way,' Phillips said as she stood up from the chair.

He recoiled. 'Is that a threat?'

'No, Archie. It's not. It's a friendly word of advice.' She stepped left and opened the door to Dooley. 'You can take him away, now.'

20

Early next morning, Phillips beckoned Entwistle into her office for an update on the case.

Jones was already in situ, sitting in one of the chairs opposite her desk.

'Are we not waiting for Bov?' he asked, stepping inside.

'He's at the doctor's this morning, so we'll just crack on,' she replied. 'Close the door, will you?'

Entwistle followed the instruction and then took the seat next to Jones.

Phillips sat forward in her chair. 'It's actually not a bad thing that we're without Bov because it means we can speak freely about our conversation with Pearson yesterday.'

Entwistle's brow wrinkled, and he appeared confused.

Phillips pressed play on her laptop and turned the screen so it was visible to Jones and Entwistle. 'This video footage shows the fire at the George and Dragon.'

Entwistle's eyes were locked on the screen. 'Bloody hell. Where'd you get that?'

'It was sent to Carter yesterday along with another video

of the Wythenshawe fire and a printed note that said, "I'm back. The Real Firestarter.'"

'You're joking?' said Entwistle. 'Scrap that, I can see you're not.'

'We believe the guy who filmed it, and can be heard laughing in the background, is our suspect for both fires.' Phillips returned the laptop to its original position and stopped the video. 'According to the fire investigator we spoke to yesterday, the device used to set fire to the George and Dragon function room was an exact copy of the devices Pearson used in the mid-noughties. And when we say exact, we mean it; they're identical.'

'Really? So we *could* be looking at a copycat, then, guv?'

'We don't think so, and here's why. The details of Pearson's devices were never made public at trial, and the only people who had eyes on them were Pearson himself, as well as the cops and the lawyers involved in the case.'

Entwistle's eyes narrowed. 'Right...'

'Which means the guy we're after either knows Pearson and maybe served time with him, or he worked as part of the original investigations, which would seem unlikely, or...' She paused as she glanced at Jones for a moment before turning her attention back to Entwistle. 'Or the guy who burned down Wythenshawe Social Club and the George and Dragon is actually responsible for *all* the fires where those devices were used, including the original fires Pearson went down for seventeen years ago.'

Entwistle's eyes widened now. 'You mean Pearson might actually be innocent?'

'Yeah, and there's more.' Phillips turned to Jones. 'Do you want to tell him?'

Jones cleared his throat as he shifted in his seat. 'Well, it turns out that Detective Chief Inspector Fox – as she was back then – was the SIO in charge of the Pearson investigation and – according to Pearson – Fox was also the one who found the smoking gun that sent him down: his DNA on a lighter unearthed at the scene.'

'I don't understand?' said Entwistle, casting a questioning glance back and forth between them both.

Phillips cut back in now. 'The more we look at this, the more it really is beginning to look like Pearson is innocent, and the self-styled Real Firestarter is the man responsible for everything. If that's true, it raises some serious questions around Fox's role in the original investigations and, more worryingly, the chain of evidence that convicted Pearson in the first place. He claims she planted his DNA – and Jones and I are starting to think there's some truth in that claim.'

'Jesus.' Entwistle swallowed hard.

'As terrifying a thought as it is, it's one we can't ignore,' said Phillips. 'And unfortunately, we all know what she's capable of.'

The room fell silent for a moment as her words landed.

Eventually, Entwistle was the first to speak. 'But why start again now? The Real Firestarter, I mean. It's been seventeen years.'

'We don't know,' replied Phillips, 'but one explanation could be that we're dealing with a man who, since setting the original fires, has served a long sentence himself.'

'So he's been in prison all this time?' said Entwistle.

'It would certainly explain his absence.'

'Okay, but what now, guv?' asked Jones.

'Now we leave no stone unturned until we find out whether Pearson is telling the truth, because if he is, then the guy who sent these videos is the person who actually killed all those cops eighteen years ago, and he has to be brought to justice for those crimes.'

'Even if it means exposing Fox in the process?' asked Jones.

'Yes,' Phillips said firmly. '*Especially* if it means exposing her. Look, I don't need to tell you how sensitive this investigation has suddenly become and the damage it could do to the whole of the Greater Manchester Police if any of this is true. But, that said, our job is to always seek the truth, no matter what the consequences.'

The room fell silent again as each of them took in the enormity of her words.

'What do you need me to do?' asked Entwistle, breaking the silence at last.

'Start by looking at any prison leavers who got out in the last six months and may fit the profile of our so-called Firestarter.'

Entwistle nodded thoughtfully as he said, 'But I'm not sure I know what that profile looks like, guv.'

Phillips took a moment to respond. 'That's a good point, actually. It would really help if we can get a proper profile done on this guy. I'll talk to Carter and persuade him to sign off on the budget to get one done properly. In the meantime, start by looking for anyone with a conviction for arson who was released from prison in the last six months.'

'Just northwest prisons?'

'No, look nationally, but with a focus on those who have settled in Manchester or the surrounding areas.'

Entwistle scribbled in his notepad.

'I also want you to request the case files for Pearson's trial,' she added. 'Get everything we have and look for anything that seems too good to be true in the chain of evidence.'

'On it.'

'There's something else we need to be mindful of too,' Phillips continued. 'Don Townsend was sniffing around the George and Dragon this afternoon, asking questions about a copycat for the Pearson fires, and it seems he's also been trying to get access to Pearson himself in Hawk Green. Now, Don may be many things, but he's not stupid. It won't be long before he starts putting two and two together and getting twenty-two, so as ever time is of the essence.'

Jones and Entwistle nodded.

'And with that in mind, Whistler, you'd best get cracking.'

Entwistle closed his pad and jumped up from the chair.

'Close the door on the way out, will you?' said Jones.

'Sure,' he replied as he left the room.

'What's on your mind?' Phillips asked when they were alone.

'Bov, and how he fits into all this. He's the only one who doesn't know about Fox being crooked, and I think it's time we told him.'

'Ordinarily I'd agree with you, but at the moment he's got a lot on his plate at home. I think the less he has to worry about, the better.'

Jones tilted his head to one side. 'What's *really* going on with him, guv? I can't see issues with Izzie's sisters as enough of a reason to treat him with kid gloves or keep him in the dark about stuff as important as this.'

Phillips exhaled loudly through her nose. 'I promised I wouldn't say anything.'

'Guv, seriously. This is Bov we're talking about. If there's something going on with him, then I'd like to know. He's one of my best mates.'

'I know he is.' Phillips glanced out towards the office. 'This goes no further, okay?'

'Goes without saying.'

'It's not Izzie's sisters that are the issue. It's Izzie herself. She found a lump, and her doctor is concerned it could be breast cancer.'

Jones's shoulders immediately sagged. 'Oh, shit.'

'Yeah. That's why he's at the doctor's this morning; he's taking Izzie for more tests.'

'No wonder he's not seemed himself lately.'

Phillips shook her head, upset at the thought. 'Anyway,' she said as firmly as she could, 'I told him to take as much time off as he needs to be with her, but he said he prefers to be at work. Helps take his mind off things, and apparently Izzie's sisters are spending a lot of time at the house, so she's being well looked after.'

'Having met them, I can see why he'd rather be here. They're pretty full on, like.'

'Yeah, I can imagine the atmosphere is quite intense,' said Phillips. 'So, for now, we just need to carry on as normal and hope the tests come back negative.'

'The poor buggers.' Jones sighed. 'They've been through so much in the last few years.'

'Yeah, they have, and I promise we'll bring him into the loop when the time is right. But till then, not a word.' Phillips checked her watch. 'I'd better get upstairs and see if Carter's in. I'd like to get this profile sorted ASAP.'

'Yeah, I'd better get on myself.' Jones stepped up from the chair.

And a few seconds later, Phillips followed him out.

21

C arter shook his head slowly. 'This is a bloody mess, Jane.'

'I know, sir.'

'Do you really think there's any truth in what Pearson is claiming?'

'Ordinarily, I'd say no, as most prisoners continue to protest their innocence throughout their sentence, but as she's already got form for tampering with evidence in the Crowther case, I wouldn't put anything past her.'

Carter frowned. 'Needless to say, we need to tread incredibly carefully.'

'I've just said the same thing to the team downstairs. This is need-to-know stuff only.'

'How did they take it? The allegations against Fox, I mean?'

'I'd like to say they were surprised, but the truth is they weren't. After what she did to Whistler in the Crowther investigation, it's not hard to believe she could have done something like this.'

'Quite,' he replied.

'That said, Bovalino still doesn't know. He missed the briefing, as he has some personal stuff going on at home, but we'll bring him into the loop when the time is right.'

'So what are the next steps?'

Phillips pushed a lock of hair behind her right ear. 'Entwistle is requesting access to the original Pearson case files so we can go back through and see if there's any issues with the chain of evidence – in particular, the DNA samples and how they were managed by Fox. Once we have the files, I'll get the new boy Mac to take a look.'

'Can he be trusted?'

'I have no idea, but he doesn't need to know *why* we're looking, just what we're looking for.'

'Jesus, Jane,' said Carter, nodding to confirm her thinking around Mac. 'If there are any evidence irregularities connected to Fox, can you imagine the fallout for the force? It doesn't bear thinking about.'

'I know, sir. It'll be a media feeding frenzy. Don Townsend will think it's his birthday and Christmas all rolled into one.'

'You mentioned he'd been sniffing around trying to link the latest fires to Pearson. Could he be a potential issue for us?'

'Right this minute no, but he is starting to put two and two together,' she replied. 'So I've taken steps to ensure the governor at Hawk Green will block all attempts from anyone in the press to speak to Pearson directly. That should keep him out of Don's clutches and buy us some time, but probably not for long.'

'Well, that's something, I suppose,' Carter said, not sounding entirely convinced.

'And because time is of the essence, I was hoping to bring in Siobhan Harris if she's available. To help create a profile of the firestarter.'

'Sounds like a great idea,' Carter agreed enthusiastically. 'Do you need anything from me to make that happen?'

'Just approval on the budget to pay for her.'

'Consider it approved.'

'Thank you, sir. I'll call her as soon as we're done.'

Just then there was a knock on the door as Diane popped her head in. 'Sorry to disturb your meeting, but Ms Blair has just been on the phone. Apparently, the chief constable is back and wants to see you both immediately.'

Phillips and Carter exchanged despairing glances.

'Thank you, Di,' he said as he swiftly ejected the pen drive from his PC. 'Tell Ms Blair we're on our way.'

A FEW MINUTES LATER, as they stepped into Fox's office, they were confronted by a very tanned chief constable. Fox was sitting behind her desk, dressed in full, immaculate uniform, and staring at her computer monitor through the glasses perched on the end of her nose.

'Welcome back, ma'am,' said Carter with forced gusto. 'I trust your time in Florida was a success?'

Fox's austere expression suggested she was not in a good mood. *No surprise there*, thought Phillips.

'It was too hot,' she said flatly. 'I have no idea how people live in that humidity all year round. It's completely oppressive.'

'Well, I must say you're looking very well and suitably refreshed,' Carter added, not letting go of his gusto just yet.

'Tell that to my jetlag,' Fox snapped as she gestured to the two chairs opposite her desk. 'Take a seat. We have a lot to catch up on.'

Phillips and Carter did as requested.

'So where are we at with these fires?' said Fox. 'Any developments?'

'I'm afraid there are.' Carter leaned forward and handed her the pen drive. 'I received these files in the post yesterday. This is a copy; the original drive is with forensics.'

Fox frowned as she took it from him and inserted it into her computer.

'You'll see there are two videos that we believe were filmed by the person responsible for setting both fires.'

Fox took a moment to navigate the files before locking her eyes on-screen as the first video played, accompanied by the unmistakable lyrics of 'Firestarter' by the Prodigy, which boomed out from the speakers.

'The person you can hear laughing is most likely our suspect,' added Carter.

When the first video had come to an end, Fox said nothing before playing the second one in full. Once again the loud music, laughter and distant screams and shouts filled the room.

Carter continued, 'He included a typed note, which is also with forensics. It simply said, "I'm back. The Real Firestarter."'

Fox flinched and appeared momentarily shaken. 'What the hell does that mean?'

'We're not sure at this stage, ma'am,' Carter lied. 'We're looking into it.'

'Who else has seen this video?' she asked.

'Just us three,' Carter smoothly lied again.

'Well, I suggest we keep it that way.' Fox closed the video down. 'Are we any closer to catching this guy?'

'The current focus is on CCTV, ma'am,' said Phillips. 'We're working our way through footage from cameras at the two venues, as well as council cameras and footage from the bus routes around the areas. Seeing if we can trace where the suspect went.'

'What about forensics?'

'The CSI team have found nothing of any significance so far due to the fire damage.' Phillips paused as she chose her words carefully. She needed to keep Fox abreast of all developments, but she had no intention of alerting her to the level of work going on in the background concerning the chief constable's involvement in the original Pearson investigation. 'However, we understand the fire investigators discovered a small homemade incendiary device that they believe was used in the fire at the George and Dragon pub.'

Fox's left eye appeared to twitch ever so slightly. It was a tiny movement, but Phillips had spotted it.

'And is that significant?' Fox asked.

It was Phillips's turn to lie now. 'We're not sure at this stage, ma'am, but we're not pinning our hopes on it due to the fact it was so badly damaged in the fire.'

Fox nodded but remained silent for a beat or two. 'So by the sounds of it, very little has changed since we spoke last week.'

'The investigation is progressing slower than we'd like, ma'am,' said Carter. 'But I can assure you, the team are doing everything they can to find this guy.'

In that moment, to give Fox something else to worry about and to divert some of her venom away from herself and the team, Phillips decided she would set off a small incendiary device of her own. 'There is another thing you should be aware of, ma'am.'

Carter shot her a panicked glance, evidently wondering what she was about to say.

Fox fixed her with a steely gaze. 'And what's that, Chief Inspector?'

'I found Don Townsend hanging around the crime scene at the George and Dragon yesterday.'

The chief constable's jaw clenched at the mention of his name.

Phillips continued, 'He was asking all sorts of questions about the similarities between these two fires and those Archie Pearson was convicted of setting. Said he thought they were somehow connected.'

Fox visibly stiffened. 'I hope you put him straight on that.'

'I told him there was no connection whatsoever,' Phillips lied again, clocking her boss's reactions.

'Good! It's utter nonsense to even think there is. The last thing we need is that moron whipping the public up into a frenzy.' Fox picked up the phone on her desk – her direct link through to Ms Blair in the outer office. 'Get Rupert Dudley up here now,' she snapped. 'I need to speak to him urgently about a press release.' She replaced the handset, then turned her attention back to Phillips and Carter.

'Would you like me to stay and brief Rupert with you, ma'am?' asked Carter.

'No need.' She waved him away. 'I can handle the press on this one. It's my officers who are being targeted, after all.'

'Very good, ma'am.'

'I want updates as soon as you have them,' added Fox, as

crisp and imperious as ever. 'And nobody speaks to Townsend without my express permission, okay?'

'Of course,' said Carter.

Phillips nodded. 'Understood.'

'Right. Well, it looks like you've got a lot of work to be getting on with, so don't let me keep you.'

Neither Phillips nor Carter needed to be told twice, and they were both out of their chairs and heading for the door in a flash.

'What was all that about?' Carter said in a low voice as they made their way swiftly down the corridor a minute later. 'Telling her about Townsend?'

'Call it a sleight of hand,' replied Phillips. 'While Fox is focused on trying to second-guess what our intrepid reporter is up to, she'll be too busy to notice what we're really doing here.'

'Clever.'

Phillips flashed a satisfied grin. 'Plus, if truth be told, I quite enjoy winding her up when the chance arises.'

22

P hillips was soon back in her office. With the door firmly shut, she pulled out her phone and called Mac.

He answered promptly. 'This is O'Shea.'

'Mac, it's DCI Phillips.'

'And to what do I owe the pleasure?' he asked smoothly.

'I need your opinion on the forensics of an old case.'

'Which one?'

'Archie Pearson's conviction for multiple arson attacks back in 2006.'

'That *is* old,' he replied. 'Can I ask what you're looking for?'

'I'm not sure, in all honesty.' Phillips wasn't ready to share the full reasons for her request just yet. Not when she didn't really know Mac. 'I paid a visit to Pearson yesterday in Hawk Green, and he made a few comments questioning the validity of the evidence against him. I'd love to get a professional eye on the forensics; see how they stack up against modern techniques.'

'Is this to do with *our* fires?'

'Kind of, but not directly.'

'Sure, if it'll help,' said Mac after a short pause. 'Send me the files, and I'll take a look at them when I get a spare moment.'

'You're a star. I'll email them to you in the next hour,' she said, then ended the call.

Next, she called Dr Siobhan Harris, one of the UK's leading forensic psychologists whose expertise she had relied on in previous investigations. They'd originally been introduced by Carter some years ago, and Harris had been a very valuable asset to her and the team ever since.

As the phone began ringing at the other end, Phillips detected an overseas dial tone.

'Hello,' said Harris eventually.

'Siobhan, it's Jane Phillips.'

'Jane? How lovely to hear from you.' Harris's soft tone belied her razor-sharp mind.

'Have I caught you at a bad time?' said Phillips. 'Sounds like you're overseas.'

'Rome, actually, but don't worry, I'm doing some lecturing at the university. It's not a holiday.'

'Oh, that's good news, well, for me at least.' Knowing how petite and stylish Harris was, Phillips could imagine her strolling through the streets of the Italian capital, looking every bit the chic, intelligent woman about town. 'Are you free to talk?'

'Sure. How can I help?'

'I'm hoping you can do some profiling for me – paid work, of course.'

'What are we looking at?'

'A fire setter targeting police personnel.'

'Wow. Really?'

'Yes,' replied Phillips. 'So far we've had one fatality and several seriously injured in the last week alone.'

'Sounds urgent.'

'It is.'

'Well, I'm just heading out to deliver a lecture for a few hours, but if you send me over what you have, I can have a look at it this evening.'

'Are you sure?'

'Positive. I'm here alone, and my Italian's not great, so it'll give me something to read over dinner.'

'Thanks, Siobhan. You're a life saver.'

'My pleasure. Look, I'd better dash; my car to the college will be arriving soon.'

'No problem. I'll send everything over as soon as I can. And good luck with the lecture,' added Phillips.

Jones tapped on her closed office door before opening it and stepping inside just as she hung up. 'How'd it go with Carter?'

'Good and bad news.'

'Really? In what way?'

'The good news is he's signed off on Harris doing some profiling for us.' Phillips paused for a second as Jones looked at her expectantly. 'I also spoke to Mac, and he's agreed to have a look at the forensics reports on the Pearson cases.'

'Great.' Jones raised a quizzical eyebrow. 'Does he know why we're looking at them again?'

'Not really, no. I gave him enough to get him involved but not enough that it might compromise us.'

'Sounds very sensible.' Jones put his hands in his pockets. 'So what was the bad news?'

'We got dragged into an impromptu meeting with Fox.'

Jones winced. 'Ouch. How was she?'

'Her usual miserable self, with added jetlag,' she shot back.

'Sounds like a fun combo.'

'Yeah, it was. So I got my own back by telling her that Townsend had been sniffing around Pearson and trying to connect his crimes with our fire setter.' Phillips chuckled. 'She almost shit a brick.'

Jones laughed. 'I wish I'd seen that.'

'It was good,' Phillips confirmed. 'So,' she went on, 'Dudley has been summoned to help manage the fallout if anything around that makes it into the media. He's probably copping it as we speak.'

'That guy has *all* the fun.'

Phillips glanced over his shoulder out towards the office. 'What about Bov? How's he been since he got back?'

'Quiet, by his standards. Had his head down the whole time.'

'Understandable in the circumstances,' said Phillips. 'Okay, let's remember he did say he wants us to treat him normally. With that in mind, let's see if he and Whistler have got any updates for us.'

'Sounds like a plan.'

'After you.' Phillips gestured towards the office before following him out.

A moment later, Jones took a seat at his desk as Phillips dropped into the spare chair.

'How're you getting on with those arsonist prison leavers?' she asked Entwistle.

'I've spoken to my mate in the probation office, and she's compiling a list of all prison leavers convicted of arson and released in the last six months who either served their time in the area or settled in the northwest after being released.'

'How long will that take to come through?' Phillips asked.

'I explained the urgency, so she's working on it as we speak.'

'Good job. As soon as you get the details, we're going to need full backgrounds as well as cross-referencing all of them against the CCTV from the two fires.'

'That's a big job,' Bovalino cut in.

'Yeah, I know, but right now it's necessary. Draft in some help from the support team if you need it.'

The big man nodded as Phillips continued, 'And as they're prison leavers and will all still be on licence, we're free to check their phone records. See if any of them have contracted phones we might be able to track on the night of each fire.'

'More likely to be pay-as-you-go, guv,' said Jones.

'I know, but it's worth a shot.'

Entwistle made a note. 'I'll get onto that as soon as the list arrives.'

Bovalino pulled his notepad closer. 'I just got an interesting hit on the ANPR cameras, boss.'

Phillips raised her eyebrows. 'Interesting how?'

'About half a mile from the Wythenshawe club on the night of the fire, a car belonging to Alex Vasilyev popped up at seven p.m., two hours before it all kicked off.'

'And who is he?' Jones asked.

'One of Podgorski's alibis for that night.'

'So...what are we thinking? Vasilyev was lying about playing cards with him?'

'Maybe.' Bovalino shrugged. 'I mean, given the timelines, it's possible that he could have made it back to the Comrades Club in Cheetham Hill, but it does seem a bit odd that he just so happens to be in the area within a few hours before the fire.'

'Yeah, it does,' she replied. 'We should check him out. As a matter of urgency.'

'Do you want to head there now?' asked Jones.

'No. You and Bov go,' replied Phillips. 'I've got a bucket load of decision logs to update.'

Jones smiled and tossed the big man the keys to the squad car. 'Looks like you're driving.'

'Just one more thing before you go,' Phillips added. 'I've asked Siobhan Harris to run a profile on our firestarter. Hopefully she can give us a better idea of the type of person we're after.'

'Siobhan?' Entwistle appeared to sit to attention. It was widely known among the team that he had a soft spot for the beautiful psychologist. 'Is she coming in?'

'Unfortunately for you, no,' said Phillips with a smile. 'She's in Rome at the moment, so she'll be doing the work remotely.'

Entwistle's shoulders sagged.

'Never mind,' said Bovalino before leaning across and patting Entwistle on the shoulder with his meaty hand. '*La prossima volta sarai più fortunato.*'

'What the hell does that mean?' Entwistle asked.

'Better luck next time. Roughly speaking!'

Jones laughed as Entwistle blushed slightly.

Phillips allowed herself a smile; it was good to see the big man getting involved in banter again. 'Oh, and Jonesy,' she added, 'while you're out, you'd better bring Bov up to speed on the videos.'

He nodded as he pulled on his coat. 'Will do, boss.'

'Right, guys,' said Phillips as she clapped her hands together. 'As ever, we've lots to do, so let's get cracking.'

23

'**E**verything all right, Bov?' asked Jones as they headed anticlockwise around the M60, which acted as Manchester's outer ring road.

'Yeah, why?'

Jones glanced out the window as he attempted to hide the fact he was fully aware of what was going on. 'You've just not seemed yourself lately.'

The car fell silent momentarily.

Bovalino let out a deep, audible breath. 'I *was* going to tell you everything's all right, but I can't lie to you, Jonesy. We've been mates for too long.'

'That's true,' Jones said kindly as he turned sideways to his friend. 'So what's going on?'

'Izzie found a lump,' Bov replied, his grip on the steering wheel tightening, 'and they think it could be breast cancer.'

'Oh mate. I'm really sorry.'

'That's where I was this morning, at the doctor's with her, getting the results of the MRI.'

'And what have they said?'

'They can't rule it out,' – he took in a long breath – 'so they need to do a biopsy.'

Jones nodded, turning to look at his friend. 'I'm sure she'll be fine, Bov,' he said. 'My sister had a scare last year, and that turned out to be nothing in the end.'

'But what if it's *not* fine?' Bov countered, an edge of panic cutting through his voice. 'What if it is cancer? I can't lose her, Jonesy. I just can't.'

'You won't,' said Jones, meaning it. 'Whatever happens, you'll get through it, just like you did when *you* got injured.'

Bovalino nodded silently.

'I take it you've told the guv?'

'Not about the biopsy – I was going to tell her when we get back – but she knows about everything else.'

'Well, it goes without saying, whatever help we can give you, it's yours, and if you need time off at all, just shout. You know that.'

'Thanks, Jonesy.'

'You're stronger than you realise, big man. You've got this. Izzie has too.'

Bovalino pulled the car into the left-hand lane as he prepared to leave the motorway at the next exit. 'Right, I hope this guy Vasilyev's in at this time of day.'

Jones took the hint: Bovalino was done talking about Izzie. 'Yeah, me too.'

Five minutes later, they arrived at the address on file and parked up outside a block of nondescript redbrick flats, which appeared to have been built in or around the sixties.

'He's number thirteen according to the file,' said Bovalino as he killed the engine.

Jones pulled up Vasilyev's mugshot on his phone, which he flashed to his partner. 'Not what you call one of life's lookers, is he?'

'Probably got a lovely personality, though,' quipped Bov. 'A real sweetheart.'

'He'd have to be looking like that,' Jones added with a laugh before opening the passenger door and jumping out.

As they made their way up the short path from the road towards the communal front door, Jones spotted the car that had been captured on ANPR – a scarlet BMW M3 – pulling into the carpark adjacent to the block. 'Looks like we're in luck.'

Bovalino followed his line of sight and smiled. 'Bingo.'

Jones led the way across the carpark and took up a position next to the car.

'Can I help you?' asked Vasilyev, frowning as he stepped out and closed the driver's door. He appeared to be somewhere in his forties; a large man, as tall as he was wide, he was wearing a blue Adidas tracksuit whose white stripes on the sleeves and legs matched his white trainers. As with most gangsters, his neck, fingers and wrists were covered in gaudy gold jewellery.

Jones held up his credentials. 'Alex Vasilyev?'

Vasilyev moved a few steps closer to examine his badge. 'What's this about?'

'We just need to ask you a few questions, if that's okay?' said Jones. 'Mind if we come in for a chat?'

Vasilyev folded his arms across his powerfully built chest. 'I do, actually.'

Jones made a show of scanning the carpark and surrounding flats. 'Do you really want to have this chat out here?'

'I got nothing to hide,' came the abrupt response.

'Suit yourself,' replied Jones, seeing no reason to waste any more time. 'We spotted this car – *your* car – last Wednesday night on the ANPR cameras in Wythenshawe.'

'A crime to drive round south Manchester now, is it?'

'So you admit that you *were* driving it at that time?' asked Jones.

Vasilyev shrugged. 'I'll need to consult my diary.'

'The thing is,' Jones continued, 'two hours after this car was spotted on that camera, someone set fire to the Wythenshawe Social Club.'

'And what? You think I had something to do with that?'

'You still with the Red Army?' Bovalino cut in.

'No, mate. I gave all that up a long time ago.'

'You sure?' pressed Bov. 'Because from what I hear, you boys had a bit of a reputation for playing with fire back in the day.' He paused. 'In particular, Molotov cocktails.'

'Not me.' Vasilyev shook his head. 'Play with fire and you'll get your fingers burned.'

Jones nodded. 'So what were you doing in Wythenshawe last Wednesday?'

Vasilyev sniffed with contempt and remained silent for a moment before a wide grin spread across his face. 'Wednesday, you say? I was over at the hospital. Took my mum up there for a follow-up appointment. Had her hip replaced a couple of months ago.'

'And she'll vouch for you, will she?' asked Bovalino.

'Oh, yeah. She'll vouch for me.'

'Of course she will,' said Jones sardonically. 'And where did you go after you took your mum to the hospital?'

'Can't remember,' he shot back.

'Really?' Jones raised his eyebrows as he glanced at

Bovalino and then back to Vasilyev. 'Because according to what you told our colleague DC Entwistle, you were playing cards with Maxim Podgorski at the Cheetham Hill Comrades Club.'

Vasilyev's eyes widened for a moment before he regained his composure. 'Oh, yeah, that's right. It's coming back to me now.'

'Do you often forget where you were?' asked Jones.

'From time to time. What can I tell you? I'm a busy man.'

Jones exhaled sharply. 'And what about this Monday just gone? Any chance you might remember where you were that night?'

'Why?' Vasilyev glared back defiantly. 'Got my car on camera that night too, have you?'

Jones held his gaze but didn't reply.

'No. I didn't think so.'

'Tell us about your beef with Sergeant Armstrong,' said Bovalino.

Vasilyev turned his attention to the big Italian. 'Never heard of him.'

'Okay. Well, what about the Serious Crimes Unit?' Bov continued. 'Ever had any run-ins with those boys that we should know about?'

'Nope. Nothing. I'm a good law-abiding citizen, I am.'

'Of course you are,' said Jones flatly.

'Anything else I can do for you?' Vasilyev checked his watch. 'Like I say, I'm a busy man, and to be honest, it's a bit too cold for me standing out here.'

'No. That's it for now,' said Jones.

'Good stuff,' Vasilyev replied as he rubbed his hands together vigorously, his cement-grey eyes glinting. 'Time to get indoors and in front of a roaring *fire*.'

Jones didn't react. 'We'll be seeing you, Alex,' he said before turning to Bov and signalling for him to lead them back to the squad car.

24

Early the next morning, Phillips was sitting in her office as Jones debriefed her on the encounter with Vasilyev.

'See if his alibi stacks up,' she said as she took a sip of her freshly made coffee. 'I've no doubt it will, but it doesn't mean his mother is telling the truth either.'

'I've asked Bov to run another check on his car and see if it pops up anywhere near Hazel Grove and the George and Dragon in the last week.'

'Good idea. And get him to take a look at his phone records too while he's at it. See if his handset pings off any of the nearby towers at the times of the fires.'

Jones sipped at his peppermint tea. 'I'm sure he'll be glad to do it. The more work I give him, the happier he seems at the minute.'

'How was he yesterday?'

'Well, he finally opened up to me about Izzie, which was a bit of a relief. I hated pretending I didn't know.'

'Did he mention the biopsy?' she asked.

'Yeah, he did.'

'Called me last night on my way home to update me too. Sounded quite upset.'

Jones nodded. 'It's really hit him hard, which is understandable.'

'Yeah, totally, but like you say, let's just make sure he stays busy; it'll help keep his mind off things.'

Just then, there was a knock at the door.

Phillips flinched slightly, surprised as she was to see Mac standing in the doorway. Seeing him up close in the daylight – and out of his forensic overalls – she realised for the first time how athletically built he was: his toned torso and muscular arms straining against his tight, police-issue black T-shirt. He also seemed taller than she had realised, at least six feet two, maybe six three.

'I'm not interrupting, am I?' he asked, flashing his perfect white teeth.

'Not at all,' said Phillips, setting her coffee cup down on the desk.

Jones shot her a knowing look as he cleared his throat and shifted in his seat.

Phillips glared at him for a split second before turning her attention back to Mac.

'I've had a look at the forensics on the Pearson case.' Mac raised the folder in his right hand as he stepped inside before perching on the edge of the office drawers adjacent to Phillips's desk. 'It certainly makes for interesting reading.'

Reclining in her chair, she attempted to appear as casual as possible. 'In what way?'

'It's the chain of evidence.' He handed the folder across. 'Specifically, the collection and identification of the DNA evidence by way of a blood sample. It was the only thing that conclusively tied Pearson to the fire at the police house in East Didsbury and essentially led to his conviction for all of the fires he was alleged to have set.'

'So in what way was it interesting?' Phillips opened the folder and began scanning the documents.

'The DNA was harvested almost a week after the scene had first been examined.'

'And what's unusual about that?'

Mac folded his arms across his chest. 'Well, it means that it had been missed by every single member of the forensics team – most of them pretty experienced, by the looks of it – for five days straight before the most junior member of forensics, alongside one of the investigating detectives, found it on day six.'

'Seems unlikely,' said Jones.

'Yeah, it does, and there's something else as well. The blood sample itself was in incredibly good condition considering it had been taken from the scene of a fire. Granted, it was from the periphery of the room and not from where the fire had been at its most fierce, but still, I would have expected it to be more fire-damaged than it was.' He pointed at the folder on the desk. 'I mean, the sample included in there did show signs of degradation as well as oxygenation of the haemoglobin, but not to the levels you'd expect from a fire of that size and ferocity.'

Phillips looked up from the folder. 'Which means what?'

'Which means, the sample *was* exposed to fire, but at a much *lower* temperature than the other blood samples taken from the room.'

'Could that be because, as you say, it was on the periphery?'

Mac pursed his lips. 'Maybe, but there were a fair

number of blood samples harvested from the scene during those first five days of the forensic sweep of the house. Now, it's worth noting that several of those samples were harvested from different areas of the room – and all at similar distances from the source of the fire as Pearson's sample – but as you'll see on page fourteen of the report, the degradation and oxygenation of the haemoglobin in each of those samples was far greater than Pearson's blood sample.' He paused, looking at both of them in turn. 'Which, in my experience, simply doesn't make sense.'

Phillips felt her brow furrow. 'So if I'm understanding this correctly, the blood attributed to Pearson *was* damaged by fire, but the heat from the fire that caused that damage was significantly less than the fire that destroyed the police house in East Didsbury.'

'That's about the size of it, yeah.' Mac nodded, his face impassive.

'So how was this not picked up by the defence team?'

'I haven't read the court transcript,' he told her, 'so it might well have been. That said, even if it was, back then it would have been unlikely to sway a jury away from a guilty verdict when DNA was still relatively new. We didn't have the same understanding or the level of control thresholds that exist today.'

Phillips tapped her finger on the file on her desk. 'Pearson claims that his blood samples were planted. Let me ask you this: if this blood evidence was presented today, would it get past those same control thresholds?'

'Not a cat in hell's chance,' he replied flatly.

'And in your opinion, do the discrepancies in the degradation of the different samples support Pearson's claims the blood was planted?'

'That's really not for me to say,' replied Mac carefully. 'But if *I* were his lawyer looking at that data, I'd seriously fancy my chances in the court of appeal.'

Phillips glanced at Jones, whose grave expression matched her own.

'There is one more thing I should mention, which is – shall we say – of a delicate nature,' Mac added.

'Go on.'

'The detective who purportedly picked up on Pearson's sample at the scene alongside the junior CSI—'

Phillips sensed what was coming.

'—was DCI Fox, or – as we know her today – *Chief Constable* Fox.'

A powerful surge of adrenaline shot through Phillips's body as her suspicions were finally realised. 'Have you spoken to anybody else about this?'

Mac shook his head. 'I brought it straight here.'

'Good. And I'd suggest keeping it that way for the time being.'

Mac flashed a smile. 'I've only just got here, guys. I wasn't planning on taking on the big boss *just yet*.'

Phillips closed the folder. 'Thanks for this, Mac; we really appreciate it.'

'Happy to help.' He stood now. 'Well, as much as I've enjoyed this walk down memory lane, I'd better get back to some proper forensics.'

'Thanks again,' said Phillips. 'I mean it.'

'Yeah, thanks, mate,' Jones added.

Mac doffed an imaginary cap. 'I'll be seeing ya,' he told them theatrically before strolling out of the room.

CARTER'S EYES widened as he stared down at the folder, which was now on his desk. 'As in *planted*?'

'Potentially yes,' said Phillips. 'And I'm afraid it gets worse.'

'Why doesn't that surprise me?'

'The sample in question – essentially the nail in the coffin for Pearson – was found *six* days after the fire, by a junior forensic scientist and the SIO leading the investigation.'

Carter closed his eyes for a moment before sighing as he opened them again. 'And let me guess, the SIO was Fox?'

'Yes, sir.'

'Oh shit,' he muttered. 'Shit. Shit. *Shit.*'

'I really think it's time to take a proper look at the Pearson case, sir.'

Carter held her gaze for a few seconds before passing across a clear evidence bag. 'This arrived about an hour ago in the post. I bagged it as soon as I realised what it was.'

Phillips turned the bag round in her hands as she examined the contents.

Carter continued, 'It's another note from our guy, plus a printout of a newspaper story from the day Pearson was convicted.'

'Pearson is innocent.' Phillips began reading the note aloud. 'He was set up by senior cops now hiding in plain sight, and I intend to prove it. You haven't heard the last from me. The Real Firestarter.' Next, she read the headline out loud. 'Cop Killer Firestarter Jailed for Life.'

'Thankfully there was no video this time round,' added Carter.

'So what do we do, sir?' Phillips asked as she handed the bag to Jones so he could take a closer look for himself.

The room fell silent as Carter scanned the forensic report for a minute or so. 'And Mac is sure about this, is he?'

'Yes, he is.'

Carter held her gaze as he asked, 'Can we trust him?'

'*Him*, I don't know yet,' said Phillips, honestly. 'But from what I've seen of his work so far – and based on his background up to this point – I think his expertise is right up there, sir. Evans was good, but this guy's on another level.'

'You've been very quiet, Jonesy,' said Carter. 'Where's your head at with all this?'

Jones reached forward and placed the evidence bag on the desk before returning to his seat. 'Well, based on Mac's take on the forensics and this Real Firestarter's crusade to prove Pearson's innocence, I agree with the guv; I think it's time to take another look at Pearson's case.'

Carter exhaled sharply as he sat forward, linking his fingers together, his elbows resting on the desk. 'Well, as much as we can't let an innocent man rot in prison any longer than necessary, we also only get one chance at this. So we need to tread very, *very* carefully. If Mac's conclusions are correct and the blood samples *were* planted by Fox, then it's up to us to prove it. If we can find the evidence to corroborate your theory, then I'll personally deliver it to the PCC myself. But there can be no doubt, nothing at all.'

Phillips felt her pulse quicken. She could hardly believe what she was hearing. 'Does that mean we're actually going after Fox, then, sir?'

'Yes, DCI Phillips,' replied Carter. '*Yes, we are.*'

25

The following morning, after a fitful night's sleep, Phillips showered and made her way downstairs, where she found Adam asleep on the couch, still dressed in his green surgical scrubs from a late shift the previous night. Keen to get out of the house as quickly as possible and in no mood for a chat, she headed into the kitchen and set about making herself a coffee for the journey into the city, while debating whether breakfast would be a good idea ahead of a postmortem. After considering what lay ahead in the next few hours, she decided starting the day on an empty stomach would be the best option.

Five minutes later with her travel cup in one hand and her car keys in the other, she was about to head out when Adam wandered in, stopping her in her tracks.

'What time is it?' he groaned with a yawn, rubbing the back of his neck.

'Half-seven,' she replied.

'I must have crashed out when I got home. We were crazy busy last night.'

'Yeah. I figured you must have been, seeing as you didn't reply to any of my texts.'

'I didn't get any messages last night,' he mumbled as he fished his phone from his trouser pocket.

'Really?' she shot back. 'I checked on WhatsApp, and it said they'd landed last night.'

Adam scanned his phone and frowned. 'Oh, shit, you're right. I didn't even see those.'

'That's something, I suppose. At least you weren't deliberately ignoring me.'

'I'm sorry, babe. There was a massive pile-up on the M62 and—'

'Don't worry about it,' she said, cutting him off. 'Look. I've got to go. I'm due to meet Tan for a postmortem at eight thirty.'

'Ah, Dr Death,' he joked. 'Give her my love.'

Phillips ignored the remark. 'I'll see you later,' she said flatly before marching out of the room towards the front door.

———

Based on the circumstances of her death, and expecting it to be a fairly straightforward process, she'd suggested Jones head into the office as opposed to joining her for Violet Williams's postmortem. She knew how much he detested the process, and, besides, having been given the green light from Carter, his time would be far better served pulling together everything they would need to put their case against Fox to the PCC.

It was approaching 9 a.m. by the time she eased the Mini

Cooper into a space on the top floor of the already packed multistorey carpark attached to the Manchester Royal Infirmary as the rain lashed down once more. Jumping out, she pulled the collar of her coat up against the weather and set off in the direction of the main building.

Ten minutes later she descended the stairs to the basement, then moved at pace along the corridor before reaching her final destination, the mortuary. Pressing the intercom on the wall, she waited twenty seconds or so for the audible buzz as the magnetic lock was released to allow her access. Pushing the door open, she stepped inside and made her way to Dr Tanvi Chakrabortty's office – the chief pathologist. No matter how many times she visited this place, she could never get used to the smell, a bizarre mixture of the pervasive odour of strong disinfectant found in regular hospital wards, coupled with the sickly stench of an old-fashioned butcher's shop. It was no wonder Jonesy couldn't stand the place.

When Phillips eventually found her, Chakrabortty appeared lost in her work, sitting at her desk, eyes narrow as she stared at the computer screen in front of her, her jet-black hair tied back in a bun.

'Knock, knock,' said Phillips, rapping her knuckle on the open door.

Chakrabortty glanced up. 'Hi, Jane,' she said, then checked her watch. 'God, is that the time? I hadn't realised.'

'Busy?' asked Phillips.

'Always. Funnily enough, I was just looking at the PM reports you sent through last night for the Pearson case.' Chakrabortty pushed her chair back and stepped up, revealing her long, elegant frame, which, as ever, was covered in pristinely pressed green surgical scrubs. 'We can have a chat about them after this if you have time.'

'That'd be great.'

Chakrabortty glanced over Phillips's shoulder. 'Are we waiting for Jonesy to join us?'

'Not this morning. Seeing as it's a basic PM, I figured I'd let him off the hook for today.'

'You're all heart,' said Chakrabortty as she moved around the desk.

Phillips smiled. 'Well, doesn't hurt to be nice once in a while now, does it?'

'Not at all.' Chakrabortty gestured towards the door. 'She's in room two. After you.'

Five minutes later Phillips – now wearing a plastic apron and latex gloves – took her position standing opposite Chakrabortty, the mottled greying-white body of Violet Williams lying on the surgical table between them, her torso covered with a crisp green sheet, the nostrils and lips black.

'You ready?' asked Chakrabortty, holding a large scalpel in her gloved hand.

'As I'll ever be,' Phillips replied before exhaling loudly.

Time almost seemed to evaporate watching Chakrabortty at work, her gracious movements quite mesmerising despite the gruesome nature of the task in hand. As they approached the hour mark, Chakrabortty, using both hands, reached into the chest cavity and removed the blackened lungs, which she placed on a separate metal table next to Violet's body.

'Wow.' Phillips stared down at the large charcoal-coloured organ. 'Is that from the fire?'

Chakrabortty shook her head. 'No. This level of discolouration is consistent with that of a life-long smoker.'

She tapped her scalpel against the upper right side of the right lung. 'See this white lump here.'

Phillips leaned in to get a closer look.

'That's cancer.'

'Really? D'you know, I've never actually seen cancer in the flesh, no pun intended.'

Chakrabortty continued, 'Based on the shape and size of it, it looks like she must have had it for quite some time, and it's never been treated.'

'When Jonesy and I spoke to her daughter, she never mentioned her mum being sick, so I'm assuming she probably didn't even know she had it.'

'That would be my guess, too.'

'Who'd be a smoker, hey?' Phillips mused.

'Having seen literally hundreds of lungs just like this one, not me, that's for sure.'

Next up, using a large pair of surgical scissors, Chakrabortty separated the trachea from the lungs and oesophagus before cutting it open along its centre and laying it flat down. 'As expected, see – it's thick with soot.'

'I can't believe how black it is. Is that smoking too?'

'No,' replied Chakrabortty. 'This is down to the fire alone, and by the looks of it, she took in a large amount of smoke.'

'As I understand it, she was trapped inside the burning function room for at least three to four minutes after the fire really took hold. She had to be carried outside by two of the other guests when they finally got the door open.'

'Poor thing must have been terrified faced with all that heat and smoke.'

Phillips shuddered at the thought: a woman in her seventies, trapped inside a burning building. It didn't bear thinking about.

Next Chakrabortty began the dissection of the damaged lungs and started by slicing through the right lobe. 'There it is, as expected,' she said a moment later as she pulled it open with both hands.

'What am I looking at?'

'Soot around the bronchioles,' replied Chakrabortty. 'Consistent with inhaling a considerable amount of smoke.'

Phillips once again moved closer to get a better look. 'How can you tell what's what? It *all* looks black to me.'

Chakrabortty used the scalpel to guide Phillips once more. 'This sticky black stuff is tar from the cigarettes, this browny-black staining here is consistent with nicotine, and these patches of black spots around these small tubes are the soot.'

'Stupid question, I guess,' Phillips mused, 'given what we're looking at, but is that what killed her? Smoke inhalation?'

'I have a few more tests to do to sign it off officially, but so far there's nothing to indicate she died of anything else like a heart attack or a stroke, which can happen when older or less healthy people are faced with traumatic situations such as a fire. Plus, the blood work displayed high levels of carbon monoxide in the body. Based on all those things together, I think it's safe to say she died of smoke inhalation.'

'Okay, that's good to know,' Phillips replied.

The remainder of the postmortem took just over an hour, and with all the tests complete and smoke inhalation finally rubber-stamped as the cause of death, they headed back to Chakrabortty's office.

'So what did you think about the Pearson info I sent through?' asked Phillips as she took a seat opposite Chakrabortty's desk.

'To be honest, pretty lightweight.'

Phillips raised her eyebrows. 'Really? In what way?'

Chakrabortty unlocked her computer screen. 'Look, I've not had a chance to do a deep dive into the various reports, but I've been doing this long enough to spot when the bare minimum has been done in a postmortem, which appears to have been the case with all the victims I looked at, but especially so with Bradley Wells.'

'He was the last victim supposedly killed by Pearson,' said Phillips.

Chakrabortty's eyes narrowed. 'Supposedly? I looked at the case notes, and he was convicted by a unanimous verdict.'

'Yeah, he was, but based on new evidence, I'm starting to have my doubts about that.'

'New evidence?' Chakrabortty sat forward. 'What have you found?'

Phillips trusted Chakrabortty implicitly, but it was way too early to share *exactly* what she had on Fox. At the same time, based on the fact they were effectively trying to bring down the chief constable, she was also keen to sense-check herself and valued her friend's opinion. 'I had the new CSI guy, Mac, take a look at the forensics—'

'Bit of a dish, isn't he?' cut in Chakrabortty with a glint in her eye.

'I hadn't noticed,' said Phillips, knowing the opposite to be true. 'Anyway, he seems to think the DNA evidence presented at trial wasn't quite as robust as it should have been.'

'In what way?'

'Some of the blood samples taken from the scene look to

have been affected differently by the same fire. Is that possible?'

Chakrabortty pursed her lips. 'I guess so, if the fire was more intense in different parts of the room.'

'That's just it,' said Phillips. 'The whole house in the East Didsbury fire was gutted. There was almost nothing left.'

'Well, if that's the case, I think he's right to question the validity of the DNA.'

Hearing that response, Phillips felt her pulse quicken once more, aware they were on the right track and closing in on Fox. Knowing Chakrabortty as well as she did, she decided to take a leap of faith. 'Can we speak confidentially, Tan?'

'Of course.'

'There's a bigger issue at play here.'

'Oh? And what's that?'

'The senior officer in charge of the Pearson case at the time – and ultimately the person who submitted the questionable DNA evidence – was DCI Fox.'

Chakrabortty recoiled. 'As in *Chief Constable* Fox?'

'Yes.'

'Wow,' murmured Chakrabortty.

Phillips nodded. 'I know.'

'Are you sure you want to rattle that cage, Jane?'

'Do I have a choice? I mean, if Mac's right and the evidence isn't sound, then there's a good chance Pearson has served seventeen years in a maximum-security prison for a spate of crimes he didn't commit. I can't just sit back and do nothing.'

'Of course not.' Chakrabortty folded her arms across her chest. 'But I don't envy you. Fox won't take kindly to you challenging her work. You know how protective she is of her precious reputation.'

'Yeah, I do, so I'm going to have to be very careful around all this.' Phillips sighed heavily. 'Look, thanks for hearing me out, Tan. I really appreciate an extra pair of ears on this one.'

'Anytime, Jane. You know that.'

'And it stays between us, right?'

'Goes without saying.'

Phillips offered a faint smile. 'Thank you.'

'One of the team will email Violet's report over this afternoon,' said Chakrabortty.

'Perfect. Any plans for the weekend?'

'With my backlog of cases, probably working. How about you?'

'Same here, I think,' replied Phillips. 'Adam's working *again*, so I may as well use the time to myself to catch up on paperwork.'

'Oh, yeah.' Chakrabortty leaned back in her chair. 'How's he getting on with the new job?'

'Loves it.'

'That's good to hear.'

'Yeah,' said Phillips with zero enthusiasm.

'You don't sound convinced.'

Phillips shrugged. 'Honestly, Tan, I'm really pleased he's enjoying it—'

'I sense a but coming?'

'I just wish he'd occasionally talk about something else at home. At the minute it's like nothing else exists outside of the HEMS unit.'

Chakrabortty smiled. 'Boys and helicopters, hey? The ultimate toys.'

'Something like that.' Phillips stood up. 'Anyway, I really should be getting back to the office.'

'I'd better crack on too,' said Chakrabortty. 'Well, whatever you end up doing, I hope you find at least some time to relax this weekend.'

'You too, Tan,' said Phillips.

26

'I 'm a firestarter, twisted firestarter,' he sang loudly in time to the music, which was once again blasting out through the Bluetooth speaker. 'I'm a firestarter, twisted firestarter!' Picking up the roll-up from the ashtray on the kitchen table, he took a long drag as he continued to read the article on his phone, posted just yesterday. 'So far, police are yet to make any arrests,' he said out loud. 'Of course they haven't, cos they're all too fucking stupid.'

Just then there was a loud banging on the wall to his left, accompanied a moment later by muffled shouts from the man he recognised as his irate neighbour. 'Switch that shit off!'

He laughed and turned the volume up even higher as he closed the article on his phone and went in search of more stories that might feature his handiwork.

Sometime later – how long he wasn't entirely sure, as he'd lost himself reading a series of online articles about the recent spate of fires – he heard a banging noise coming from his front door. Glancing up from his screen, he felt his jaw clench. 'Piss off!' he shouted before returning his gaze to the phone.

As 'Firestarter' continued to play on loop at full volume, the banging came again, louder and more rapid this time.

'Right, that's it,' he muttered as he jumped up from the chair, grabbing his Zippo as well as a can of air freshener, which was sitting on the side. The banging continued unabated as he marched towards the door. 'I'll bloody show you,' he mumbled as he released the chain, grabbed the handle and yanked it open – stopping in his tracks a split second later.

Standing there in front of him were two uniformed police officers, one tall, well-built male, and one short but stocky female. Taking in the name badges on their chests, he noted they were Officers Howard and Shabir respectively.

'There's been a noise complaint,' said Howard, glancing in towards the room where the music still boomed loudly.

Surreptitiously slipping the Zippo into the pocket of his jeans, he decided the best course of action was to feign deference, something he'd become accustomed to in prison over the years. 'Sorry, Officers,' he said sheepishly. 'I've been doing some cleaning and didn't realise how loud it was. I'll turn it down. Just give me one sec.'

Moving back into the kitchen, he pressed pause on the phone and placed the air freshener on the table before heading back to the front door, where Officers Howard and Shabir still stood.

'These are small units,' Howard said as he stepped back and took in the flats around them. 'So I'd suggest keeping the volume at a more suitable level from now on to avoid upsetting your neighbours, okay?'

'Of course, Officer.' He nodded vigorously. 'I'll make sure it doesn't happen again.'

'Good, because next time we'll nick you for disturbing the peace, understood?'

'Yes. Understood,' he replied, taking a mental note of the numbers on each of their shoulders.

'Right,' said Howard, turning to Shabir, 'we'll be off, then.'

He watched them walk along the landing before they turned left down the staircase and out of sight.

Closing the front door now, he headed back into the kitchen and took a seat at the table before grabbing a scrap of paper. 'Officer Howard, 4583, and Officer Shabir, 4527. I'll be seeing you again,' he said as he scribbled the names down. 'And next time, I'll be the one giving the orders.'

27

P hillips's weekend had panned out pretty much as she thought it would. With Adam working right through and with not much of a social life outside of their relationship, she'd opted to spend the majority of Saturday and Sunday in the office as she attempted to get ahead on the investigation.

Having spoken to almost no one for two days straight, by the time the team arrived at eight o'clock on Monday morning, she was eager to get the early morning briefing started without delay. So with a coffee in hand – the initial pleasantries out of the way – and everyone sitting around the table in the MCU conference room, she jumped straight in. 'So, team, where are we at with everything?'

Entwistle, whose laptop was connected to the big screen at the end of the room, was first up. 'We got a couple of reports back over the weekend, which I scanned through yesterday. The first was from digital forensics, who've been looking at the pen drive sent to the chief super. Frustratingly, it looks like there's no digital footprint and nothing on there that can help us identify the sender.'

Phillips took a mouthful of her coffee. 'That's annoying, but it was always going to be a long shot. Our fire setter would have to be either stupid or incredibly lax to leave anything behind.'

Entwistle continued, 'Mac has also sent through the forensic profile for the ink that was used on the note sent to Carter.'

'Anything of value?'

'Sorry, guv. No. It appears to have come from a standard HP inkjet printer, which are ten a penny and completely untraceable.'

'Of course they are.' Phillips's tone was sardonic.

'However, I think *I* might have found something of interest.'

'Really?' Phillips raised her eyebrows. 'What?'

Entwistle opened a folder on his laptop, which now appeared on the big screen. 'I had a few hours to myself over the weekend, so I started working my way through the list of prison leavers and thought this guy would be worth a closer look.' A prison mugshot flashed up on-screen of a gaunt, thin man with dark shadows around his eyes wearing the ubiquitous prison-issue grey sweatshirt. The left side of his neck carried what appeared to be extensive burn scarring. 'Bruce McDonnell, aged fifty-six. Got out on licence six months ago after serving seven years of a fourteen-year stretch for arson. He set fire to a boarding kennel in Stockport that was well known for housing retired police dogs. According to his file, the fire took hold so quickly there was no way to save any of the dogs, and all ten animals housed there were killed that night.'

'What kind of monster could do that to innocent animals?' Bovalino asked.

'Sounds like a total scumbag,' added Jones.

Entwistle continued, 'He served the first three years of his sentence up in Durham at HMP Frankland.'

'Wasn't that where the Yorkshire Ripper, Peter Sutcliffe, was held before he died?' asked Jones.

'Yeah, it was. Ian Huntley's in there too,' Entwistle replied, referring to the man behind the notorious Soham murders of 2002.

'A veritable rogues gallery,' said Phillips.

'What's really interesting, though,' Entwistle continued, 'is that McDonnell finished his sentence in Hawk Green.'

'Was he anywhere near Pearson?' Phillips asked.

'Yeah. The same block.'

'Now that *is* interesting.' Phillips took another drink of coffee.

'I haven't had a chance to check him against the CCTV from around the fires yet, and I need to find out if he has a mobile, but I do have an address for him if we want to pay him a visit.'

'We do,' said Phillips. 'Especially given what he did to those police dogs.'

'Shall we go take a look, guv?' Jones asked.

But before she could answer, a chorus of beeps filled the air as each of their phones vibrated.

Entwistle grabbed his. 'Looks like a notification from the *MEN*.'

Phillips had already opened the link on-screen, and her stomach churned as she read the headline aloud. '"Cops Chasing Archie Pearson Copycat?" Oh shit. Fox will have a coronary when she sees this.'

Entwistle scanned the story further. 'Looks like he's really gone for us on this one, boss. Saying we're struggling for leads as we hunt for a copycat killer.'

Phillips was already up and out of her chair. 'I need to go and see Carter.'

'What about McDonnell?' asked Jones.

'You and Bov go,' she shot back over her shoulder. 'I'm needed upstairs,' she added before almost running out of the room.

PHILLIPS WAS ATTEMPTING to read the story on her phone as she rushed up the back stairs towards the fifth floor. Reaching the penultimate landing, she turned back on herself and was met by Carter coming the other way, worry etched on his face.

'I was just on my way to see you. Have you read it?' he asked.

'The main bits, yes.'

'This is all we need right now, Townsend making waves.' Carter lowered his voice to a whisper and glanced furtively down the stairs. 'With everything else we're trying to do, the last thing we want is the chief constable's profile any higher than it needs to be at the moment. Plus, it'll only make her even harder to manage.'

'I know, sir, but what can we do? Don Townsend's a law unto himself.'

Carter checked the stairs once more. 'Out of all of us, you've got the closest relationship to him. Is it worth you trying to talk to him?'

'I can try, but to what end? The piece is already out there now. The damage is done.'

'From this article, yes, but I'm sure there'll be a follow-up piece or pieces. It might be worth trying to get him to hold off on those.'

Phillips exhaled sharply. 'I can give it a try, but I can't promise he'll listen to me. That said, Don does love to make a deal, so I guess if I could offer some kind of quid pro quo to rein it in, that might tempt him.'

'What did you have in mind?'

'To be honest, right now I have no idea, but I'm sure I can figure something out.'

'Great,' said Carter.

'Do we need to go and speak to Fox?' Phillips queried.

'No. It's fine. I'll spare you that. I can do it on my own.'

'Are you sure, sir?'

'Definitely. I'd much rather you stay out of her way and concentrate on the investigation and see if you can muzzle Townsend.'

'Okay.' She nodded her agreement. 'Well, in that case, I'd better get going.'

'And I should go and see Fox.' Carter offered a weak smile. 'Wish me luck. Somehow I think I'm going to need it.'

28

Sometime later, Jones and Bovalino walked side by side down the exposed balcony that led to McDonnell's second-floor council flat. The wind was blowing hard once more, and rain wasn't far away.

'Charming spot,' said the big man.

Up ahead a small, slightly built man with what appeared to be shopping bags sitting around his feet and wearing a thick anorak was unlocking the door to McDonnell's address, but with his back to them, they couldn't be sure it was him.

'Bruce McDonnell?' said Jones.

The man turned and frowned. 'Who's asking?'

Jones presented his credentials. 'DI Jones and DC Bovalino from the Major Crimes Unit.'

'I didn't do it,' the man said with a smile.

'So you are Bruce McDonnell?'

He nodded.

Up close now, the scarring to his neck was even more prominent, and Jones noted it extended up the back of his left ear, as well as marking both hands. 'Can we come in?' he asked, slipping his ID into the inside pocket of his coat.

McDonnell looked Bovalino up and down, then turned his attention back to Jones. 'What's this about?'

'It's probably better we speak inside – out of this wind,' said Jones.

McDonnell took a moment to respond, then nodded reluctantly before pushing open the front door and stepping inside.

Following him in, the stench of stale tobacco was the first thing that hit Jones, who glanced back at Bovalino just behind.

His expression suggested his senses were being assaulted by the smell as well.

'Lived here long, have you?' Jones asked as they reached the sparsely furnished living room, which was equipped with nothing more than an ancient television set and a small two-seater sofa facing it. Scanning the room, he spotted at least four ashtrays placed around the space, each of them full to the brim with what appeared to be roll-up butts.

'About five months, I think it is now,' replied McDonnell, placing his shopping bags on the table in the kitchen area adjacent to the room they occupied now. 'Since I left the halfway house.'

Jones had little desire to spend any more time than was completely necessary in this dank, depressing space, so he cut to the chase. 'Where were you last Wednesday night – the eleventh of October?'

McDonnell picked up a pouch of rolling tobacco and some cigarette papers from the table next to him. 'Mind if I smoke?'

'If you must,' said Jones flatly.

McDonnell took less than thirty seconds to fashion a slim white cigarette, and a moment later he placed it between his thin lips and lit it. The end glowed orange as he took a long drag before exhaling thick smoke from his mouth and nostrils. 'What time on Wednesday night?'

'Around nine o'clock,' Jones replied.

McDonnell produced a wide grin, revealing crooked, tobacco-stained teeth. 'I'd have been here. I rarely go out after seven p.m.'

'You still on tag?' Bovalino asked.

'No, it came off last month, but when I was, I got into the habit of being in before seven, and it's kinda stuck.'

'Can anyone vouch for you?' said Jones.

McDonnell took another long drag, exhaling smoke as he spoke. 'My mum. She's staying here with me at the moment.'

Jones felt his eyes narrow. 'I thought the council only provided one-bed flats for single blokes?'

'They do,' McDonnell replied. 'I've been sleeping on the couch.'

Bovalino glanced at the small sofa. 'Can't be very comfortable for you.'

McDonnell shrugged before taking another drag. 'Beats a prison cell.'

'So can we speak to your mum?' Jones cut back in.

'Not today. She's in Southport on a day trip. The local Methodist church organised it.'

'I see. And when will she be back?' asked Jones.

'Not till later this evening. I've got to go and pick her up from the church at nine.'

'I thought you didn't go out after seven?' said Bovalino.

McDonnell smiled again. 'I'm happy to make an exception for Mum. She'll be here all day tomorrow, if you want to come back.'

'We will,' Jones replied. 'And what about Monday night, just gone? Where were you then?'

'Same. Here with Mum.'

Jones scrutinised the man's face for any signs he was lying, but if he was, it didn't show. He changed tack now. 'Tell us about Archie Pearson.'

'Archie?' McDonnell appeared to flinch slightly. 'What do you want to know about *him*?'

'You did time with him, didn't you?' Jones replied.

'Yeah, why?'

'What was he like?'

'Nothing special,' said McDonnell. 'Quiet, kept himself to himself.'

'Seventeen years inside and he still claims to be innocent,' said Jones. 'What do you make of that?'

'*No one's* guilty in prison, DI Jones.' McDonnell laughed. 'We all just needed better lawyers.'

Jones said nothing for a moment as he studied the scarring on McDonnell's neck. 'Did you get those burns from the fires you set?'

At this, McDonnell's posture visibly stiffened. 'No. They were someone else's handiwork.'

'Really? Who?'

'Thankfully I don't remember. I was too young when it happened.'

'So you got them as a kid?'

'Yeah. I was about five or six at the time.'

'I'm sorry to hear that,' said Jones.

McDonnell suddenly stood to attention. 'Where are my manners? Can I get you both a cup of tea or a coffee?'

'No, thanks,' Jones replied.

'Are you sure? I got some biscuits from the shop.'

'No, we'd better be going.' Jones looked at Bovalino and then glanced in the direction of the front door.

The big Italian nodded his agreement.

'We'll be back tomorrow morning to speak to your mother,' said Jones.

'What time can I expect you?' McDonnell finally stubbed out his cigarette. 'I'll make sure she's ready.'

'Probably around ten.'

McDonnell laughed nervously. 'I really hope she's not having one of her bad days and can't remember. She has early onset dementia, you see.'

'Just make sure you're both here,' replied Jones, his voice entirely neutral.

'Where else am I going to go?' said McDonnell. 'With the paltry amount of benefits they give me each week, the only thing I can afford to do is sit in the flat and watch telly.'

Jones nodded without feeling. 'We'll see you tomorrow,' he said before following Bovalino out.

29

'I thought I might be hearing from you today,' said Townsend, flicking his cigarette stub to the ground as Phillips drew closer to the revolving-door entrance of the *Manchester Evening News* main building. 'Although it's not often you come all the way into the city to see me.'

Despite the overwhelming urge she felt to give him a piece of her mind, Phillips knew Townsend would be far easier to negotiate with if she stroked his ego as opposed to taking him down a peg or two. 'I need your help, Don.'

Townsend raised his eyebrows. 'Really? This sounds like fun.'

'Is there somewhere more private we can talk?'

'Well, now I'm really intrigued.' He gestured away from the building. 'Let's take a walk in St John's Gardens.'

A few minutes later, Phillips found herself walking side by side with Townsend through the small inner-city park located just a few hundred metres from Spinningfields, one of the city's main business districts. She was more than familiar with her surroundings, having investigated a fatal stabbing that had taken place in this popular public space just a few short months ago. The park was also strongly connected to Townsend and his former lover, Victoria Carpenter. Several years ago, she had fought to protect the park from greedy Realtors connected to the Chinese mafia, and that battle had ultimately cost her her life.

'Any news on when they'll be putting up Vicky's memorial plaque?' asked Phillips.

'Spring next year,' he said in a low voice. 'Everything seems to take forever when you're dealing with the council.'

'I can imagine.'

'It's ironic, really. Aaron, as the supposed grieving widower, will be the guest of honour at the official ceremony, when it was always me she loved, and it was my baby she was carrying.'

Phillips didn't know how to respond to his candour, so thought it best to say nothing.

Thankfully Townsend appeared just as keen to change the subject as she was. 'So, what can I do for you, Jane?'

'I need you to take a step back from publishing any more content on the arson attacks.'

Townsend stopped in his tracks. 'You've got to be kidding?'

She looked him square in the face. 'I'm deadly serious, Don.'

'Now, why would I want to do that? The article has already had close to half a million views since it landed this morning and almost two hundred thousand shares. My editor is over the moon.'

Phillips scanned her surroundings to ensure she couldn't be overheard before speaking in a low voice. 'Look, Don. I can't get into the details just now, but I need you to trust me on this one. I'm working on something big that's connected to these investigations, and your stories could seriously jeopardise the outcome.'

'Sorry, Jane, but you're going to have to give me more than that.'

'I can't. Not yet.'

Townsend shrugged as he turned back in the direction of his offices. 'Well then, I can't help you.'

She placed her hand on his wrist as she attempted to stop him leaving. 'I promise you'll get the exclusive once I can share it.' She held his gaze. 'And it'll be big, Don, far bigger than this story now.'

'Really?' His eyes narrowed. 'How much bigger?'

'Bigger than *anything* I've ever given you before.'

'Okay. I'm still listening.'

'All I need you to do is hold off on printing anything further connecting Pearson to the recent arson attacks.'

'Why?' he asked.

'I can't say at the moment, but I promise it'll all make sense in time. And it'll be worth it.'

Townsend scratched his stubbly chin. 'So what do I do in the meantime? Like I say, my editor is chomping at the bit to get more content out.'

She took a moment before answering. While she hated divulging operational information, she knew she had to give him a bone of some sort. 'Look, I can't promise it'll be today – or even tomorrow for that matter, but I've drafted in a specialist to help me create a psychological profile of the arsonist. Once I have it confirmed, I'll share it with you.'

'And I can print it?'

Phillips nodded reluctantly. 'Yes.'

'And just to be clear, you've got no issue with me doing a

follow-up on the fires as long as I stay away from the Pearson link?'

'None at all,' she conceded.

'Okay,' said Townsend. 'I can live with that. As long as I still get the exclusive when the time comes.'

'You will,' she said.

'Sounds like a win-win to me.'

As the wind suddenly picked up and blew across the park, Phillips shoved her hands deep into her coat pockets. 'I'd better be getting back.'

Townsend pulled a pack of cigarettes from his pocket. 'Think I'll have another smoke to celebrate our deal.'

Phillips nodded. 'I'll be in touch,' she said, then set off back to the car.

30

Phillips removed her coat and hung it on the back of her office door before resetting her ponytail, then heading out into the main office to check in on the rest of the team. 'How did you get on with McDonnell?' she asked as she took her usual position at the spare desk.

Jones leaned back in his chair. 'He was a funny little guy, to be honest.'

'How do you mean, funny?'

'Well, he was just a bit odd. Bov and I were saying on the drive back, considering he's in his mid-fifties, he seemed a lot older. Very small and slight with almost translucent skin. To be honest, he didn't look well to me.'

'Not surprising considering how much he smokes,' added Bovalino. 'The place reeked of stale fags.'

'So, what did he have to say for himself about his where-abouts on the nights of the fires?'

'Reckons he was at home with his mum, who's staying with him at the moment,' Jones replied.

'And did she vouch for him?'

Jones shook his head. 'She wasn't there. Out for the day apparently on a trip to Southport with the local church. We've arranged to go back tomorrow morning and speak to her. He made some remark before we left about her having early onset dementia, so we'll have to wait and see how reliable she is.'

Phillips rolled her eyes. 'It's never straightforward, is it?'

'No.' Jones chuckled. 'Never.'

Just then Phillips's phone vibrated in her pocket. Fishing it out, she could see it was Dr Siobhan Harris calling. 'Siobhan, how's it going?'

'Good, Jane. I've had a look at the info you sent through and worked up a profile.'

'Great,' said Phillips. 'I'm just going to put you on speaker if that's okay? I'm here with the guys.'

'No problem.'

Phillips activated the speaker function and held the phone out in front of her mouth. 'Ready when you are, Siobhan.'

'Hi, guys,' she said.

A chorus of hellos filled the air a second later.

With the room silent once more, Harris continued, 'Okay. Well, first things first, generally speaking, we can separate fire setters into two main groups – there are actually *five* groups, but to get into that level of detail, I'd need to examine the subject face to face. So for the purpose of a profile such as this, we'll look at the main two. Group one is made up of those who *like* fire, and group two is those who use it as a convenient tool for interpersonal violence. I'd say your guy is in the first group. Based on the information you gave me, we can presume he has a strong relationship with fire, a sense of connection that has developed over time. He may even become aroused when he's in contact with fire.'

'Sexually?' said Phillips, the note of surprise clear in her voice.

'Not necessarily. More likely his adrenaline will spike when he sees it, and his heart starts pumping. It's a living thing – one that will get him excited, the smell of the smoke, the colour and movement of the flames. They all mean something to him.'

'Okay. What else can you tell us about him?'

'Well, he likely started his relationship with fire at an early age. It would have been playful and inquisitive at first, such as setting fire to dry grass and leaves in the summer months, but he would probably have graduated quite quickly to bigger objects once he realised the destructive power of fire. Looking at the device he used for the second blaze, I would say he has a deep understanding of fire and how it can be harnessed to his own ends.' She paused for a moment, allowing the officers present to consider her insights.

'Hi Siobhan, it's Jonesy.' He spoke in a loud voice, sitting forward so he was closer to the phone. 'On the method of fire setting, I've got a question.'

'Hi, Jonesy. Sure.'

'Is there anything significant in the fact he used a Molotov cocktail on the first fire and the small incendiary device on the second?'

'I think there is, actually,' replied Harris. 'Obviously, I can't say for certain, but one of the dominant traits in fire setters is a desire for control. I think the fact he started the fire *outside* of the first building could suggest it was his first time setting a fire of this size – or at the very least, his first time in a long time. Once he had confidence in his ability, he was then able to set the second fire up close and personal, so to speak.'

Jones nodded. 'Makes sense.'

'So do we have any idea of what kind of man we're looking for, physically and mentally, for example?' asked Phillips.

'Again, profiling isn't an exact science, but I'd say your man is somewhat of a loner, someone who keeps himself to himself. He's unlikely to be married or in a relationship and probably lives alone. Alternatively, he could also share a home but with someone who leaves him to his own devices, such as an elderly relative. Outwardly he's likely to be polite and mild mannered, subservient even, but this will mask his inner rage, which will probably have been building steadily since he was a kid, when he likely experienced some form of significant trauma. That's usually the root cause of fire setting: events from childhood.'

Phillips spotted Jones and Bovalino exchanging knowing glances. 'What is it?' she asked.

'It might be nothing, guv,' said Jones, 'but the doc's profile sounds a lot like McDonnell: single, lives with an elderly parent and very polite and mild mannered.'

'He also said he'd got those burn scars from a fire when he was just a young kid,' added Bov.

'Who are we talking about?' Harris cut in.

'A person of interest the guys spoke to today. He's out on licence after serving seven years for setting fire to a boarding kennel for dogs. Killed ten animals in one night. He also spent time on the same block of Hawk Green prison as Archie Pearson.'

'Sounds like a very strong match for the profile,' said Harris.

Phillips nodded. 'I agree.' She turned her attention to Bovalino. 'Get the car keys,' she instructed. 'We're not waiting until tomorrow; we need to bring him in now.'

The big man nodded, then stepped up from the chair.

Phillips matched him. 'Thanks, Siobhan. First-rate work as ever. Look, we'd better go, but we'll keep you posted.'

'Please do,' Harris replied. 'And good luck.'

nder blues and twos, and with Bovalino at the
wheel – an amateur rally driver on the weekends
– the twenty-minute journey to Burnage took just
over ten. Jumping out of the squad car in unison, Jones led
the way as they raced up the concrete stairs to the third floor,
turning right onto the exposed landing a minute later.

'It's that one at the end, guv.' Jones pointed towards
McDonnell's flat, which was cloaked in darkness.

'Doesn't look like he's in,' surmised Phillips.

'I wouldn't put it past this fella to be sitting in the dark,'
added Bovalino. 'He was a bit of a weirdo, like.'

Jones stepped forward and banged heavily on the flat's
front door.

Just as Phillips had feared, there was no answer, so she
dropped to her haunches and pushed open the letter box
before shouting her instructions. 'Open up; it's the police.'

No response.

She repeated the process, shouting louder this time.

Again, nothing.

Phillips stood.

'What time did he say he was picking up his mother from her trip?' said Jones.

'Nine, I think,' Bovalino replied.

Phillips checked her watch. 'It's not even five o'clock yet.'

Just then a door behind them opened. 'Are you the police?' a male voice asked.

Each of them turned to face the large man with a shaven head.

Phillips produced her ID. 'DCI Phillips. And you are?'

'Eric Stephens.' The burly man nodded towards McDonnell's door. 'Have you come to sort him out? He's a bloody nuisance.'

'In what way?' Phillips asked.

'The noise. Playing that sodding "Firestarter" song, day and night.'

Phillips felt herself flinch slightly. '"Firestarter"?'

'Yeah. You know the one by the Prodigy? He plays it on loop constantly, and these walls are paper-thin. It's all we can hear most of the time. I thought your lot had sorted him out the other day, but he just carried on once they'd gone.'

'How'd you mean, "our lot"?' said Jones.

'Police. They were here on Saturday after I complained. For all the good it did. An hour after they left, he just started again.'

'And they didn't come back?' asked Phillips.

'No. I called them again, but the guy on the switchboard said it was busy, and they might not get to it that night, so I just gave up.'

'I see,' said Phillips. 'And what about his mother? Does he play that song when she's at home?'

Eric Stephens frowned. 'His mother?'

'Yeah. She lives with him,' added Jones.

'Not that I've ever seen,' replied the man. 'It's always just been him ever since he moved in.'

Phillips locked eyes with Jones for a split second, then turned her attention back to the neighbour. 'You wouldn't happen to know where he is now, would you?'

The man shook his head. 'No idea. I've only spoken to him once when I first asked him to turn the music down. The fucking maniac threatened to pour petrol through my letter box and set me and my missus on fire. That's why I got your lot involved. He's a total psycho.'

Phillips's pulse quickened. 'Do you know what time he left the flat today?'

Stephens shrugged. 'Dunno, probably around two, I think. The music stopped, and I heard him bang the front door shut when I was having my breakfast. I work nights, you see. That's why the music is such a pain in the arse.'

'That's about an hour after we spoke to him, guv,' Jones cut in.

'That figures,' said Phillips. 'Well, thank you for your help, Mr Stephens. We can take it from here with regard to your noise complaint.'

'I bloody hope so; the guy's a menace,' said Stephens as he stepped back inside and closed his front door a moment later.

Phillips turned her attention back to Jones and Bovalino. 'It *has* to be McDonnell, and now the slippery bugger's done a runner.'

'Shit. Sorry, guv,' said Bovalino. 'We didn't know.'

Phillips's mind raced, picturing their number one suspect going to ground now that he knew they were closing in on him.

'What do you want to do?' asked Jones.

'Get a force-wide alert out on McDonnell and find out which officers attended the noise complaint on Saturday. Let's see if they have anything of value to share.' She thumbed over her shoulder towards the flat. 'And I want this place locked down and searched inch by inch. We need forensics in there ASAP.'

Jones was already pulling his phone from his pocket. 'I'll speak to Whistler to organise a warrant, and then I'll get onto Mac.'

'And tell them both to cancel any plans they might have had. I sense it's going to be a long night.'

———

TWO HOURS LATER, the place was teeming with people as Phillips, Jones and Bovalino – each wearing blue latex gloves and shoe coverings – alongside Mac and his forensic team, set about examining the contents of the small flat.

'I see what you mean about the stench of cigarettes.' Phillips wrinkled her nose as they stepped into the small, dank bedroom. 'Reminds me of when I was a kid growing up in Hong Kong and my dad used to take me to the Mahjong clubs on Kowloon; all the old boys chain-smoking as they played for hours on end. It was like moving through fog walking round those places.'

'As an ex-smoker, it turns my stomach,' replied Jones.

Bovalino stepped in through the door, carrying a piece of paper in his gloved hand. 'I just found this in the rubbish bin, guv.' He handed it across.

Phillips examined the contents.

'It's an appointment reminder from his doctor's for tomorrow,' said Bov. 'The surgery's just round the corner.'

Jones stepped to Phillips's shoulder to get a better look.

'Says he needs to get his blood checked before they can approve his outstanding prescription for cyclophosphamide,' she said.

'What the hell's that?' asked Jones.

Bov pulled out his phone. 'How do you spell it?'

Phillips held up the letter so he could see for himself.

'Let's see what Google has to say.' He tapped into his phone and a moment later turned the screen to face Phillips and Jones. 'Oral chemotherapy tablets, by the looks of it.'

'So McDonnell's got cancer,' said Phillips.

'Well, if he has,' Jones replied, 'it hasn't stopped him smoking and would certainly explain his sallow appearance.'

Phillips checked her watch, then turned her attention to Bovalino. 'It's after half-six, so they may well be closed now, but get yourself round to the surgery and see what you can find out about McDonnell and these meds.' She handed back the letter. 'If they're overdue and keeping him upright, then he may have no choice but to be at that appointment tomorrow. And if he is, we'll be waiting for him.'

'Will do, boss,' said the big man before heading out of the room, passing Mac, who was coming the other way.

'Well, he's no hoarder, that's for sure,' said Mac, pulling down his face mask. 'Aside from a load of tab-ends, empty Pot Noodle containers and a bunch of used cup-a-soup sachets, there's nothing in the kitchen that's of any use to us.'

'The standard diet of the long-term prison inmate,' quipped Jones.

'Quite.' Mac flashed a smile. 'We'll get started in here next if that's okay with you?'

'Sure,' replied Phillips. 'We've had no joy, but hopefully your guys will have better luck. We'll get out of the way.'

A few minutes later, Phillips and Jones stood next to each other in the small living space as the forensic team began moving their equipment through to the bedroom.

Jones's voice was low when he spoke. 'I'm really sorry, guv. Bov and I should have collared him when we had the chance.'

'Based on what?' she shot back. 'Without Siobhan's profile, we'd still be none the wiser, so there's no way you could've known just by talking to him.'

'But it's so obvious now. McDonnell's a perfect fit for our fire setter.'

'Yeah, like you say. He is *now*, but this afternoon he was just another ex-con on a long list we were investigating.'

'If he sets another fire before we find him...' Jones's words tailed off.

'Look, there's no point beating yourself up about it,' said Phillips. 'The best thing any of us can do right now is focus on finding him. Okay?'

Jones nodded. 'Okay, guv.'

'Right. First things first, we need to find out when we can expect Bov back, cos he's got the squad car, and without him, we'll be stuck in this dump for the rest of evening.'

32

The following morning, he woke up to the sound of vacuuming in the next room. Slipping out of bed, he rubbed his arms to keep warm as he tiptoed across the floor and opened the door just enough to see out onto the landing of the small hotel. Checking to ensure the 'Do Not Disturb' sign was still hanging on the handle where he'd left it last night, he pushed the door to and placed the small chain into place.

'It's bloody freezing,' he muttered before slipping on a pair of tracksuit bottoms, followed by a thick jumper. 'The joys of a dirt-cheap hotel,' he added as he filled the kettle and set it to boil.

The vacuuming continued next door as he made himself a cup of tea before rolling a cigarette. Despite the No Smoking signs plastered all around the building from reception on the ground floor all the way through to his room in the attic, it was evident from the yellowing wallpaper and smell in the air that both current residents as well as former guests felt free to ignore the directive. He certainly had no plans to curb the one thing he had left that brought him any pleasure. Well, the one thing apart from setting coppers on fire.

Pulling out his trusty Zippo, he placed the roll-up between his lips and sparked up, taking a long drag before exhaling a satisfying, smoky breath.

Despite his many years in prison, thanks to a continuous stream of young prisoners through HMP Hawk Green – many in their late teens and early twenties – he had managed to maintain a decent grasp of technology and, in particular, the power of social media. Unlike many of his fellow older inmates who saw it as something only relevant to their kids or grandkids, he had developed a fascination for the various platforms and, above all, X – commonly known by its former moniker, Twitter. He loved the fact anyone could have an account, and you could pretty much say what you liked to whomever you liked, without the slightest recourse. Free speech for everyone and no comebacks. He liked the idea of that, and during the long nights in prison, it was one of the many things he dreamed of enjoying once he finally got out.

Sitting on the edge of the bed, he opened the X app on his untraceable pay-as-you-go smartphone and began the process of deleting his existing account. He'd set it up a few months back in order to get used to the platform and figure out how to navigate the various functions available to each user, but it was of no use to him now. Now he was ready to create a brand-new handle to unleash click-worthy content the likes of which the people of Manchester – or even the world, he mused – had never seen before.

'Username?' he said aloud when prompted on-screen – a wide grin spreading across his face as he typed in his reply. '@realfirestartermanchester.'

He took another long drag of his cigarette, blowing out a thick plume of smoke as he went in search of a suitable image for his profile picture. Scrolling through his photos, he found what he was looking for: a still shot he'd captured of the function room at the George and Dragon engulfed in flames. 'Perfect,' he said before stubbing out the roll-up on the saucer resting on the bed next to his knee.

The vacuuming outside grew louder now – the cleaner had evidently moved out onto the landing, butting the head of the Hoover up against the base of his door as she pushed it back and forth across the carpet.

Trying his best to ignore her, he turned his attention back to his phone as he began to pull together his first post under his new handle.

It didn't take him long to find a mugshot of Archie Pearson, taken from an article written at the time of his conviction, detailing his sentence – a life term with a minimum of seventeen years to be served before he'd be eligible for parole. He shook his head. 'And they call us criminals,' he said under his breath.

With the photo attached, he spent the next ten minutes crafting the text, which was not easy with only 280 characters to play with. After a few false starts, he decided less was more and cut the message down to its simplest form. 'An innocent man rots in jail! The police are corrupt!' he read aloud, but quietly enough that he wouldn't be overheard by the cleaner. 'A cartel of senior officers continues to turn a blind eye to injustice to protect their places at the trough.

Time for change – time to expose the pigs hiding in plain sight. #realfirestartermanchester #fire #corruptGMP #pigs.'

With his finger hovering above the screen, he took one last look, then pressed the post button.

A moment later, it went live.

33

Phillips had been updating her decision logs for three hours straight by the time Bov knocked on her open door just after 11 a.m.

'Hi, guv. You got a minute?' His hair and the top half of his shirt were soaking wet.

Phillips frowned. 'You look like you've just stepped out of the shower.'

'I have. It's pissing it down outside.' He rubbed his hair with his hands as he attempted to shake off some of the water. 'This is just from walking across our carpark.'

Phillips gestured for him to take a seat. 'At least the rain makes it harder to start fires.'

Bovalino sat down opposite. 'On that. I've been to see McDonnell's doctor, Dr Sharmin.'

'Any joy?' Phillips leaned back in her seat.

'Well, she wouldn't tell me directly what's wrong with him – patient confidentiality and all that – but after a bit of persuasion on my part, she *did* admit McDonnell is a very sick man.'

'How sick?'

'Again, she kind of skirted around it, but by the sounds of it, he's not going to be around for very long.'

'What are we talking? Years, months?'

'She wouldn't say, but judging by her grave expression when we were speaking about him, I'd say sooner rather than later.'

Phillips blew out through her lips. 'Which means McDonnell has nothing to lose, making him even more dangerous.'

'That's what I was thinking too,' said Bovalino. 'His blood test appointment is scheduled for one o'clock today. I'm going to head back to the doctor's and see if he shows up.'

'Good idea, but I have a feeling he won't. If he knows we're onto him, he'll probably go to ground. When was the last time anyone checked the force-wide alert on him?'

'I looked it up it on my phone just before I came into the building, and there was no sign of McDonnell, not even anyone resembling him, I'm afraid.'

'Damn it.' Phillips sat forward now. 'Well, stay on uniform's back. We need to make sure finding him doesn't drop down their list of priorities.'

'Of course, guv. I'll chase them up now.'

'Speaking of uniform, did we get anywhere with the officers who handled the noise complaint at McDonnell's?'

Bov pulled his notepad from his pocket. 'PCs Howard and Shabir, ma'am. I spoke to Howard first thing this morning on my way to the doctor's, but he had very little to say. According to him, they were only with McDonnell for a few minutes and didn't actually go inside the flat.'

Phillips sighed. 'Another dead end,'

'Sorry, guv.'

'Don't be daft,' she replied with earnest. 'It's not your fault.'

Bov offered a faint smile. 'I'd better crack on,' he said before stepping up from the chair.

'Before you do.' Phillips motioned for him to retake his seat. 'How are things with you?'

Bovalino glanced over his shoulder out towards the office, where Jones and Entwistle appeared lost in worlds of their own, before turning back to Phillips, his expression suddenly serious. 'She's got a biopsy booked in for next Wednesday at Christie's.'

'Well, that's good, isn't it? The fact they're not wasting any time.'

'Yeah, maybe, but I can't help thinking that the fact it's so quick is because it's serious.'

'I understand why you'd think like that, but in my experience, it's best not to speculate as to what it might be until they tell you one way or the other.'

'I guess.'

'And the good thing is, Izzie's young, fit and healthy. Even if they do find a tumour, there's no reason why she won't make a full recovery. The treatments these days are incredible.'

Bovalino said nothing and appeared deep in thought.

'What time is the procedure on Wednesday?'

'She's up first, nine a.m. So I'll be back in the office by eleven.'

'No, you bloody won't,' Phillips shot back. 'You'll take the day off and look after your wife.'

'Honestly, I'd rather be at work, boss.'

'I'm sure you would, but Izzie needs you, and whether you like it or not, I won't support you burying your head in the sand on this. Unless you stand up and face what's going on, this will come back to bite you.'

Bovalino's shoulders sagged as he stared back at her in silence.

'I know Izzie's got her sisters, but right now, she needs you more than anybody. You've always been her rock, Bov, and you've got to put aside any of your own fears and be there for her right now when it really matters. Do you understand?'

'Yeah, I do,' he said as he nodded.

'Good. Because the Bovalino I know and love can handle anything.'

'Thanks, guv.' He glanced back towards the office. 'I'm okay with Jonesy knowing about why I'm off that day, but can we still keep this between the three of us? I'd rather not talk to Whistler about it just yet. The less people know, the better.'

'Of course. We don't have to tell each other *everything*.' Considering the secret Entwistle was carrying around on a daily basis, Phillips had no issue keeping him out of the loop on something such as this. 'Speaking of what Whistler knows, let's go and see how he's getting on with McDonnell's background check.'

A minute later Bovalino returned to his desk as Phillips moved to Entwistle's shoulder.

'Any updates on McDonnell?' she asked.

Entwistle pointed to his screen with his pen. 'I'm glad you asked, cos based on this little lot, he's a very close match to Siobhan's psych profile.'

'In what way?' Phillips bent forward to get a closer look.

'Turns out McDonnell's mother died when he was five years old, and he went to live with his aunt, Mary McIntyre, in Urmston. By the looks of it, he was with her for a few years before becoming a ward of the state and being put into care. Once in the system, his name pops up a lot in police and social services files; it looks like he quickly became a handful. A year or so later, and after several arrests for petty theft and malicious damage, he was finally sent to Borstal – for twelve months when he was just thirteen. He served the full twelve months and, on his release, went back into care, but it wasn't long before he was in trouble again, and he was arrested six months later for arson. He did two years that time, for setting fire to a car that belonged to one of the carers at the children's home.'

'Bloody hell, that's some record for a kid that age.'

'It gets worse,' said Entwistle. 'Three months after getting out of Borstal that time, and while back in care, he was arrested again for burning down a prefab building at the school he was attending. He got three years for that, starting his sentence in Borstal before transferring to prison when he was seventeen. He's been in and out of the nick ever since and each time for setting fires.'

Phillips stared at the information on-screen for a moment before responding, 'Do you know how he got the scars?'

'No, boss. There's no details regarding that on file, but I'm guessing they have something to do with his fire setting.'

'Yeah, I think you might be right,' Phillips replied. 'And on that, check the dates of each of his incarcerations as an adult against the Pearson fires. If McDonnell was on the outside each time they were set, then he's looking more and more likely to be the real firestarter, as he claims to be.'

Entwistle made a note in his pad.

'Is the aunt still alive?' Jones cut in.

'I dunno. I haven't had a chance to check.'

'What was her name?' asked Bovalino.

'Mary McIntyre,' Entwistle replied.

At that moment, Phillips's phone began to ring in her pocket. Pulling it out, she groaned seeing Townsend's number on-screen. 'What the hell does he want now?'

'Who is it, guv?' said Jones.

Phillips showed him her phone screen before hitting the answer button. 'Don, what's up?'

'Have you seen Twitter this morning?'

'No. I don't use it.'

'Well, I suggest you speak to someone who does,' he said, his tone laced with mischief.

'Seriously, Don. I don't have time for games, and I know you're dying to tell me, so why don't you just share what's so important.'

'Get on Twitter and search for the hashtag realfirestartermanchester. You'll see what I mean.'

She stood to attention now. 'What did you say?'

'You heard me; look up hashtag realfirestartermanchester,' he repeated. 'It's quite something, and once you've had a look, call me back. I'll be needing a quote.'

She hung up without responding, then turned to Entwistle. 'Pull up Twitter, will you?'

'You mean X?' he corrected.

'Twitter, X. I don't care, just get it up on-screen now.'

'What's going on?' asked Jones.

'I don't know yet, but based on what Don just said, I have a horrible feeling our firestarter has gone viral.'

'I'm on X,' said Entwistle.

Phillips moved back to his shoulder. 'Search for hashtag realfirestartermanchester.'

He typed in the details as requested, and a second later the same live video that had been sent to Carter appeared on the screen.

'Oh, God,' mumbled Phillips.

'Holy shit, look at these comments,' said Entwistle a second later.

Jones and Bovalino were out of their seats in a flash, moving next to Phillips as they all stared at the video playing on-screen.

Entwistle began reading out loud through the list of comments attached to the post:

Filthy pigs deserve what they get.

Corrupt bastards – let them burn.

Let's have scumbag BBQ.

Bring on the revolution.

'It's hardly the outrage I would have expected considering the video shows people trapped in a burning building,' said Jones.

'Not *people*,' Phillips replied. '*Cops*. And that's the difference.'

Jones straightened. 'I know we're not the most popular folk on the planet, but this is a bit strong, isn't it?'

'Whatever it is, it's in the public domain now. When was this posted?' she asked.

Entwistle took a moment to find the answer. 'Two hours ago.'

'Okay. Send it over to Siobhan.'

'Yes, guv.'

Phillips continued, 'And get digital forensics onto Twitter – or whatever the hell it's called – and see if we can get hold of an IP address for the person behind that account.'

Entwistle was already copying the link details from his browser.

Phillips turned to Jones and Bovalino. 'We need to track down McDonnell ASAP – as in right now – so let's put some serious screws on uniform to see if they can help us find him.'

Both men nodded.

And in the meantime I really need to talk to Carter before Fox sees this. If this tweet blows up like I think it will – like I think it already *is* doing – she may well panic and start going all out to hide her involvement.'

'We'll lose everything we've got on her if she does.' Jones nodded. 'And I'd put money on it that she'll soon be flinging shit left, right and centre to cover her tracks.'

'Cover her tracks?' Bov frowned now. 'How do you mean?'

Phillips turned to Jones. 'You can tell him. I really need to get upstairs,' she said before turning on her heel and almost sprinting out of the room.

34

P hillips's hopes that they could somehow manage the Real Firestarter fallout ahead of Fox getting wind of the tweet were dashed before she'd even reached the back stairs, when Carter called to say they were both needed in the chief constable's office immediately. So it was with a strong sense of trepidation a few minutes later that she walked past Ms Blair's now – and unusually – empty desk and straight into the inner sanctum of Fox's office to find Carter and the comms director, Rupert Dudley, sitting opposite the chief constable.

'Close the door and take a seat,' Fox barked.

Phillips did as requested and took her position to Carter's left.

Fox held up an A4 printed copy of the tweet in question. 'What are we doing about this hashtag realfirestarter nonsense? I'm told it's trending on Twitter.'

'The platform's called X now, ma'am,' offered Dudley meekly – appearing to regret his intervention immediately.

Fox glowered at him as she placed the printout flat down

on her desk. 'I don't give a monkey's what it's called. All I know is hashtag corruptGMP is now being seen all over the world alongside it!'

'We think it's been posted by a man we've identified as Bruce McDonnell, ma'am,' said Phillips.

'And who the hell is he?'

'A recent prison leaver with a long history of fire setting, including burning down a home for retired police dogs.'

Fox recoiled. 'He set *dogs* on fire?'

'Yes, ma'am.'

'That's barbaric.'

Phillips continued, 'We drafted in the forensic psychologist, Dr Siobhan Harris, to create a profile; it's one he seems to fit perfectly.'

'And where is this McDonnell now?' Fox asked.

'There's a force-wide alert out for him as we speak.' Phillips was dreading sharing the next piece of information. 'We believe he may already know he's a suspect.'

Fox's brow furrowed. 'How?'

'He was on a list of prison leavers with convictions for arson that we'd started having initial conversations with.'

'We've *already* spoken to him?'

'Yes, ma'am.'

'And we let him go?'

Phillips shifted in her seat. 'I wouldn't say we let him go as such. When we first spoke to him, we hadn't yet received the psychological profile, and because he claimed to have a solid alibi, there was no reason for us to suspect him above any of the others on what is quite an extensive list.'

'You say he *claimed* to have an alibi? What do you mean by that exactly?'

Without realising, Phillips had walked herself deeper

into trouble. She cleared her throat. 'Well, ma'am, when Jones and Bovalino first spoke to him, he said his elderly mother could vouch for his movements on the nights of the fires, but that she was away on a church trip that day, so we would have to come back to speak to her another day. Now, having looked into his background, we now know his mother died when he was a small child.'

Fox shook her head. 'So DI Jones – one of MCU's most senior officers – fell for the oldest trick in the book?'

Phillips felt her jaw clench in frustration. 'Ma'am, I don't think that's a fair assessment of the situation.'

'Regardless of fair,' Fox almost snarled, 'do we have any idea where this guy might actually be?'

Even though she knew he was unlikely to show, Phillips decided to inflate the importance of McDonnell's potential visit to the doctor's. Anything to get out of this meeting as quickly as humanly possible. 'When we searched his flat in Moss Side last night, we found a letter that included details of a doctor's appointment for this afternoon. Having spoken to the surgery, we believe the appointment may be of vital importance to him. He has terminal cancer and needs his bloods checking in order to get the chemo meds he needs, so we're hoping he may still attend. Bovalino will be watching at a distance, ready to grab him if he does.'

'I see. You've sent the largest, most conspicuous officer in the GMP to stake him out. That sounds sensible.' Fox's tone oozed sarcasm.

Phillips curled her toes tightly in her boots in an attempt to stop herself from responding in the way she really wanted to. 'He'll be discreet. I have no doubt about that, ma'am.'

Fox tapped the printout with her finger. 'And who's he

referring to when he says, "an innocent man is rotting in prison"?'

'We believe he may be talking about Archie Pearson.'

'Archie Pearson?' Fox was incredulous. 'He's as guilty as they come. I should know, I put him there.'

Phillips fought to suppress the urge to share what she knew about the weakness of the DNA samples that had been key to Pearson's conviction. As tempting as it was to knock Fox down a peg or two in the moment, she knew that would have to wait until they had all their ducks in a row. If the chief constable was given even the slightest hint they had something connecting her to Pearson's potentially false conviction, she'd soon find a way to distance herself from the entire investigation and pin any irregularities on someone else. There was no way that could be allowed to happen. *Not this time.*

Fox turned her attention to Dudley. 'I want a rock-solid plan of how we're going to manage this with the media within the hour, Rupert.'

'Of course, ma'am,' he replied.

She looked at Phillips and Carter in turn. 'And you two had better catch this McDonnell fella ASAP. If I get hauled over the coals by the PCC, I won't be going in there alone. Do I make myself clear?'

'Perfectly,' said Carter.

'Yes, ma'am,' Phillips added.

'Dismissed.'

PHILLIPS AND CARTER huddled together on the now empty fifth-floor corridor.

'The doctor's appointment sounds promising,' said Carter.

'I wouldn't get your hopes up,' Phillips replied. 'It's true, but I just said that to placate her. If McDonnell is our Real Firestarter, then I think he's smart enough to know we may have found the letter.'

'So Bov isn't really going, then?'

'Oh, no, that's happening just in case. What I'm saying is I don't think McDonnell will show.'

'So what's next?' asked Carter.

'Whistler has done a background check on him, and it turns out he lived with an aunt after his mum died. We're hoping she's still alive and may be able to give us a bit more insight into who he is and how we might eventually be able to track him down. I've tasked digital forensics with contacting Twitter – X, whatever – to locate an IP address for the realfirestartermanchester account.'

Carter lowered his voice to a whisper. 'And where are we at with reviewing the Pearson case?'

'I've got Whistler cross-referencing the dates of all of McDonnell's prison terms against the dates of the fires that Pearson was convicted of. If he was on the outside each time, then it's looking more and more likely that he was responsible for them and not Pearson, which could be the nail in the coffin for Fox.'

Carter glanced along the corridor, then nodded sagely. 'Be careful, Jane. She has eyes and spies everywhere.'

'I will be, sir.'

'And keep me posted on everything, won't you?'

'Of course.'

Carter straightened. 'Right, then. I'd better let you crack on.'

'Thank you, sir,' said Phillips before turning and setting off towards the stairs.

Five minutes later as she strode into MCU, Entwistle beckoned her over.

'What have you got?' she asked as she approached his desk.

'Bov's gone to stake out the doctor's, but he left this for you.' He handed across a Post-it with the address scribbled on it. 'McDonnell's aunt is still alive and living in sheltered housing in Salford.'

'Well, that's a start at least.' Phillips turned to Jones. 'You can drive.'

He picked up the keys from his desk and grabbed his coat.

'Oh, and I checked in with digital forensics,' added Entwistle. 'They've put in a request to X, but there's been a bit of a hold-up. Apparently the info we're after requires approval from someone higher up the chain, so they're still waiting for a response.'

Phillips let out a frustrated sigh. 'Just make sure they make it a priority to get that IP address, okay?'

'I will.'

Jones moved next to her now. 'You ready?'

'Yeah, let's go.'

A moment later, just as they reached the door to MCU, Entwistle shouted from behind them, 'Oh shit!'

Turning, Phillips found him staring at his laptop screen, open-mouthed.

'What is it?' she asked, rushing back to his desk with Jones at her back.

'The video of the second fire.' He tapped the screen with his finger. 'It's just this second been posted on X.'

Phillips and Jones huddled together behind Entwistle in order to see his screen.

Entwistle continued, 'It's the same handle, @real-firestartermanchester, and this time he's asking for suggestions of which cop hangout he should burn down next.'

Jones let out a low breath. 'That's not good,' he said.

'And look at this,' Entwistle added. 'Some fucking weirdos are actually answering him.'

Phillips watched the feed refresh.

'Bloody hell.' Entwistle sank his head into his hands.

The next comment that came up was a photo.

Of Ashton House. The building they were all in right now.

35

'I want three firearms units covering this building until further notice,' said Phillips. 'Two on the main gate coming into the carpark and one in reception.' She looked hard at her colleagues. 'Just in case McDonnell is stupid enough to follow that idiot's suggestion and tries to firebomb this place.'

'On it,' said Entwistle, reaching for the phone.

A second later, she and Jones made their way out to the car.

Phillips spent the majority of the twenty-minute journey on the phone to Carter, bringing him up to speed on the raised threat level and subsequent security measures she'd asked to be put in place at Ashton House, as well as the reason for their visit to Salford. When she was finally done, she was keen to find out how his conversation with Bovalino had gone regarding their plan to bring down Fox.

'As expected, really,' said Jones in answer to her question. 'Shocked initially, but not really that surprised, knowing her as we all do.'

'And you told him to keep it to himself, right?'

'Absolutely,' Jones replied before indicating left as they approached the turnoff leading to the sheltered housing block where they hoped to find Mary McIntyre at home. 'Bov won't say a word.'

After parking out front, and with the wind once again blowing in sideways, Phillips and Jones made their way along the short path and rang the bell next to the front door.

Aware of Mary's age, they waited patiently for her to answer.

It was almost two minutes by the time they finally heard the door being unlocked before it was opened on the chain.

'Hello?' came the shrill reply from a diminutive grey-haired lady leaning on an NHS walking frame.

Phillips smiled warmly and placed her badge next to the gap in the door. 'DCI Phillips and DI Jones from Major Crimes Unit. Are you Mary McIntyre?'

The lady nodded. 'What's this about?'

'Could we come inside?' asked Phillips. 'We'd like to talk to you about your nephew, Bruce.'

'Been in trouble again, has he?'

Phillips maintained her smile. 'It really would be easier if we could talk inside out of this bitter wind, Mrs McIntyre.'

The door closed momentarily as she released the chain, and then opened once again. 'Wipe your feet,' said Mary before turning slowly on the walker and shuffling back towards the living room.

As they entered the small lounge at the rear of the property, Phillips was struck by the stifling heat emanating from the gas heater placed in the corner of the room. She felt her cheeks instantly flush.

Having reached her high-backed armchair, Mary placed

the walker to the side and very slowly eased herself down into the seat.

Phillips and Jones dropped onto the small couch adjacent to her.

'So what's he done this time?' asked Mary before continuing without waiting for an answer. It was evident she liked to talk. 'He's been in trouble his whole life, that boy. In and out of prison, but then it's not surprising. I mean, you know what they say, "once a bastard, always a bastard".'

Phillips moved forward to the edge of her seat, resting her wrists on her knees, her fingers linked together. 'What exactly do you mean by that?'

'That he was a bastard, abandoned by his father, like.'

'And you think that affected him?' asked Phillips.

Mary nodded. 'Oh yeah. It affected them both. I mean, it broke poor Annie's heart when Norman buggered off. It was all flowers and dinners at the beginning, telling her how much he loved her and how they were going to spend the rest of their lives together, but he was just saying that to get her into bed. And when she fell pregnant, well, he was off like a shot, back to his wife and kids.'

'He was married?' asked Jones.

'Oh yeah. Of course, Annie didn't know that, not until after she'd tried to reason with him one night after they'd split. She tackled him on his way out of work, and by all accounts, he was livid. Called her all the names under the sun and said it was just a bit of fun – and that he already had kids of his own with his wife. She was absolutely destroyed, and I'm convinced that's what caused her breakdown.'

'Tell us about that,' said Phillips.

'It was a bad business. When Norman left her, she was only nineteen, and despite the fact my mother and father told her to have an abortion, she decided to keep the boy. I think she thought Norman would come to his senses once he met the little guy, but he was having none of it. So there she was a year later, living in a flat on her own and bringing up a baby with no money and no future.'

Phillips nodded along, happy to let the old lady talk.

Mary continued her story without drawing breath. 'Well, it wasn't long before she started smoking and drinking heavily and eventually started taking tranquillisers that she got off a local fella; said they helped her sleep. I tried to get her to stop, and more often than not, I'd take Bruce home with me if she was in a bad way, but the night she died, I'd worked a few extra hours – cos we were short-staffed – and by the time I got to her place, it was too late.' She paused, and Phillips saw how her eyes glistened now, tears not far from the surface, and her face pale with remembered shock. 'The whole place was on fire.'

Out of respect, Phillips allowed a long silence to descend before continuing, her voice soft when she spoke. 'Is that how Bruce got those scars?'

'Yes. Poor lad was in bed when Annie passed out with a cigarette in her hand and set fire to the couch she was lying on. Furniture wasn't as safe as it is now, and the whole thing went up in a flash. At least that's what the coroner's report said.'

'So how did Bruce survive?' Jones asked.

'A neighbour saw the smoke and managed to break down the door and save him, but not before he'd suffered terrible burns thanks to those bloody cheap pyjamas she used to buy him from the market, but they were all she could afford.'

'That must have been awful for him,' Phillips said gently.

'It was. He was in hospital for a very long time, and it was a lot for him to deal with at such a young age, losing his mum and then all the surgery to try to heal the burns. Not to mention the fact he always looked different to the other kids thanks to the scars.' She stopped for a moment, lost in her memories, before adding, 'That's why I think he ended up going off the rails as a teenager.'

'We understand he lived with you for a while after his mum passed,' said Phillips.

'I tried my best with him, but I wasn't married either, and I didn't meet my late husband until years after. I even tried to get his father to take an interest given what had happened, but he point-blank refused. Said the kid had nowt to do with him.' Mary shook her head in disgust. 'One o' your lot, n'all.'

Phillips frowned. 'One of our lot, how do you mean?'

'A copper. Plain clothes like you two.'

'Bruce's dad was in the *police*?'

'Yes. CID if I remember rightly and a right arrogant bugger with it.' She sighed heavily. 'I think that's why our Annie fell for him. All that bravado.'

Phillips glanced at Jones. His expression suggested he had come to the same conclusion as her: so that's why Bruce McDonnell hated cops so much.

But Mary wasn't finished. 'So in the end, it all got too much for me, and I thought it best he go to a foster family who could give him a more normal life.'

Phillips nodded her understanding, but she was keen to get back to the fact McDonnell's dad had been a cop. 'I don't suppose you remember Norman's last name, do you?'

'Clarke,' replied Mary without hesitation. Then, 'At least I think it was. Annie said everyone called him Clarkey, but she preferred Norman.'

'And you're sure he was plain clothes?'

'Yeah. Worked out of the old Bootle Street nick. Annie used to meet him there after work when they first started seeing each other. I met him once or twice myself, but like I say, I never really took to him. Too flash for my liking, but Annie was besotted.'

'And did Bruce know who his father was?' said Phillips.

'Hard not to. His mother never stopped talking about him and how one day they'd be a happy family together, but any fool could see that would never happen.'

'And when was the last time you saw your nephew?' Jones asked.

Mary took a moment to think. 'Must be twenty years or more now. He turned up at our old house one night in Salford. A right mess he was, bloodied and covered in bruises. Funnily enough, that was because of his father.'

Phillips raised an eyebrow. 'Oh really?'

'He'd managed to track him down and found out he drank in a pub in Salford most nights. It was only about a fifteen-minute walk from our house. Apparently, Bruce confronted Norman and explained who he was – hoping somehow that his dad would welcome him with open arms.' The old lady rolled her eyes at this, as if in despair. 'Instead he beat the living daylights out of him.'

'Norman beat him up?'

'Yes, along with a bunch of pals. Told him his mum was a slut and that she'd slept with half the coppers in Manchester, so any one of them could be his dad, which of course was all lies. But Bruce was in a right state by the time he got to our house. Crying and shouting. It was as if he'd lost another parent all over again.'

Phillips shifted in her seat; this awful story made her

uncomfortable even as it brought them closer to the truth. 'Do you remember what year that was?'

'The year? No.' Mary shook her head. 'But I do remember the World Cup was on, and England had lost to Portugal that afternoon. My husband was going nuts cos he was a City fan and that prat from United, Wayne Rooney, had got himself sent off.'

'That was in 2006,' said Jones.

'That's the one!' Mary smiled. 'He cleaned himself up a bit, and then Bruce left here raging an hour or so later. Saying he was going to make Norman and his mates pay for what they did.'

'And what was he planning to do?' Phillips asked.

'I don't know, and I didn't ask,' replied Mary. 'I learned a long time ago to stay out of other people's business.'

Phillips had to stop herself smiling at the irony of that after all Mary had just told them. 'I don't suppose Bruce had a place that he liked to go when he was a kid, did he? Somewhere he felt safe?' she said.

'Not that I remember, no.'

They sat for a moment, and then Mary's brow furrowed. 'Here I am telling you our life story, and I still don't know what you want with Bruce. What kind of trouble is he in?'

'We're investigating a series of arson attacks, and we believe Bruce may have been involved.'

Mary shook her head sombrely. 'I've seen his name pop up in the court section of the papers over the years; it was the only way I could keep track of him. Every time it always had something to do with arson. I've never understood that. After what happened to him and his mum, why would he want to mess about with fire?'

'I'm afraid we don't know, but we do need to track him

down urgently.' Phillips pulled a business card from her pocket as she stood up from the chair and walked over to the phone plugged into the wall. 'I'll leave my card next to the phone. If Bruce shows up or gets in contact, be sure to give us a call immediately, won't you?'

'Pfft.' Mary scoffed. 'I doubt he'll come looking for me after all this time. And besides, he has no idea where I live.'

'Well, from what we understand, he's a resourceful man, so you never know,' said Phillips. 'Thank you for your time, Mrs McIntyre.'

'It's been nice to have a bit of company,' replied Mary. 'I hope you find him soon.'

'You take care of yourself,' added Phillips, gesturing for Jones to lead them out.

Outside, as they walked back towards the car, they debriefed on the cascade of information Mary had offered them. 'If she's right and his old man was CID, then it would certainly go some way to explaining why he hates cops so much,' said Phillips.

'But why the obsession with fire, guv?' Jones said as he deactivated the central locking. 'I mean, after what happened to him and his mum?'

'I don't know.' She held up her phone. 'But I know a woman who might.'

'Harris?'

'Exactly,' said Phillips as she pulled open the car door before dropping down into the passenger seat.

36

The reaction to his two social media posts had been way beyond anything he could have hoped for, and while he wasn't one hundred percent sure exactly what it meant to be trending, he knew from previous conversations with some of the Hawk Green younger inmates that, in regard to achieving his ultimate goal, it was a very good thing indeed. Reading through some of the hundreds of comments prompted by his posts, he was struck by how vitriolic they were. He had always known the police were unpopular, especially within some of the poorer and/or ethnic communities across the city, but he had not expected the comments that had come from people who – by looking at their profiles – appeared to be white and, to some degree, middle-class and business professionals.

After quickly rolling a cigarette, he lit it with the Zippo, then inhaled deeply as he read one of the more acerbic comments aloud. 'Stick all the pigs inside Old Trafford, then burn the fucking place to the ground.' He laughed out loud, picturing Manchester United's seventy-five-thousand-seat stadium filled to the brim with cops all fighting to get away from a deadly inferno.

He continued scanning the comments until he had finished his cigarette, stubbing it out onto the now over-flowing saucer he'd been using for an ashtray since his arrival at the hotel. Then, without warning, he began to cough, lightly at first, but he very quickly found himself struggling for breath as he hacked and retched uncontrol-lably until eventually a large lump of phlegm travelled from his throat up into his mouth. Grabbing a tissue, he spat it out, staring down at the dark red mucus on the paper. The doctor had warned him this would happen more and more frequently as the tumours in his lungs grew and that his best, most immediate chance of relieving his symptoms would be to quit smoking, but what would be the point in doing that? His condition was terminal. He was essentially a dead man walking; no sense in depriving himself of one of the few pleasures he still had left in life.

Throwing the bloodied tissue into the waste bin, he took a moment to roll himself another cigarette before switching from the X app back to the article he'd started reading earlier about Chief Constable Fox's appointment to the role two years ago, a one-to-one interview with – as the journalist put it, 'Manchester's Top Cop'. As part of the piece, Fox had set out her manifesto for the job, promising to reduce crime rates, tackle gang violence and the associated drug wars, as well as her desire to create a more open, transparent force, capable of effective policing in a modern-day Manchester.

'What a load of bollocks,' he muttered as he stared at the headshot of the chief constable taken outside the main entrance of the Greater Manchester Police HQ in Failsworth. 'Never mind Manchester's Top Cop – Manchester's most

corrupt cop, more like.' Having read a raft of more recent articles, it was evident that in the two years since her appointment nothing had significantly changed, and her promises
to make the city a safer place had failed to materialise. A
broad grin spread across his face as he contemplated what
was to come for her after years of patient planning. If Fox
thought she could continue to hide in plain sight, she had
another think coming. He was about to set a fire under the
chief constable that would burn for years to come. And the
best bit about it was, by the time she realised what was going
on, it'd be too late for her – or any of her cronies for that
matter – to do the slightest thing about it.

37

'We knew it was a long shot,' said Phillips as the team took their seats around the large table in MCU's conference room the following morning.

'I waited for three hours, but there was no sign of McDonnell,' said Bovalino. 'So I went in and spoke to the doctor, who confirmed he was a no-show for his appointment.'

Phillips exhaled loudly as she fought to hide her frustration.

'How did it go with the aunt?' the big man asked.

'Well, we've now got a pretty good idea of why McDonnell hates coppers so much.'

'Really?' said Entwistle.

'Oh yeah,' Phillips replied, and for the next few minutes she and Jones debriefed the guys on their conversation with Mary McIntyre – including the fact his dad, Norman Clarke, was once a CID detective.

When they were finished, Entwistle was frowning. 'That

name rings a bell,' he said as he began searching through folders on his laptop, the feed from which was being projected onto the screen at the opposite end of the room. 'Here we are,' he added a few moments later.

A photo of a dated police ID appeared on-screen of a man Phillips would have put in his fifties at the time the picture was taken.

'This is Norman Clarke,' said Entwistle.

'And why do we have photos of him?' Jones asked.

'Because he was one of the officers caught up in the very first fire set by Pearson at the Ship Inn in Salford,' he replied. 'Suffered severe burn injuries and was pensioned off as a result.'

'What was the date of that fire?' said Phillips.

Entwistle scanned through the details for a second. 'Saturday the first of July, 2006.'

Phillips sat forward in her chair. 'What day did England play Portugal in the World Cup that year?'

Bovalino frowned. 'That's a bit random, isn't it, boss?'

'There's method in my madness.'

'Give me a sec.' Entwistle opened Google on his laptop, which again appeared on the big screen. 'Saturday, first of July.'

'That's the day – the match when Rooney got a red card – that Mary told us McDonnell got a good hiding off his old man,' said Jones.

Phillips nodded. 'And the day *he* said he'd make Clarke and his mates pay for what they did to him.'

'By setting fire to the pub,' Jones continued.

Phillips was ahead of him, her eyes locked on Entwistle. 'Where did you get to with cross-referencing the dates of the Pearson fires against McDonnell's time inside?'

'That was my main update for the meeting, guv; he was on the outside for *all* of them.'

'If that's the case, then he has to be the real firestarter.' Phillips banged her hand down hard on the table. 'Pearson has been telling the truth all along. He really could be innocent.'

Just then, Entwistle's phone beeped on the desk, and Phillips felt hers vibrate in her pocket.

Whistler glanced at the screen, and his eyes widened. 'Oh, shit.'

'What is it?' asked Jones.

Phillips grabbed her phone from her pocket.

'Looks like another social media post from the Real Firestarter,' said Entwistle.

'Bring it up on the screen, will you?' she asked.

A second later the feed appeared in full Technicolor for all to see.

Jones read the contents of the new post out loud: 'Thank you for all your wonderful suggestions. Next target confirmed. Soon you will see with your own eyes the true level of police corruption in Manchester.'

'What the hell does he mean by that?' asked Bovalino.

Phillips stared at the screen in silence for a few seconds before responding. 'Whatever he's alluding to, we can be pretty sure it means that more cops are in danger. We've got to find McDonnell, and we've got to find him *now*.' She turned to Bovalino. 'Get onto uniform and see where they're at with the force-wide alert.'

'On it,' he replied.

'And get the comms team to raise the alert level to high. I want every officer in the city watching each other's backs. They need to know what McDonnell looks like, and they need to be aware of what he's capable of. No doubt they'll have heard about the fires for themselves, but we know how hard of thinking some of them can be. I'll draft up a briefing note now. I want to know that every cop in Manchester has read it by the time they clock off their shift today.'

'I'll make it happen, boss,' said Bovalino.

Phillips turned her attention to Entwistle now. 'Check with McDonnell's bank and see if we can monitor his movements in real time. He left the flat in a hurry, so with a bit of luck, he'll at least need to buy some more smokes soon. And speak to Rupert Dudley. It's time we shared McDonnell's mugshot with the public.'

'Are you sure, guv?' asked Jones. 'We could end up with every crazy in the city claiming he's hiding in their garden shed.'

'I know, but right now, McDonnell could actually be *in* one of those garden sheds.'

'There is another thing to consider,' said Entwistle. 'If we put an appeal out to the public, as he's so active on Twitter, he's likely to see it, which means he'll know we're onto him – more than he does already, I mean.'

'I get that,' she replied, 'but it might work in our favour. If McDonnell feels paranoid that everyone's looking for him, he may start to do things differently and out of his current routine, which is the quickest way for him to slip up.'

'I hadn't thought of it like that.'

'That's why the guv gets paid the big bucks,' said Jones with a grin.

'I wish,' replied Phillips. 'I'd better get that briefing note sorted,' she added before striding out of the conference room and heading back to her office.

38

Seeing his mugshot suddenly plastered all over the internet had been a new experience for him. Despite his long list of convictions, he'd managed to fly under the radar for most of his life and avoided the fame or notoriety that many of his fellow inmates had enjoyed – or endured, depending on your point of view – throughout their criminal careers. Initially he'd been filled with a mild sense of panic that his plans were now in jeopardy, but all it took was a single glance in the mirror to realise he was unlikely to be recognised in the street. Cancer is a cruel disease that slowly eats away at the body, and in his case, it had changed his appearance significantly compared to the old mugshot that had been shared on the GMP's X feed. Staring at the image now, he reasoned it must have been taken three or four years ago, around the time he had been relocated from HMP Frankland to Hawk Green. Having lost in the region of a couple of stone since then and with his hair much thinner and patchier, it was fair to say he looked very different. That said, he would still need to take precautions – just to be on the safe side.

He decided it would be best to shave off what was left of his hair completely. Matching his gaunt features and grey skin with a bald head would make him almost unrecognisable next to the mugshot, and the pair of almost zero-strength prescription specs he'd bought for cash at the pharmacy down the street would only add to his anonymity.

And so, with hand soap on his scalp and a disposable razor in hand, he set to work.

Thirty minutes later, with his backpack on his shoulder and his new look in place, he left the hotel room and set off confidently down the street.

The car-rental garage was less than a ten-minute walk away. Thankfully, a fine mist of rain was blowing off the road, which allowed him to drop his head and move gingerly towards his destination without looking in any way suspicious. Luck was on his side today; he could feel it.

As he stepped into the small but spotless rental office, his pulse quickened knowing his chances of being recognised would be much greater standing toe-to-toe with whoever was manning the office. In an attempt to calm his nerves and appear relaxed, he removed his damp glasses and made a point of stopping to dry the lenses before placing them back on his nose and smiling widely at the woman working behind the counter.

She was slim and blonde – probably in her twenties – and returned his smile as she looked up. 'Good morning and welcome to M12 Car Rentals. How can I help?'

He noted the name badge on her chest. 'Good morning, Tiffany, I have a car booked for the next couple of days.'

'What name is it under?' she asked.

'O'Malley. Michael O'Malley.'

The girl's brow furrowed as she set about locating the booking on the system, tapping into the computer on the other side of the desk, all the time repeating the surname under her breath as she did. A minute or so later, she smiled again. 'Here it is. Michael O'Malley. We have you in a Ford Focus, booked from four o'clock today through to Saturday the twenty-eighth at ten a.m. Is that correct?'

'Perfect.'

She glanced back at her screen. 'Now I can see from the booking you've opted for the standard insurance, which covers you for all damage, accidental or otherwise. However, it does come with a £500 excess. Would you like to add an excess cover for twenty-five pounds a day and remove all liability in the event of an accident or theft?'

'No, thank you. I'm not planning on going far. I think I'll be all right.'

'Are you sure? Most of our customers do prefer that extra piece of mind.'

'No, thank you,' he said as he flashed a smile. 'I'll be just fine without it.'

'Not a problem,' said Tiffany as she began typing again.

Still very much on high alert, he glanced around the office in search of CCTV cameras while all the time trying his best to appear casual.

'I'll just need a copy of your driving licence.'

'Of course.' Pulling the wallet from his jeans pocket, he took a moment to locate the fake ID he'd bought a few months ago. Thanks to one of his mates in Hawk Green, when he first got out, he'd been able to connect to a guy known only as Mr C, who'd provided a faultless replica of a genuine licence belonging to the real Michael O'Malley that now included his picture.

'And I'll need a credit card,' she added.

'Not a problem,' he said, passing across the cloned Visa card he'd also bought from Mr C.

'Thank you,' she said as she busied herself finalising the booking.

The printer to her rear burst into life, and a second later she stepped close enough to remove the printed pages before turning back and laying them flat on the countertop. After marking Xs on a number of pages throughout the document, she handed him the pen. 'If you can sign where I've indicated.'

He nodded as he scribbled his version of Michael O'Malley's signature on each of the pages, then handed the document and pen back.

'I'll just show you how everything works, and you can be on your way.' Tiffany led the way outside, and after a quick explanation of where the fuel cap was located and how to open it if needed, she handed over the keys. 'She's all yours, Mr O'Malley.'

'Thank you,' he said, now itching to get away.

'Well, have fun,' she said with one final, professional smile before turning on her heel and heading back to the office.

A broad grin spread across his face as he watched her go. 'Oh, I will, Tiffany,' he muttered. 'I will.'

39

With the public appeal for information on McDonnell's whereabouts launched early afternoon and the threat level to police personnel raised to high, it was with a heavy heart that Phillips logged off her laptop just after 8 p.m. It had been a frustrating afternoon, and they were still no closer to locating McDonnell despite several possible sightings, which had ultimately come to nothing. As Jonesy had predicted, 'the crazies' had started seeing him everywhere, from their local McDonald's in Stretford to the toilets of a large supermarket in Ashton-under-Lyne, as well as a post office in the small village of Shotwick located on the Welsh border. *The joys of social media wannabes*, thought Phillips. Crazies was about right.

The rest of the team had called it a night an hour earlier, and as she locked up her office, she racked her brain for anything else they could put in place to expedite the search for Manchester's most wanted man. But the reality was she'd done everything within her power up to that point, and there

was still no sign of him. No genuine sightings, no card trans-
actions or cash withdrawals, and no further threats or online
activity from the man himself since his most recent post that
morning. She was well aware that at that very moment
McDonnell could be readying himself to attack his next
target anywhere in the sprawling city, and it terrified her to
know she hadn't the faintest idea how to stop him.

Switching off the lights, she made her way out of the
main office, then downstairs towards the carpark. The wind
and rain had started again in earnest a few hours ago, and as
she moved out through the revolving door at the front of
Ashton House, she pulled up her coat collar, then made a
run for it to her Mini Cooper parked just a few metres away.

After struggling with the old-school lock, she yanked
open the door, then dropped down into the driver's seat
before pulling the door closed against the pounding rain.
'Bloody weather,' she muttered as she fired the engine.

A minute later she slipped out into the relatively light
traffic and headed south towards home.

Time seemed to pass by in a blur, her mind whirring as
she ran McDonnell's most recent X post over and over in her
mind. Who or what was the target he'd identified? Why had
he chosen them, and how soon would he actually strike? She
could feel a stress headache building around her temples as
the answers refused to come – the throbbing pain in her
head only made worse by the Mini's low driving position,
which meant the headlights of the cars behind were almost
dazzling in her rear-view mirror.

Turning off the Mancunian Way – Manchester's inner
ring road – she made her way through the suburbs of Hulme
and Whalley Range, with Chorlton just beyond.

'I need to get a bigger car,' she grumbled as the lights

from the car behind continued to dazzle in her mirrors, as it had since following her off the ring road. The torrential rain battering the tiny windscreen wipers only added to her stress.

Eventually, after what felt like an eternity, she spotted her road coming up, then pulled off the main drag and away from the blinding lights of the car in tow.

Parking on the drive a few minutes later, she was surprised to see Adam's car missing. 'That's odd,' she mumbled as she turned off the engine and headed inside.

After Floss met her at the door, purring around her ankles, she made her way into the kitchen, where she spotted a note from Adam on the countertop. Picking it up, she scanned the contents.

Playing squash with Tony, back about ten. Love A xx

Phillips sighed. She had a vague recollection of him mentioning it, but unsurprisingly, she'd totally forgotten. Glancing down at her watch, she could see it was after nine. With no real appetite and her head still pounding, she decided to forgo dinner and instead kicked off her shoes, picked up Floss and made her way into the lounge. The couch was calling, and she wanted nothing more than to crash out and attempt to quieten her racing mind.

40

He'd never really been a fan of driving, especially at night, and he had always hated doing it in the rain, but to be fair, the Ford Focus made it a lot easier than he remembered. With plenty of time to spare after picking up the car, he'd followed his phone's map app to find the exact location of his next target. Of course, the car had its own navigation system built in that he could have used, but he knew only too well that the police could trace that route back to him in time, and he had no intention of making their lives easy. Not at all. Plus, it was a lot simpler to burn a pay-as-you-go mobile without drawing attention to yourself, as opposed to torching and destroying a brand-new rental car.

While he waited for her to show herself, he sat in the shadows, parked out of sight, and scrolled through the screeds of comments attached to his latest post. Once again, he was amazed by the level of hatred and mistrust that appeared to exist for the people who were paid to protect the public. It seemed the chief constable had failed spectacularly in her quest to win back the hearts and minds of the people of Manchester. Hardly a shock, given her own lack of integrity.

In spite of the stickers attached to the dashboard stating the opposite, he pulled out his tobacco papers and rolled himself a cigarette, which he settled down to enjoy inside the car. He had no need to reclaim the deposit he'd paid and had no intention of getting out to smoke. He now knew only too well how much CCTV had proliferated in society during the last few years – the sheer volume of people in Hawk Green caught on both public and private cameras was evidence enough of that, and while he had no real fear of being caught, he was determined to finish without interruption what he had started.

Finally, after what felt like an age, he spotted her hastening through the rain towards her car parked outside the main entrance. 'Here we go,' he said softly as he fired the ignition.

A couple of minutes later, as she pulled out onto the main road, he slipped into gear and set off after her at a distance.

Keeping track of her in the torrential weather was not as easy as he had imagined it would be, and on more than one occasion, he cursed himself as cars pulled in in front of him, obscuring his view. Having planned to stay at a safe distance, he soon realised that in this amount of rain, he could easily get a lot closer without drawing attention to himself and so accelerated into the outside lane of the dual carriageway as he chased her down. Just as she pulled off onto the slip road, he tucked in behind and followed her down the ramp.

For the next ten minutes he found himself sitting directly behind her, but as the sheer volume of cars made traffic slow anyway, he felt confident she would have no idea she was being followed; to her he would simply be another commuter in a long line of traffic attempting to get home after a long day.

Finally, after indicating left, she pulled off the main carriageway and down the quiet road to what he guessed must be her home.

A moment later, having stopped to park up at the side of the tree-lined street about thirty feet further along, he jumped out, simultaneously triggering the automatic boot release with the key fob as he did. Then, sheltering from the rain as best he could, he slipped the backpack onto his shoulder, closed the boot and set off at pace down the road in search of her car.

He arrived soon after, just in time to catch a glimpse of her stepping through the front door of the well-appointed house. He stood for a moment in the shadows of the tall trees, taking in the scene as he surveyed the surrounding area. When he was happy no one was watching, he took off his backpack, pulled out a black ski-mask, which he immediately slipped on, then set off towards the narrow lane that ran parallel with the houses to the rear.

The rain continued to pour as he walked slowly down the back of her house. Thankfully, there were no streetlights nearby, and he moved into what he guessed would be the best position unnoticed. With one final glance left and right, and feeling confident no one could see him, he took a few steps backwards before launching himself at the seven-foot fence, lifting himself up with surprising ease. While the cancer had already robbed him of some bulk, his muscle mass had so far remained relatively unchanged, and being that little bit lighter now gave him a distinct advantage when it came to climbing; something he'd always been good at, even as a kid.

Pulling himself over the fence, he dropped softly onto the flowerbed below, crouching down onto his haunches as he did so.

Glancing across the large garden, he could see her moving around the kitchen; he felt amazed that someone doing her job would allow themselves to be so easily exposed. Why would she leave the blinds open at night?

For the next ten minutes he remained in the same position, the rain soaking him to the skin as water dripped from the end of his nose at an almost frenetic pace. That didn't matter, of course.

Petrol was flammable whatever the weather.

Just as he was about to make his move, he heard what he thought sounded like a car pulling up to the front of the house. A second later the engine died, and the sound of a car door being banged shut filled the air.

Turning his attention back to the view through the kitchen window, he watched on as a minute later she turned to face the man who had wandered into the space; he was wearing gym gear darkened at the shoulders by the rain.

He cursed himself now. For all his planning and preparation over the last few days since deciding on her as his next target, somehow he'd neglected to factor in her partner's role – which now meant he'd need to seriously rethink how it would all play out. As he sat and watched what appeared to be a relatively frosty exchange between the pair, it suddenly struck him: her partner could add a whole new dimension to the attack – offering him a unique leverage that had so far been missing. It was time to regroup and rework a new plan.

With a renewed energy, he allowed himself a smile as he stood up.

Remaining out of sight in the shadows, he moved quietly across the far edge of the garden to the base of a beech tree located less than fifteen metres away. Standing next to its large trunk – with the backpack still on his shoulders – he placed his left foot on the fence, grabbed a low-hanging branch with both hands, and then – after jamming his right foot against a large protrusion in the tree trunk – hoisted himself up and over the fence in one fluid movement.

Landing gently and, thanks to the rain, almost silently on the other side, he scanned his surroundings again. Once he was happy no one had heard or seen him, he set off back to the car, stopping just in front of the house to take a quick picture that would be perfect for his next social media post.

41

After very little sleep, Phillips made her way into the office early in the hope there would be some form of update on McDonnell's whereabouts.

Arriving just after 7.30 a.m., she made herself a coffee before firing up her laptop, ready for the day ahead. Whatever hope she had when she sat down faded fast as she began scanning the list of potential sightings that had come in from the uniformed patrols overnight. Much to her frustration, they had all been checked and dismissed, which meant they were still no closer to locating McDonnell. 'Damn it,' she growled as she stared bleakly at the screen ahead.

'Like that, is it?' said Jones as he stepped through the door to her office.

She shook her head wearily. 'Fifteen potential sightings of McDonnell overnight, and every single one of them was a dead end.'

'He's a slippery bugger.' Jones dropped into the seat opposite. 'I'll give him that much.'

'You're not kidding.' Phillips reclined in the chair for a moment before continuing, 'If you were in his shoes, and knowing we were onto him, where would you go?'

Jones shrugged. 'Somewhere with no CCTV that didn't require a credit card, for starters.'

'Like one of those dodgy B&Bs the asylum seekers are put up in?'

'They'd be as good a place to start as any. He could easily blend in unnoticed with a bunch of people who are glad to have a roof over their heads.'

'Maybe we start there? Get uniform to start canvassing those types of places?'

'That's a big job, guv. There must be hundreds of dodgy hotels like that across the city.'

Phillips sighed in frustration just before her phone beeped. Glancing down, she could see a notification had flashed up on-screen. Unlocking it, she frowned. 'What the hell?' she muttered.

'What is it?' asked Jones, sitting to attention.

'Another post from the Real Firestarter.' She turned the screen so he could see it.

Leaning forward, he took the phone to get a closer look.

'Apparently another photo, which has some relevance to his next target.'

Jones scrutinised the image. 'Where on earth is it?' He turned the phone sideways, and his eyes narrowed. 'I can't make it out.'

'Me either,' she replied.

Just then the phone began to ring. 'It's Whistler,' Jones said as he passed it back.

'Whistler, what's up?'

'Have you seen Twitter, guv?'

'Yeah,' said Phillips. 'Jonesy and I are looking at it now.'

'Any idea what it is in that image?'

'No idea. How about you?'

'Not a clue.'

'Give me a second,' she said as she pulled X up on her laptop and took another long look at the post. 'I can't say why, but I feel like I should know it. There's something vaguely familiar about it.'

'I'm looking at it now on my tablet,' he replied. 'But for the life of me, I can't make it out.'

'How quickly can you get in?' she asked. 'We need to identify what this means as a matter of urgency.'

'If I leave now, I'll be there in half an hour.'

'Great. As quick as you can.' Phillips turned her attention back to Jones. 'I wonder if Fox has seen this yet?'

'Well, if she has, we'll find out soon enough, I'm sure.'

Phillips sat in silence for a moment as she continued to stare at the image on-screen. 'I've had an idea,' she said before scrolling through the contacts in her phone.

A second later, she was making a call, and Jones watched on as she activated the speaker function.

'DCI Flannery,' came the sharp response as it was answered.

'Danny. Jane Phillips.'

'Jane? How you doing? Your number didn't come up.'

'My way of protecting myself from strange men,' she joked.

'I hope you're not referring to me,' he said with a laugh. 'Anyway, what can I do for you at this hour on a Thursday morning?'

'I'm wondering if you might have some specialist kit that can help me.'

'What did you have in mind?'

'I'm trying to trace a structure that's been posted online, and wondered if you have anything that might scan the image, then locate where it is?'

'What do you mean by a structure?' he asked.

'Probably best if I send it to you. Give me a second.' Phillips placed the phone down on the desk as she emailed the image from her laptop to Flannery. 'It should be landing any second,' she said, picking up the phone once more.

'Here it is.' Flannery fell silent for a moment as he opened the message. 'What the devil is that?'

'That's what we're hoping you can help us find out. We think it's part of a police building.'

Flannery blew out a breath. 'Unless we know specifically what we're looking at in the first place, it'd be impossible to trace it. Sorry, Jane.'

'Not to worry, Danny.' Phillips felt her shoulders sag as she locked eyes with Jones. 'It was worth a shot.'

'If you can maybe get more of the image, we might be able to do something, but even then, it depends what images we have stored on our databases to reference against. Alternatively, you could maybe try Google images. See if you can find a match on there.'

Phillips dropped her chin to her chest. 'Needle in a haystack springs to mind.'

'Sorry I can't give you better news,' Flannery said, sensing her despair. 'You know I'd help if I could.'

'I do, yeah.' Phillips raised her head once more. 'Look, I'd better go. This one's super urgent.'

'Good luck with it,' said Flannery. 'And shout if you need anything else.'

'Will do,' Phillips replied, ending the call.

'Like you say, guv,' offered Jones. 'It was always going to be a long shot. What now?'

'We do what Danny suggested; get online and start looking at photos of every major police building in Manchester to see if we can figure out where the bloody hell he's going to strike next.'

An hour later, after splitting up the city's police properties into three segments dependent on location, Phillips, Jones and Entwistle began frantically searching Google for anything that remotely resembled the mysterious image posted by @therealfirestartermanchester. Bovalino would be in later after taking Izzie to her latest doctor's appointment.

It was approaching midday by the time the big man strode into the office, carrying a cardboard tray filled with hot drinks and sandwiches, which he quickly handed out. 'I thought the least I could do was fetch some supplies, seeing I wasn't here first thing.'

'You all right, big man?' asked Entwistle playfully as he took the lid off his coffee. 'You've been bunking off a lot lately, haven't you?'

Bovalino produced a tight smile. 'A few things at home to deal with.'

'Any news on Norman Clarke?' Phillips asked, keen to change the subject on his behalf.

'Yeah,' said Bov as he took a seat. 'He's definitely *not* the next target.'

'And what makes you say that?' asked Jones.

'Because he's dead. Died of a stroke a few years after leaving the force.'

Phillips didn't know whether to feel relieved or frustrated that such an obvious target was no longer in the frame. 'Which means we really have nothing to go on right now.' She sighed as she dropped her pen on the desk and exhaled sharply.

'No luck figuring out what that post last night was all about, then?' Bovalino asked.

'Nope.' Phillips glanced at the clock on the wall. 'The three of us have spent the last three hours reviewing God knows how many pictures of police buildings in Manchester, and the reality is we haven't got a clue.'

'Have you thought about putting it out on our social media?' Bovalino asked, unwrapping his sandwich.

Phillips frowned. 'Ours? As in the GMP?'

Bovalino took a bite before replying. 'Yeah. I'm no expert, but last time I checked, we had over half a million followers on there. You never know, one of them might recognise it.'

Phillips sat to attention. 'That's a bloody great idea.'

'He has one every now and again,' said Entwistle with a grin.

Bovalino flashed him the V-sign before grinning back.

'Thanks for the brainwave, Bov – and the coffee.' Phillips paused for a moment. 'I need to go and see Dudley,' she said, jumping up from the chair before rushing out of the room.

Five minutes later she found Rupert Dudley sitting behind his desk in the small office on the fourth floor that he called home. He appeared to be grimacing as he stared intently at the computer screen in front of him.

'Everything all right?' she asked as she tapped on his open door.

Dudley glanced up, and his posture visibly softened. 'Sorry, Jane. I was miles away. Just trying to get ahead of things with the latest Firestarter posts that went up last night and this morning.'

'Is Fox giving you a hard time over them?'

'That's just it,' he replied. 'She's not mentioned it at all. In fact, I've not heard from her since the aftermath of the Townsend article, which is quite unnerving. She's rarely quiet when it comes to anything like this.'

Phillips shrugged. 'It's probably still the jetlag. It always knocks me out of kilter.'

'Yeah, maybe.'

'Anyway.' Phillips handed him her phone. 'I need you to put this out on our social media pages.'

Dudley's eyes narrowed. 'That's the image from the Firestarter post that landed this morning.'

'Yeah, it is.'

'Why would you want to put *that* out?' Dudley was incredulous.

'Because we're having no luck figuring out what it is, and time is running out before he strikes again. If we can get this out in front of *our* followers – people who actually *support* the police – one of them might be able to tell us where we should be looking.'

'I'm not convinced, Jane, and I'm not sure Fox will go for it either.'

'Let me deal with her,' she replied briskly. 'And besides, if she's out of action like you say, then Carter can probably give us the go-ahead on it instead.'

Dudley fell silent for a moment, evidently deep in thought.

'Come on, Rupert. All you need to do is draft up the post. I can deal with the politics. Okay?'

'Okay.' He nodded finally, but still a little hesitant. 'When do you want it to go out?'

'As quick as you can.'

'I'll work it up, and as soon as Fox or Carter signs off on it, I can post it.'

'You're a legend, Rupert,' said Phillips before turning around and setting off towards the fifth floor.

Ten minutes later, after sharing her plan to post the image with the chief superintendent, she waited impatiently for him to give her the green light.

'Something like this really should go through Fox,' said Carter, running his hand through his salt-and-pepper hair. 'I'm authorised to sign off on general posts, but this one is a little more contentious.'

'I know that, sir,' Phillips replied, 'but the truth is, I don't think she'll go for it. And as we're running out of time, I figured it might be better to ask for forgiveness rather than permission on this one.'

Carter pursed his lips and remained silent for a long moment before his face wrinkled. 'Come to think of it, she might be off this afternoon; something to do with her son's school, according to Diane. I can always use that as my excuse for not running it past her in the first instance.' He picked up the phone on his desk. 'I'll call Dudley and give him the green light.'

'Brilliant. Thank you.' As Phillips stood, her phone began to vibrate in her hand. Bov was calling. 'I'd better take this, sir?'

Carter gave her the thumbs-up before waving her away.

'What's up?' she asked Bovalino as she marched past Diane in the outer office.

'There's been a sighting of McDonnell in Longsight, guv.'

'Is it credible?' Phillips picked up speed as she turned out onto the corridor.

'Yeah, the manager of an independent hotel has called it in. Reckons McDonnell is staying there.'

Phillips's pulse quickened. 'Tell Jones to get the car ready. I'll meet him in the carpark.'

42

W ith their anti-stab vests in place under their coats and with Jones driving under blues and twos, Phillips and Jones raced through the afternoon traffic from Ashton House to Longsight – a multi-cultural suburb located three miles southeast of the city centre. As the world zoomed by the window in a blur, Phillips felt her phone vibrate once again as Dudley's post of the mysterious structure flashed up in a notification. With her eyes locked on the image, she wondered again what about it appeared so familiar. Despite having no idea what she was looking at, she couldn't shake the fact she had at some point seen it before.

Just then her phone rang through the car's central console. She could see from the display it was Entwistle and hit the green answer icon. 'What's the update?'

'The tactical team are en route, guv,' he replied. 'I've briefed Andrews, and they should be at Lionsgate Villas in ten minutes.'

'Same as us,' said Jones as they accelerated past a line of

cars that had pulled to the side of the road to let them through.

'Have you seen the comments on the post?' asked Entwistle. 'Bov was right; it's getting quite a positive response. Very different to those on the Real Firestarter's post.'

'I'm looking at them now,' Phillips replied. 'Can you and Bov start cross-referencing the suggestions with images online?'

'We'll get straight on it.'

'Great, thanks. And have the phone on standby in case we need you.'

'Goes without saying, boss.'

Phillips turned her focus back to the image on her phone screen.

Exactly ten minutes later, Jones pulled the car up to the kerb about a hundred feet down the road from the hotel next to the tactical unit's large van.

Jumping out, she was met by the team leader, Sergeant Louise Andrews, a six-foot, physically imposing cop with a fierce reputation for kicking down doors on behalf of the GMP, and someone Phillips had worked with on many occasions over the years. 'Lou,' said Phillips as they approached the four-person team.

'How do you want to play it, ma'am?' asked Andrews.

'If the target is in there, I don't want to spook him, so we need to be discreet initially.'

'What did you have in mind?'

'Jones and I will go in and speak to the manager, and I'll need two of your team ready to follow us in and the other two covering the back of the building.'

'Of course,' said Andrews.

Phillips continued, 'If McDonnell *is* inside, then as soon as we identify which room he's in, and based on the threat to life he poses, we'll need you to go in with full screens and Tasers.'

'Not a problem.' Andrews passed across two police radios. 'The frequencies are all set to channel B, which is scrambled and untraceable to any scanners.'

Phillips took hers. 'Everybody ready?'

Andrews and Jones nodded in unison.

'Let's go,' Phillips added before setting off down the street with Jones at her back.

As they approached the hotel, it was evident that the converted, redbrick Victorian villa had seen better days; its paint was peeling, and the neon 'vacancies' sign in the front window was broken. Now it intermittently flashed out the word 'acancies'.

'It's exactly the sort of place you said he'd pick, Jonesy,' Phillips whispered as she led the way up the short path to the battered front door. As they stepped inside, they found themselves in a familiar setting. The team had hunted down criminals in buildings such as this many times before. Again, it seemed that the majority of the hotel owners offering the city's cheapest accommodation shared a common view on the renovation and upkeep of their properties; namely, that it was an unnecessary expense.

The unmistakable smell of damp filled the air, and despite the No Smoking signs, Phillips noted that the wood-chip wallpaper was heavily nicotine-stained and peeling back from the walls where it connected with the ceiling. The threadbare carpet resting underfoot was a trip hazard waiting to happen.

Fixed to the wall to the right of the small reception

counter was a doorbell with a sticker underneath that read 'Press for assistance'. Phillips followed the instruction, then waited. When no one appeared, she pressed it again. A minute or so later, a door behind the counter finally opened, and a rotund woman with frizzy, greying hair and glasses hanging on a cord around her neck stepped through with a quizzical look fixed to her face. 'Yes?' The accent was undoubtedly Eastern European.

Phillips pulled out her ID and kept her voice low as she turned her phone screen so the woman could see the mugshot of McDonnell displayed on it. 'We were told you may have this man staying with you.'

The woman's eyes narrowed as she pulled on her glasses and leaned forward to get a closer look at the photo. 'Room eleven – top of house,' she said in broken English.

'Is he in the room currently?'

The woman shrugged. 'Don't know. He come and go. Unless he need something, I don't see him.'

'Are you the one who called to tell us he was here?' Jones asked.

'No. My sister, Agnes,' the woman replied gruffly. 'I told her not to. It bring trouble.'

'In that case, please take another look at the picture.' Phillips pushed the phone closer. 'Are you *sure* this is the man in room eleven?'

'I think. Yes.'

That was all the encouragement Phillips needed as she pulled her radio from her coat pocket. 'Alpha team, this is Mike-Charlie-One...'

Jones turned to the woman. 'Best you go back inside the office and close the door. It's about to get very busy round here.'

The radio crackled into life. 'This is Alpha team,' Andrews replied.

'Alpha team, we are clear,' Phillips barked into the handset. 'Strike, strike, strike!'

At that, the frizzy-haired woman disappeared back where she'd come from, and twenty seconds later, Andrews and PC Nelson arrived wearing helmets and visors as they rushed through the front door. Andrews also carried a transparent plastic shield while Nelson gripped a single-person door ram in both gloved hands.

'Top floor, room eleven,' said Phillips, pointing the way.

Andrews didn't need telling twice as she and Nelson took the stairs two at a time with Phillips and Jones tucking in behind.

As they reached the top-floor landing, Andrews stood back, holding the shield in her left hand, before drawing her Taser in the right.

Nelson took his lead from her, banging heavily on the door. 'Police, open the door!'

The space fell silent.

Nelson banged once more and repeated the instruction. 'Police, open the door!'

Again, no response.

Andrews turned to Phillips. 'It's your call, ma'am.'

'Break it down,' she said flatly.

With a loud crack, Nelson slammed the battering ram into the door just below the handle, splintering the frame as the door flung open on its hinges. As he stepped back, Andrews moved forward with the shield and Taser ready.

'Armed police!' she shouted as she moved into the room, stopping in her tracks seconds later, before turning back to Phillips. 'It's empty, ma'am. He's not here.'

Phillips followed her in and was immediately struck by the stench of stale tobacco and the condition of the room, which was in total disarray.

Jones followed her in. 'God, it stinks in here.'

'What a mess,' said Phillips.

'It's in the same state as his house,' added Jones.

Andrews activated the radio fixed to her chest. 'Lewis, this is Andrews. Any sign of the target at the back door?'

'No, boss. All clear.'

'Looks like we missed him, ma'am,' said Andrews.

'Shit.' Phillips rubbed her hand down her face, causing it to redden.

'What would you like us to do?'

As Phillips took a moment to review their options, her attention was momentarily drawn to a piece of paper resting on the small table that contained the kettle. 'What's that?' Picking it up, she read the handwritten notes aloud. 'Officer Howard, 4583, and Officer Shabir, 4527.'

'The two officers who told McDonnell to turn his music down,' said Jones. 'Could they be on his list of targets?'

'God only knows,' Phillips replied. 'But if he bothered to bring their names and badge numbers with him when he did a runner, they obviously mean *something* to him. Given his claims that he's already picked his next target, we need to get them into protective custody ASAP.'

'Leave it with me,' said Andrews. 'I'll sort it out with Control.'

'Thanks, Lou. And it's probably best you head back to the van for the time being.'

'Will do.'

'Make sure you keep an eye on the front door in case he comes back,' Phillips instructed as she pulled on a pair of blue latex gloves. 'In the meantime, Jones and I will have a good look round in here.'

Andrews nodded, then signalled for Nelson to lead the way out.

Phillips turned to Jones now. 'If you check the chest of drawers, I'll start with the wardrobe.'

'Sure,' said Jones, twanging the latex glove noisily against his wrist.

As soon as she opened the wardrobe door, Phillips spotted a large camouflage-print rucksack sitting upright against the back of the space. Getting down on her haunches, she dragged it towards her. As she pulled open the top, a strong smell of petrol wafted upwards. 'Wow,' she muttered.

Jones stopped what he was doing. 'What is it?'

She reached inside and pulled out a green jerry can. 'I think we can safely assume this is how he's been transporting the petrol around.'

'Phew.' Jones winced. 'I can smell it from here.'

Phillips lifted the rucksack up onto the bed and began carefully emptying its contents.

'Check this out,' said Jones a second later.

Stepping up, she moved across the room. 'What are we looking at?'

'These were in an envelope in the bottom drawer.' He passed her a bunch of dog-eared newspaper cuttings. 'Looks like our man has been keeping tabs on Fox's rise up the ranks for some time.'

Phillips frowned as she leafed through the different stories. 'Some of these must be almost five years old.'

'More like ten, I'd say.'

Phillips's mind raced as she cast her eye over picture

after picture of the chief constable. 'He's obsessed with her,' she muttered. And then it hit her. 'Oh, shit!'

Jones did a double take. 'What's up?'

Phillips didn't answer and instead opened the contacts folder in her phone and rapidly scrolled through the names.

'Guv, what's going on?'

As soon as she found what she was looking for, she copied the address and dropped it straight into Google maps. 'I think I know where I've seen McDonnell's image before.'

Jones moved to her shoulder.

With a weak signal inside the old hotel, it took a while for the location to appear on-screen, and when it finally landed, she switched to Street View and frantically zoomed in. Her eyes widened as she fixed her gaze on the screen. 'Fuck! Fuck! Fuck!' she growled. 'Holy *fuck*.'

'What is it?' asked Jones.

'The reason we couldn't find any buildings that matched McDonnell's picture in the police database is because the photo wasn't taken outside a police building. It's a snapshot of a gatepost attached to a private residence.'

'Which private residence?'

A cold shiver ran down Phillips's spine, and she swallowed hard. 'Chief Constable Fox's!'

43

Having parked the car out of sight, he'd made his way back down the rear of the house, and with the backpack slung over his shoulders, he'd once again scaled the fence before dropping down into the darkened garden beyond. Sitting in the thick shadows of the trees, he stared across at the house – which for the time being appeared empty. Not a problem, he thought; he'd waited years for this moment. A little bit longer wouldn't matter.

For the next hour, as he waited patiently for his mark, he allowed his mind to wander back to his childhood and the foggy memories he had of his mum. She had deserved so much more than being treated like garbage by that bastard Norman Clarke. He felt a deep sadness imagining the immense pain she must have felt when he had abandoned them both, a hollow emptiness, which he knew only too well himself. As his gut began to twist with the inner rage of injustice that threatened to consume him most days, he exhaled sharply and sniffed hard as he forced himself to focus on the job in hand.

Soon after, he spotted car lights casting shadows to the front of the house as the sound of a large diesel engine filled the early evening air around him before being switched off a moment later.

Welcome home, Chief Constable Fox.

He watched through the large window as the various house lights were switched on, and the family – Fox, her husband and what looked to be her young son alongside a black Labrador – moved from the front door through into the open-plan kitchen at the back of the house; right where he wanted them.

Fox looked different, dressed as she was in her civilian clothes, and for a split second he almost didn't recognise her, that is until she started barking orders in the direction of the boy.

A moment later, her son beckoned the dog towards him and then opened the back door to let it out. Thankfully he'd spotted the dog on his recce last night and – after a quick trip to the butcher's this morning – had come prepared. While simply cutting the mutt's throat would be far simpler and quicker than what he had planned, it was likely to be noisy and bloody, and he was determined to maintain the element of surprise at all costs.

Opening his backpack, he reached inside and retrieved the burger patty stuffed full with his own sleeping medication, which he'd been prescribed by his doctor to help counter the effects of his chemotherapy pills.

So far, the dog had remained close to the house, sniffing around the flower beds and shrubs, but as soon as the meat was exposed to the evening air, its head lifted and locked on his location.

'Here, girl,' he whispered as he threw the patty over onto the lawn.

Shuffling across the grass, the dog sniffed at the meat for a moment before biting down and gobbling it up a second later.

He checked his watch. It was just after 6 p.m. 'Shouldn't be too long now,' he mumbled.

Next, the dog set off on another sniffing expedition around the garden, and it was just five minutes later that it moved closer to him again, lying down and resting its head flat on the grass, which was now wet from the evening dew. A few seconds later it closed its eyes.

'Job done,' he said, standing now.

Just then the back door opened, and the boy moved outside onto the patio. 'Rosie!' he shouted into the darkness without reply. 'Rosie!' he called again. 'Come here, Rosie!'

Slowly and silently, he reached into his backpack and pulled out the carving knife he'd brought from the flat in readiness for what he was about to do.

The boy moved over the steps that led from the patio down to the lawn, causing the security lights to flood the space.

With his position still covered by the shadows of the trees, his pulse quickened as he watched the boy move closer.

'There you are, Rosie,' said the boy as he locked eyes on the prostrate Labrador. 'What you doing down there, girl?'

Taking a deep, silent breath, he exhaled slowly, and then, as the boy moved to the edge of the shadows, he pounced.

'PUT your hands where I can see them!' he shouted as he moved through the open back door, holding the knife against the boy's throat and his gloved hand over his mouth.

Fox jumped back, her eyes wide in sheer horror. 'What the fuck?' she yelled, touching her hand to her chest.

'Please don't hurt Ben,' said her husband, immediately raising both hands in surrender.

'Do exactly what I say, or I'll cut the boy in two,' he continued as he moved next to the island in the middle of the kitchen.

'I don't think you realise what a massive mistake you're making,' snarled Fox, regaining her composure. 'I'm a senior police officer in the Greater Manchester Police.'

'I know exactly who you are, Chief Constable Fox.' He placed the backpack down on the island countertop before reaching inside and retrieving a set of cable ties, which he threw across the floor towards the husband. 'Put those on your wife.'

Fox stared back in silence.

'Now!' he growled, pushing the knife harder against the kid Ben's neck.

Fox's husband bent down and quickly retrieved the ties, then straightened and moved towards her.

'That's it,' he said. 'Nice and tight.'

Fox's husband followed the instruction, and less than a minute later she stood with her hands tied.

'On your knees,' he said, gesturing with the knife.

Fox paused for a second.

He pressed the knife harder against the boy's neck. 'Do it now!'

Reluctantly, she sank to her knees.

He turned his attention back to the husband. 'Come over here.'

The husband acquiesced and walked slowly towards him.

Handing the child a second set of cable ties, he pointed towards the boy's father. 'Put these on your dad. And no funny business, got it?'

Somehow Ben did as he was told despite the fact he was visibly shaking, and so, a moment later, Fox's husband stood shackled a few feet away.

'Get on your knees next to your wife,' he said as he grabbed Ben and pulled him back towards himself.

'What do you want? Money?' asked Fox as her husband dropped slowly to the tiled kitchen floor.

'Pah,' he scoffed as he pulled out another set of cable ties. 'No, I don't want money. I want something far more valuable than that. I want justice!'

'Justice? For what?'

'For Archie Pearson,' he replied as he locked Ben's wrists together, 'and all the others like him whom you've fitted up over the years. All to feather your own nest.'

'Pearson?' The look on Fox's face was incredulous. 'What the hell has he got to do with you?'

Placing the knife down momentarily, he locked the boy's wrists in another set of cable ties, then pushed him back towards his parents. 'You too, son, on your knees.' He locked eyes with Fox now. 'I'll tell you what he's got to do with me, shall I? Archie Pearson has served seventeen years for setting a bunch of fires he had nothing to do with. And do you want to know how I know that? Because *I* set them. Those fires, all of them, were down to *me*. You see, I'm the Real Firestarter, me, Bruce McDonnell.'

Fox's mouth fell open as she stared back.

McDonnell reached into the backpack and pulled out a plastic water bottle. 'Do you know what this is, ma'am? That's what they call you at work, isn't it? *Ma'am?*'

Fox didn't respond; her eyes were fixed on the bottle.

'This is truth serum,' he said, twisting off the cap as he glanced at Fox's husband. 'I'm sorry, I never got your name.'

'T-T-Timothy,' he stuttered.

'Mind if I call you Tim?'

The man shook his head. 'No, no, that's fine.'

'Good. I like to keep things informal,' he shot back with a smile. 'As I was saying, this here is truth serum.'

'You can't think you'll get away with this,' Fox cut in, 'breaking into the home of the chief constable. I have a panic alarm around my neck, and I pressed it as soon as you burst in. Every copper in Manchester will know we have an intruder in the house by now.'

'Do I look like I care?' McDonnell coughed hoarsely for a long moment. 'The more the merrier, as far as I'm concerned,' he added before spitting loudly and grossly into the sink next to him.

Kneeling in between his parents, Ben began to cry.

'It's all right, son; everything's going to be okay,' said Tim in a hushed tone.

'Listen to your dad, Ben,' said McDonnell. 'As soon as your mother finally tells the truth, then everything will be over.'

Just then, Fox's phone, which was on a bench just a few feet away, vibrated. Glancing over, he read out the caller ID. '*DCI Phillips* ring any bells?'

Fox straightened. 'She's one of my finest detectives and no doubt, along with a firearms team, will be here in a matter of minutes.'

'We'd better get cracking, then, hadn't we?' he said with gusto, gripping the bottle in his hand as he moved next to Tim. 'Just shuffle away from the kid, will you?'

The smell of petrol from the bottle was pervasive, and Tim's eyes widened. 'What are you going to do with that?'

'Just do as you're told, and this will all be over soon enough,' he said without feeling. 'Come on, shuffle over towards me a bit. I don't want to get any of this on the boy.'

Tim followed the order and moved away from his son.

'That's it,' said McDonnell before turning his attention back to Fox. 'It's time to confess, ma'am.'

'Confess?' Fox recoiled. 'Confess to what exactly?'

'To stitching up Archie Pearson and all the other innocent people you've put away.'

'All my convictions were one hundred percent sound,' she snorted.

McDonnell chuckled. 'You and I both know that's not true, ma'am.'

'I know nothing of the sort.'

'Bullshit!' he growled as he struggled to control his mounting rage. 'And I'm not leaving here until you admit to what you've done.'

'I'm admitting to nothing!'

'Oh, I think you are,' McDonnell shot back, taking a step forward before turning the open bottle of petrol upside down so the contents drained out over Tim's head and torso.

Tim yelped, an animal noise of pure fright.

A second later, McDonnell pulled the Zippo from his

pocket and fired it up so the naked flame danced just centimetres from Tim's petrol-soaked body. 'As your friends will be joining us soon enough, it appears the clock's ticking, ma'am. Tick-tock, tick-tock.'

44

'She's not answering,' said Phillips as Jones raced down the wrong side of the road past the stationary traffic, under blues and twos. 'He must already be at the house.'

'We're about five minutes out,' said Jones.

Just then Entwistle's caller ID flashed up on the central console, and she immediately accepted the call. 'Please tell me you know where McDonnell is?'

'Sorry, guv. I don't, but Control just told me that Fox's personal panic alarm has been triggered at her home address.'

'Shit,' growled Phillips. '*I knew it.*'

'What the hell's going on, boss?'

'About ten minutes ago when we were searching his hotel room, I finally realised where I'd seen the image from his post before. It's a close-up of Fox's gatepost. It's a distinctive handmade metal structure, and I must've noticed it when she insisted on having a meeting with me, Carter and Dudley at her house during the Crowther investigation.'

'And you think that's why she's triggered the panic alarm, because McDonnell's there now?'

'Yeah, I do,' Phillips replied. 'We're en route to her place as we speak; we've got Andrews and the tactical team in tow,' said Phillips.

'Do you want firearms as well?'

'Yeah. Now we know he's there for sure, let's get them in.'

'What about uniformed units, guv? The panic protocol dictates every cop in a three-mile radius divert to Fox's location.'

'No, no. Absolutely not. Talk to Control and tell them to rescind the directive. The last thing we need is more street cops walking into trouble. I want specialist units only, and they all answer to me on this one. No one is to go in without my say-so, understood?'

'Yes, guv. I'll make it happen.'

WITH HIS LEFT hand still holding the open-flamed Zippo, McDonnell reached into the backpack and pulled out his phone before placing it down on the kitchen bench. After activating the camera, he picked it up again, switching it to video and turning it to face Fox, who remained kneeling on the floor. 'Move to your right, would you?' he asked as casually as if he were filming a bride at a wedding. 'I only want you in the shot.'

Fox didn't flinch.

'Do it now,' he snarled, pushing the open flame of the Zippo closer to her husband.

'For God's sake, darling, do what he says!' Tim yelled.

'Please, Mum,' Ben screamed a split second later.

After glaring at McDonnell for a long moment, Fox finally shuffled sideways across the tiled floor.

'That'll do,' he said as she moved to his preferred position.

He smiled now as he pointed the camera at her face. 'I'm recording you here, so it's time to start talking. State your name and rank.'

'Look, there's no need for any of this.' Fox's tone was notably different. 'If you stop now, I can get you the proper help you need to deal with everything that has led you to fire setting. And I'll speak to the CPS too. I'll make sure they go easy on the sentencing and recommend a specialist facility as opposed to general population.'

He shook his head, smiling. 'So this is the part where you negotiate, is it? Try to win me over, show me that you actually care?'

'I'm just trying to stop you making the biggest mistake of your life, Bruce.'

'Oh, first names all of a sudden, is it?'

Fox ignored the question. 'Come on, stop this madness. Before the firearms unit comes through that door armed to the teeth. Believe me, seeing this scene, they won't hesitate to shoot to kill.'

'That suits me just fine,' he said as another coughing fit hit, causing him to wheeze and hack horribly before spitting bloody phlegm into the sink. 'Instant death by police marksman beats what I've got ahead of me, that's for sure. I'm not a well man, see.'

Fox's eyes narrowed. 'What's wrong with you?'

'Stage-four lung cancer,' he replied before coughing once again. 'I've got three months at best.'

'I'm sorry to hear that,' Fox mumbled without feeling.

'No, you're not,' he snapped. 'You're just trying to get me onside.'

'Please, don't do this,' Tim cut in now, his voice trembling. 'Think of what it's doing to our son.'

McDonnell coughed and hacked for a long minute, all the time holding the Zippo next to Tim's petrol-drenched skin. 'It's not down to me, mate. As soon as your wife tells it like it actually is, this will all be over.' He focused his attention back on Fox. 'I'm a dying man, with nothing to lose, ma'am. So it really is time you started talking.'

JONES PULLED the squad car up on the main road about twenty feet away from the turnoff to Fox's house. The tactical unit parked up behind a moment later.

Phillips jumped out and walked swiftly over to talk to Sergeant Andrews with Jones at her side. 'We don't know for certain, but we strongly believe McDonnell is already at the property. As you'll have seen on the force-wide alert, Chief Constable Fox activated her personal panic alarm just over twenty minutes ago. I've tried calling her, and there's no answer, which is totally out of character and not a good sign.'

'So how do you want to play this one, ma'am?' asked Andrews.

'Super low-key,' Phillips replied. 'We all know what McDonnell is capable of, and I don't want to set him off by going in heavy handed. Not yet, anyway.'

Andrews nodded.

'I've requested a firearms team,' Phillips said as she checked her watch, 'who, according to Control, should be here in just over ten minutes.'

'My team can handle him, ma'am.'

'I'm sure you can,' Phillips replied. 'But if – as we imagine is the case – there's a serious threat to life for Fox and her family, Tasers may not cut it. We may have to shoot to kill, and I'm not taking any chances on this one.'

'Understood,' said Andrews.

'Now, McDonnell's not stupid, and I'm sure he'll be expecting company, but perhaps not just yet. That hopefully gives us the element of surprise and a few extra minutes to play with, so Jones and I will use that time to try to get a closer look around the house to see if we can locate where the occupants are. Once we know, we'll message through.' Phillips pulled her radio from her coat pocket. 'Again, let's use channel B.'

'All good, ma'am,' said Andrews. 'If you need us at any point, we'll be ready to go in at a second's notice.'

Phillips turned to Jones. 'You up for this?'

'Always.' He smiled.

A COUPLE OF MINUTES LATER, Phillips led the way as they moved carefully past the gatepost she now recognised so well and up the long driveway, stopping as they reached the bulky Volvo XC90 parked in front of the house. 'It's still warm,' she said, placing her hand on the bonnet.

Jones touched it too. 'Can't have been back that long.'

Phillips took another step forward, and in a flash the area around them was instantly illuminated by automatic security lights fixed to walls above them. Ducking down, she launched herself forward and into the relative cover of the open outer porch.

'Shit,' mumbled Jones as he followed suit, crouching down next to her.

'The whole place is probably packed full of security lights,' whispered Phillips. 'If we try to move round the side of the house, we'll be lit up like a Christmas tree.'

'So what do we do?'

Phillips shifted her body slightly so she was facing the front door. Reaching up slowly, she tried the handle, and, much to her surprise, it opened with little to no noise. Pushing it open a touch, she could hear raised voices coming from inside the house. She pointed silently inside, and Jones nodded without speaking.

A moment later, they found themselves in a darkened hallway that Phillips knew from her previous visit ran through to the kitchen at the rear of the house. Careful not to make any noise, she led the way as they moved through the house towards the voices. As they reached the end of the long hallway, it was clear that the man they could hear speaking was angry, his tone agitated. Phillips was sure she could hear Fox's voice intermittently but couldn't be totally sure. Glancing at her watch, she noted the firearms team would be arriving in approximately five minutes. And then the man who'd been doing all the talking shouted a command that made her blood run cold.

'Stop fucking me about,' he raged. 'Start talking – or I'll set this fucker on fire!'

Phillips stopped in her tracks for a moment and locked eyes with Jones.

'What now?' he mouthed silently.

Taking a very quiet step forward, she peeped around the door frame and into the kitchen. From her position, she could see Fox kneeling on the tiled floor, her hands cable-tied in front of her. To her right, a young boy she recognised as the chief constable's son was also kneeling with his hands together, his face red and distorted from crying. To his right was a man Phillips knew to be Fox's husband, Tim; he was also kneeling and shackled at the wrists, his hair and shirt soaked. Phillips guessed the liquid was petrol, given the pervasive smell in the air.

To her horror, standing next to Tim, holding a lit Zippo in one hand and a mobile in the other, was McDonnell.

'State your name for the camera,' he barked.

'Chief Constable Fox,' she replied reluctantly.

'That's better,' he continued. 'Now, for the purpose of the tape, when you were a detective chief inspector, did you manufacture DNA samples that were then presented as evidence against Archie Pearson at his trial in 2006?'

Fox nodded softly.

'I'm taking that as a yes,' said McDonnell from behind the camera. 'And did that evidence lead to his false conviction?'

Fox paused for a second.

McDonnell moved the naked flame of the lighter a fraction closer to Tim. 'I'll ask you again, did that manufactured DNA evidence lead to the false conviction of Archie Pearson?'

'Yes.'

'That's more like it,' he said smugly. 'And is it true that *you* personally recommended to the parole board earlier this year that Pearson should not be allowed out on licence, and instead that he should remain in custody indefinitely?'

'Yes.'

'So thanks to your actions, an innocent man has been

rotting in jail for seventeen years and will continue to do so unless someone proves otherwise. Is that correct?'

Fox didn't respond.

'Is that correct?' McDonnell growled.

Phillips turned back to Jones, but still they both managed to hear Fox's delayed answer filtering out from the room behind.

'Yes.'

It was the admission of guilt Phillips had been seeking for what felt like an eternity, but under the circumstances, any satisfaction she might have felt had evaporated.

Jones pointed at his watch, then held up four fingers, indicating that the firearms unit would be here in four minutes.

Phillips nodded silently as she considered the options available.

Then, quick as a flash, she removed her coat.

'What are you doing?' he mouthed, his voice barely audible.

She deftly handed her coat across and replied in the same manner. 'Wait here and have this ready. If I give the signal, use that to damp out any flames. And fast.'

His silent expression was incredulous.

Phillips took a long breath, then turned and stepped out into the doorway.

'Don't do it, Bruce,' she said calmly and levelly as she moved into the kitchen, her hands raised in surrender.

Suddenly all eyes in the room were on her.

'It doesn't have to end like this,' she added as she walked slowly forward.

'Oh, Phillips, thank God,' said Fox. 'I told you she was one of my best.'

Phillips kept her eyes locked on McDonnell.

'So you're DCI Phillips, are you?' he asked, taking a step closer to Tim now, the lighter flame still flickering dangerously close to the petrol that covered his shaking body.

'I am.' Phillips nodded. 'Put the lighter down, Bruce. This isn't the answer.'

'Every cop in the city will be here soon enough,' spat Fox. 'Give yourself up while you can.'

Phillips stopped a few feet away from McDonnell. 'She's right, Bruce. The firearms team are on their way, and they won't hesitate to use deadly force.'

'Good,' he replied. 'They'll be doing me a favour.'

'I know about the cancer,' Phillips said softly. 'Stage four. That means you have months rather than years.'

McDonnell flinched slightly.

'And I know all about your mum, and how your dad, Detective Sergeant Norman Clarke, broke her heart and abandoned you both all those years ago,' Phillips continued, her voice as gentle but unpatronising as she could make it. 'No wonder you hate coppers like you do. He may not have set the fire at the house himself, but he as good as killed your mum that night.'

McDonnell snarled. 'You're trying to get inside my head, to win me over, but it won't work. I know your tricks, and all you coppers are the same. All you fucking care about is protecting your own; you're rotten to the core.'

'We're not all the same,' Phillips said firmly.

'Bullshit.' McDonnell nodded towards Fox. 'With that corrupt bitch at the top, there's no other way to be.'

'I know all about the chief constable's previous misdemeanours. I know that they go back years,' said Phillips. 'And I have done for some time.'

Fox recoiled. 'I beg your pardon?'

Phillips kept her eyes locked on McDonnell. 'If you put down the lighter and give yourself up, you can help me put a stop to the lies for good.'

'And why would I do that when I've got this?' McDonnell held up the phone.

'What are you going to do with that?'

'I'm not going to do anything,' he said as he pointed the phone at the boy. 'He is. On your feet, lad.'

'Please leave him alone,' Tim pleaded as his son looked to him for answers.

'I'll make sure you *suffer* for this,' Fox growled through gritted teeth.

Phillips locked eyes on Fox. 'For once in your life, will you *shut up!*'

Fox's eyes widened as she opened her mouth to respond, then thought better of it.

'Come on, son,' McDonnell focused back on Ben, waving the phone gently as he did. 'On your feet, lad – or your dad's toast.'

The boy looked to his dad with terror-filled eyes, then moved his gaze to Phillips.

'Do as the man says, Ben,' she said. 'Everything's going to be okay.'

'Hurry up, son,' said McDonnell as he moved the lighter closer to Tim once more. 'Thanks to your mother, we haven't got all day.'

Reluctantly, a terrified Ben slowly lifted himself onto his feet and took a few steps towards their captor.

Phillips kept her eyes locked on the lighter flickering next to Tim's head as McDonnell handed the phone to the boy.

'D'you know how to use Twitter?' he asked. 'You know, X?'

Ben nodded weakly.

'The app's already open, so I want you to share that video using the hashtag realfirestartermanchester. You got that?'

The boy nodded silently.

Phillips's mind raced as she tried to figure out a way out of this mess. The firearms unit would be here any second now, and the last thing she wanted was a young boy to witness the horrific scenario that lay ahead if she couldn't talk McDonnell down. It was time to bite the bullet. 'This isn't the way to get justice for Archie, Bruce. Or for anyone else. It won't give you what you want.' She paused for a brief moment. 'But *I* can.'

'Really? And what do I want?'

'To expose Fox's corruption, and those like her. To ensure they get what's coming to them.'

Fox's eyes widened. 'What the hell are you talking about, Phillips?'

Phillips ignored her while wishing she really would learn to put a sock in it. 'If Ben posts that video, it'll go viral. Guaranteed. And that means it'll be seen by millions all over the world.'

'Good,' McDonnell shot back. 'That's exactly what I want.'

'No, it isn't,' she replied. 'Because that video will demonise *you* and make the chief constable look like the victim here. People don't take kindly to kids being tied up, to people making them suffer for the crimes of their parents.'

McDonnell's severe expression softened ever so slightly.

Phillips continued, 'Stand down now before it's too late, and you can help me bring her to justice for her crimes.'

'What the hell are you talking about?' Fox demanded.

Phillips resolutely ignored her and kept her eyes locked on McDonnell. 'I have evidence that proves she doctored DNA evidence in Archie's trial, and I have the testimony of a serving officer that she blackmailed him into getting rid of incriminating evidence.'

Ben turned to his mother now. 'Mum?'

'Don't be absurd, Benjamin,' snapped Fox. 'I would never do that!'

Phillips locked eyes with the chief constable now. 'I know all about what you did to Archie's blood samples and the threats you made to Entwistle. You can deny it all you like, but you won't be wriggling your way out of this one, ma'am.'

A snarl formed on Fox's top lip. 'You're finished, Phillips. I'll make sure of that.'

Phillips held her gaze in silence for a long moment as her heart pounded like a drum in her chest before she turned her focus back to McDonnell. 'Come on, Bruce. For once in your life, *you* have control. You have the power to stop this and do something good with what's left of your life.'

McDonnell's posture softened almost imperceptibly as he stared back.

'Help me end the corruption we both know exists in the force, and give yourself some peace in the time you have left,' said Phillips.

'How can I trust you?' he asked. 'How do I know you'll do what you say?'

She shook her head. 'You don't, but the alternative is you die consumed by fear and pain, just like your mother, Annie. And after speaking to your aunt Mary, I know she wouldn't have wanted that for her precious little boy.'

Incredibly, McDonnell's bottom lip began to tremble.

'Give me the lighter, Bruce.' Phillips's voice was tender now as she stepped very cautiously forward and held out her hand in front of him. 'Do it for your mum.'

A tear streaked down McDonnell's cheek.

'Please, before it's too late.'

McDonnell seemed to crumple in that instant.

His grip loosened, and he finally let go of the lighter.

Phillips exhaled sharply as it landed in her hand. 'Thank you, Bruce.'

A split second later, Jones stepped through into the kitchen, radio in hand. 'This is Mike-Charlie-One. All units stand down, stand down, stand down.'

As Ben rushed to his father's aid, Fox began barking orders, waving her wrists as she snapped, 'Get me up and out of these fucking things.'

Phillips ignored her as she fished a set of handcuffs from her pocket and spun Bruce round, so he had his back to her. Pulling his arms behind his back, she cautioned him. 'Bruce McDonnell, I'm arresting you for the murder of Violet Williams, you do not have to say anything, but it may harm your defence if you do not mention when questioned something that you later rely on in court. Anything you do say may be given in evidence.'

Having now released Fox, Jones moved next to Phillips. 'I can take it from here, guv.'

Phillips nodded as she glanced over his shoulder at the surreal scene before her, which somehow seemed to epitomise the chief constable: Tim – now wrapped in Jones's coat – was hugging Ben tightly against his body like his life depended on it. Fox, on the other hand, was standing on her own a few feet away, rubbing her reddened wrists. 'I'll pretend I didn't hear any of that, DCI Phillips.'

Phillips couldn't hide her utter contempt for the woman. After everything her family had just endured, how could her first thought be about the job, about her reputation?

Fox continued, 'I don't have to tell you how damaging making those kinds of accusations could be for your career.'

Phillips clenched her fists as she glared back at the woman who had made her life a misery for the last ten years.

'I'll expect to see you, Chief Superintendent Carter and DC Entwistle in my office first thing tomorrow morning to discuss how we move this whole thing forward.'

'Sorry, Dorothy but that won't be happening any time soon. We all know you're as bent as they come. And now I have everything I need to prove it.'

Fox stepped in closer so her nose was mere inches from Phillips's face. 'Don't ever try to fuck with me, Jane,' she growled in a low voice. 'And you will address me as ma'am.'

Phillips let out a sardonic chuckle. '*I* won't be fucking with you, *ma'am*. You did that to yourself a long time ago when you framed Archie Pearson.'

Fox's eyes widened as she snarled.

Phillips glanced towards Tim and Ben on the other side of the kitchen. 'If I were you, I'd focus on sorting out your family. Because by the time I'm finished with you, they could be all you have left.'

'How dare you talk to me like that!'

Phillips shook her head but remained silent, then turned and strode out of the room back towards the front door.

45

TWO WEEKS LATER – TUESDAY, 7 NOVEMBER

P hillips's stomach churned as she walked across Albert Square towards the Manchester Town Hall extension, a grade II listed building dating back to 1938 that in its heyday would not have looked out of place on the streets of lower Manhattan or even downtown Chicago. With a bitter wind blowing, the late afternoon sky that loomed overhead appeared as black as her mood in anticipation of the outcome of Carter's meeting with the Police and Crime Commissioner regarding Fox. Despite the rock-solid raft of evidence they'd presented to the emergency committee hurriedly convened to investigate the allegations against the chief constable, Phillips had the horrible feeling in her gut that Fox would somehow manage to wriggle her way out of facing criminal proceedings and the custodial sentence she and Carter were hoping would eventually be forthcoming. God knows, if anyone could, she could.

Out of nowhere, there was a flash of lightning, and a few seconds later the foreboding rumble of thunder filled the air as the rain began to fall. With the main entrance to the building just fifty feet away, Phillips made a run for it, rushing inside just as the heavens opened around her.

A few minutes later she took a seat on one of the leather art deco sofas positioned in the ornate double-height hallway on the ground floor as she prepared herself for the meeting with Carter. Her mind was awash with possible scenarios and outcomes, none of which she particularly relished. In that moment, she wondered if she'd done the right thing by exposing the chief constable's long list of misdemeanours. Would it have been better to leave things as they were and not rock the boat? After all, sharing the truth would only ever damage the public's faith in the police – something that would not help her or any of her fellow cops when it came to fighting crime. But, with all that said, the reality she simply couldn't turn away from was the fact that she had sworn to uphold the law, no matter what. And nobody, not even Fox, was above that law.

Letting go of a deep sigh, she allowed her gaze to settle on her phone in the hope of finding a distraction when, as if by magic, it began to ring in her hand; the caller ID announced that Bovalino was her saviour.

'Hi, Bov,' she said softly, knowing he'd been off work that morning in order to take Izzie to the oncology department at Christie's for the results of her biopsy. 'How did it go?'

'It's not cancer, boss!' he blurted, his voice rising out from the phone and up into the space around her. 'It's benign. She's in the clear!'

Phillips let out another sigh – this time, one of pure relief. 'Oh, thank God. That's brilliant news. You must be so relieved.'

'Oh, Jesus, guv. You have no idea.'

'And how is Izzie?'

'Over the moon, as you can imagine. We've just this minute told her sisters too.'

Phillips smiled at the thought. 'And how did that go?'

'Oh, you know, tears, cheers, and even more tears.'

Phillips felt her heart swell as she pictured the scene. 'Well, listen, after everything you've been through, I really think you should take a few days off, okay?'

'There's no need for that, boss. Honestly. I'll be back in first thing.'

'No, you won't. You'll take a couple of days to be with your beautiful wife, and that's an order. Got it?'

'Got it!' Bovalino laughed softly. 'If you insist, boss.'

At that moment, Phillips glanced up and spotted Carter making his way along the massive curved hallway towards her. 'Look, I've gotta go, Bov, but give Izzie my love, won't you? Tell her I'm thinking about her.'

'I will.' Phillips sensed the big man pausing for a moment. 'Thanks, boss. For everything.' His voice cracked now.

Phillips smiled softly into the phone. 'Anytime, Leonardo,' she said, referring to his rarely used first name.

Carter was just a few feet away by the time she stepped up from the sofa.

Her heart sank when she saw the grave look in his eyes. 'How did it go? Do I even need to ask?'

'Let's talk outside,' he said, gesturing towards the exit.

As they walked side by side in silence, Phillips's heart pounded in her chest, and adrenaline pulsed through her body as she waited for the update. It was a sickly feeling she knew only too well from the many times she had waited in court, praying for a guilty verdict.

A minute later they arrived at the main entrance to the

building. Open to the elements, they huddled together as rain lashed down onto the paving stones outside.

Carter pulled her to one side before checking left and right to ensure they couldn't be overheard.

'So?' said Phillips, struggling to hide her impatience.

'Look, there's good news and bad news.'

Phillips's heart sank as she dropped her head to her chest for a moment before looking up again. 'So what's the bad news?'

'They've decided against prosecuting her, Jane.'

Phillips recoiled. 'You what? You've got to be kidding me!'

Carter gestured for her to lower her voice. 'I know, I know. I feel exactly the same as you do.'

'So what *are* they doing?'

'Retiring her off.'

Phillips felt like she'd been hit with a hammer blow. 'What the f...' she seethed powerlessly.

'I tried, Jane. I really did, but the PPC said the Home Secretary was having none of it.'

'But she's a bloody crook!'

'I know she is,' Carter said in a low voice. 'But the feeling was that protecting the force was of greater importance than prosecuting a ready-to-retire chief constable.'

Phillips began pacing back and forth as she struggled to control the rage that threatened to overwhelm her. 'So Fox builds a career on lies and corruption, sending God knows how many innocent people to prison for the best years of their lives, and she walks away scot-free?'

'Not entirely scot-free,' replied Carter. 'I mean, she won't be getting an official send-off or any kind of fanfare. Plus her CBE's off the table.'

Phillips stopped in her tracks. 'Her CBE?'

Carter nodded. 'Apparently she'd been put forward for one in the New Year's Honours List.'

'Oh, well. That's all right, then, isn't it? No party and no medal from the King. That'll be punishment enough.'

Carter's shoulders sagged. 'I wish it were different, Jane, but I'm afraid there's too much at stake here.'

'And what about Pearson? Will he get the pardon he deserves?'

'No,' Carter replied flatly. 'But he will be getting out imminently as well as being offered a generous compensation package, in return for his silence of course.'

'Unbelievable. Un-*fucking*-believable.'

'Like I say, I'm sorry, Jane. I really am.'

Phillips fell silent.

'At least there is one good thing to come out of all of this mess,' ventured Carter.

'And what's that?'

'Entwistle's testimony will not prejudice his chances of promotion when they come up. To be honest, if anything, I'd say he'll be a shoo-in for detective sergeant if, and when, you think he's ready for it.'

Phillips stayed quiet as she attempted to process everything she'd just heard. 'Look, I think I need to take a few days off – if that's okay? Jonesy is up to speed on all the cases, so there shouldn't be any issues.'

'Of course.' Carter offered a weak smile. 'As long as you promise to come back.'

Phillips nodded. 'I'll be seeing you, sir,' she said, pulling her collar up and stepping out into the rain.

46

FRIDAY, 10 NOVEMBER

Phillips pulled the little Mini Cooper into the near-empty carpark of the Pig and Whistle in Congleton just after 3 p.m. Finally, for the first time in what felt like weeks, the wind and rain had subsided, and the sun was threatening to break through the clouds above. After switching off the engine, she sat in silence for a moment and cast her gaze out through the passenger window to the green fields beyond the dry-stone wall next to the car. It had been two days since Carter had shared the news that Fox would not be punished for a career built on corruption, and the injustice of it all had gnawed at her being like a relentless toothache ever since. Over the twenty-odd years of her career, she'd witnessed plenty of examples of sweeping things under the carpet, but the PPC and Home Secretary's decision to let Fox walk away without so much as a scratch was on a different level entirely. Shaking her head, she picked up the folder from the passenger seat and opened the driver's door.

A couple of minutes later she wandered into the main body of the pub and through to the snug at the rear of the bar, a cosy, intimate little spot she'd shared with Adam in the not-too-distant past on one of their rare evenings out together.

As she walked through the narrow entrance to the small nook, she spotted the person she had invited here for a drink earlier that morning.

'Hello, Jane.' Don Townsend flashed his trademark, tobacco-stained, toothy grin. 'What can I get you?' Judging by the two empty glasses sitting on the table in front of him, he'd already been here for some time.

Phillips dropped into the booth opposite him, placing the folder on the seat to her left. 'I'll have a small white wine spritzer if you're buying.'

'Coming up,' he said before shuffling out of the booth.

With the bar being virtually empty – as Phillips knew it usually was at this time of day – he quickly returned with Phillips's drink served in a tall glass, and a large whiskey for himself.

'I hope you're not expecting to drive after this.'

'Me?' He feigned shock. 'Never.'

'Seriously, Don. You'd better not be.'

Townsend raised his hands in defence. 'Relax, will you? I got one of the junior reporters to give me a lift. He's recently moved up from London, so I've sent him off on a fact-finding tour of the area to help him with his local knowledge. He'll pick me up on the way back in about an hour.'

'That's all right, then.' Phillips relaxed a little as she took a sip of her drink before placing the glass back on the table.

'Now, I'm sure you didn't drag me all the way out to the

Cheshire countryside for an afternoon chat, did you? So what's going on?'

'Have you ever wondered if it's all worth it, Don?'

Townsend's brow furrowed. 'If what's worth it?'

'The relentless pursuit of your goals?'

'I'm not following you.'

Phillips exhaled sharply through her nose. 'Well, ever since I've known you, you've only ever cared about one thing – aside from Vicky, of course...'

Townsend eyed her suspiciously as he took a mouthful of whiskey. 'And what's that?'

'...the *exclusive*, of course.'

'Doesn't every reporter?'

Phillips shook her head softly. 'Not like you, no. I mean, take Evans, for example.'

'What about him?'

'For one, the fact that you were willing to use a woman's life-threatening illness, and her doting husband's desperation to save her, just to get the inside scoop on the GMP. That's not normal.' Phillips was of course referring to the fact Townsend had for several years been paying someone on the inside for information regarding police investigations – until *she* had exposed the mole, that is.

Townsend flashed a thin smile. 'Are you trying to entrap me, Detective Chief Inspector? Is this conversation being recorded?'

'No.' Phillips took another drink. 'This conversation is one hundred percent *off the record*.'

'What you suggest was never actually proven in a court of law, but if we're speaking hypothetically, I'd say the husband in question got a good deal. His wife received the life-saving drugs she needed – not available on the NHS at the time, I might add – and all he had to do was share what was going on behind the scenes at his work. Sounds pretty fair to me.'

'Even though it ruined his career?'

'*You* did that, Jane. Not me.'

Phillips let out an ironic chuckle as she raised her glass. 'Touché.'

Townsend leaned forward and lowered his voice. 'So what's this meeting *really* about?'

'The exclusive, of course,' she replied, repeating her own words before taking a couple more mouthfuls of wine.

'What exclusive?'

'The one you've been waiting for – for your *whole* life, Don.'

Townsend raised his eyebrows as he sat back. 'Well, you've certainly got my attention now.'

Phillips placed her glass on the table, turning it in her fingers. 'It's not official yet, but Chief Constable Fox is stepping down.'

'Wow,' he replied. 'I must admit I wouldn't have seen that coming.'

'The PCC will announce the news of her retirement on Monday morning, and Fox will leave with immediate effect.'

'Why so fast?'

'Because it's not her decision.'

'Oh really?' Townsend's eyes widened. 'Tell me more.'

Phillips sighed before taking a gulp of her spritzer. 'Sadly, I can't.'

'Is this to do with the Real Firestarter investigation?'

'Like I say, I can't tell you that.'

'But it is, isn't it?'

Phillips took her time to drain her glass before setting it slowly down on the table. 'I'd better be going.'

'What?' Townsend recoiled. 'You've only just got here, and besides, you can't leave me hanging like this.'

'You're a bright boy, Don. I'm sure you'll put the pieces together soon enough.' She tapped him on the wrist before slipping out of the booth.

'Don't go just yet,' Townsend almost pleaded. 'Why don't you stay for one more?'

'No, thanks. I'm well and truly done,' she replied as she made her way towards the snug exit.

'Hey,' he shouted after her. 'You forgot your folder.'

Phillips stopped in her tracks, spinning around so she was facing him. 'Have I?' she said nonchalantly. 'You mean the folder containing classified information about the outgoing chief constable's involvement in the wrongful conviction of Archie Pearson? God, I wouldn't want that to fall into the hands of a cut-throat, exclusive-hungry hack, now, would I? Imagine what damage such a person could do to her precious reputation.'

'Wait a minute...' Townsend's words tailed off as he grabbed the folder. Taking his focus entirely off Phillips, he began leafing through its contents.

'And remember...'

Townsend glanced up.

'You always protect your sources, right?' Phillips flashed a knowing grin. 'I'm pretty sure you found *that* in a taxi or on a park bench or something...'

'Sure,' he said with a lopsided, wolfish grin. 'Course I did.'

'Do what you do best, Don,' she added with a wink.

A few minutes later as she stepped outside, the sun had

delivered on its promise, and the carpark and surrounding fields were now bathed in glorious autumnal sunshine. Suddenly the world seemed a better place, and as she walked back to the car, she found herself singing a song she'd come to know only too well in the last month. *'I'm a Firestarter, twisted Firestarter.'*

ACKNOWLEDGMENTS

This book would not have been possible without a host of amazing people.

First and always foremost, my wife, Kim, who constantly reminds me how far I've come since I started my writing journey. Thank you for encouraging me to stop and smell the roses occasionally instead of always pushing on towards the next goal on my list.

My gorgeous boy, Vaughan, you inspire me every single day when I listen to you creating your own stories when playing.

Carole Lawford, ex-CPS Prosecutor, and retired police officers, Bryn Jones and Keith James; your guidance on British Law was as robust as ever.

Dr Faye Horsley, author of New Perspectives on Arson and Firesetting: The Human-Fire Relationship. Your insights on the makeup of fire setters were invaluable in making this story as authentic as possible. And thank you Emma Walsh for allowing me into your network of experts.

My coaches, Donna Elliot and Cheryl Lee, from 'Now Is Your Time'. Your belief in me continues to inspire me every day.

Fellow author, Ceryn Rowntree. Your words of wisdom, kindness and hilarious insights helped me navigate some of the more challenging moments whilst writing this book.

Thanks to my publishing team of Jan, Brian, Garret, Claire, Alice and Lizzie. I couldn't do this without you.

And finally, thank you to my readers for reading *Deadly Inferno*. If you could spend a moment to write an honest review, no matter how short, I would be extremely grateful. They really do help readers discover my books.

www.omjryan.com

ALSO BY OMJ RYAN

The DCI Jane Phillips Crime Thriller Series

(Books listed in order)

DEADLY SECRETS (a series prequel)

DEADLY SILENCE

DEADLY WATERS

DEADLY VENGEANCE

DEADLY BETRAYAL

DEADLY OBSESSION

DEADLY CALLER

DEADLY NIGHT

DEADLY CRAVING

DEADLY JUSTICE

DEADLY VEIL

DEADLY INFERNO

DCI JANE PHILLIPS BOX SET

(Books 1-4 in the series)

Printed in Great Britain
by Amazon